GATHER

MONARCH RISING: BOOK TWO

SYLVANA CANDELA

MONARCH RISING
BOOK TWO

GATHER

A HOUSE DIVIDED AGAINST ITSELF CANNOT STAND

SYLVANA CANDELA

This is a work of fiction.

ISBN (softcover): 978-1-7376706-2-9
ISBN (ebook): 978-1-7376706-3-6

Cover design by Sweet 15 Designs
Interior design by Wendy C. Garfinkle
Edited by Leanne Sype

www.sylvanacandela.com
www.peacefulworldpublishing.com

Dedicated to those who wish to heal the divide,
and all who need the healing.

"A house divided against itself cannot stand. I believe this government cannot endure, permanently half slave and half free. I do not expect the Union to be dissolved – I do not expect the house to fall – but I do expect it will cease to be divided."[1]

~Abraham Lincoln

---

[1] *Excerpt from Abraham Lincoln's 1858 acceptance speech as candidate for president.*

Table of Contents

PART 1
PIED PIPER

Chapter 1 – Static

THE OVERSEER GROUNDSKEEPER of Lord Ekene's estate in Johannesburg, is doing his gardening. Suddenly, he looks up and sees a man falling from a third story window of the Lord's office suite. The Groundskeeper runs toward the scene, yelling in Chinese and waving his arms at the other gardeners nearby, "Hurry! Over there!" As the man falls, a tree breaks his descent before he finally lands on the grass below.

The Overseer Groundskeeper is the first one to arrive at the fallen man's side and can see the man is still breathing. "Hey man! Hang in there, brother! Help in on the way."

When he looks closer at the bruised and beaten face of the Communications Overseer, he recognizes him as Lord Ekene's right-hand man. This causes the Groundskeeper to become even more fearful and anxious than he already is, wondering what horrible thing the Communications Overseer must have just done.

Other gardeners arrive on the scene with the same look of fear on their faces.

"Call for a Cloudambulance immediately! Say that someone just jumped out of a window from Lord Ekene's office suite, and that we fear it may be a family member of the Lord."

The Buddy devices have an emergency line left open for such reporting, as long as it is regarding a medical emergency. . . of a Lord or Master, or a family member.

"Yes, sir!" says one of the gardeners. "The Cloudambulance is on its way!"

The Groundskeeper notices that the Communications Overseer is trying to lift his hand and move his lips, so he gets down close to the injured man on the grass and says, "It's okay, Communications

Overseer, sir. There is a Cloudambulance on the way right now. Should be here any moment. You just hang in there."

But the Overseer is becoming more frantic with tears forming in his eyes, trying desperately to say something to the Groundskeeper.

"It's okay, I'm here, Communications Overseer. Is there something you want me to do for you?"

The Overseer nods in the affirmative. He manages to lift his hand and hold it out to the Groundskeeper with a look of total despair on his broken face.

Putting his face right in front of the Overseer, the Groundskeeper asks him, "What is it Communications Overseer? What can I do for you, sir?"

The man is in a daze, wondering why in heaven's name he just jumped out of a window. He has never wanted to end his life before and he does not want to die now.

Looking straight into the eyes of the Groundskeeper with deep wells of sadness, the fallen man stammers out in a whisper, "P–P–Please just . . . c– call me T- T–Tafari."

"Sure thing, Tafari," the Groundskeeper whispers softly to him.

He and the other gardeners are deeply touched by Tafari's words. Knowing that this might be the last words he will ever utter to another human being on this earth, Tafari's most desperate need is to do that which is forbidden by all servants of the UC while they are on duty: to speak his name to another and ask in return that he be called by his own name. Tafari's deepest need at his darkest moment, is to be *recognized* as a human being, free to be the living spirit that he was born to be, and *worthy of life*.

The Cloudambulance arrives. The back doors of the van open and two AI paramedics emerge followed by a human Overseer Paramedic. "Okay, what happened here?" the Overseer Paramedic asks with a sarcastic tone in his voice.

The gardeners are too stunned by everything and unable to respond immediately to the Paramedic's brusque question. But it doesn't take long for the Paramedic to look at Tafari and figure out what is going on.

The Overseer Paramedic yells at the AIs, "Paramedics! Load the Lord's family member onto the stretcher. Take him into the van and run the full body-mending program. Immediately, paramedics!"

The AI paramedics quickly follow their orders.

Looking around to make sure no one is watching, the Overseer Paramedic softens his tone and lowers his voice as he turns to the Groundskeeper Overseer. "I have seen this many times, my friend. His body will be mended, but his spirit will still be badly broken for quite some time."

"I understand," says the Groundskeeper. "And thank you, Brother," he adds quietly to the Overseer Paramedic; the two men exchange knowing glances at each other.

Looking at the other gardeners, the Overseer Groundskeeper says to everyone present, "We will take care of our friend Tafari and do our best to attend to his broken spirit," and turning to the Overseer Paramedic only, he quietly finishes his sentence, "kind sir."

* * *

Lord Ekene has put the finishing touches on his Static Program for Operation Pied Piper. He is quite pleased with himself and the results of the whole program for mass suicide, which he himself has had a hand in perfecting and testing. He is enjoying the breeze from the open window his Communications Overseer jumped out of not too long ago, as well as the display of Ekene's brilliant success that the open window represents. Then the thought occurs to him. *I guess I had better get another Communications Overseer ready for this evening's broadcast.* He calls in his personal servant.

"Servant!" Lord Ekene says, speaking to the young man who has just been summoned, "Go fetch me another Overseer for tonight's Communications broadcast!"

"Yes, My Lord." The young man bows and he scurries off to complete his task.

Lord Ekene gets to work creating the script for the new Communications Overseer. The next broadcast of news and instructions on My Buddy will now be programmed with the new Static Program. All he needs now is the final approval of the Council to put it into worldwide distribution.

* * *

A monitor is flashing with an incoming message from Lord Ekene's High Overlord Contact. It is accepted by SPA somewhere in the Continental Territory of Sinopacifica.

SPA: "Greetings, HOC. What news do you have for me?"

HOC: "Greetings, Most High! The news I have for you is truly excellent!"

SPA: "Excellent, is it? Well then, let's hear about it. Without delay!"

HOC: "Yes, Most High, without delay! My Lord Ekene feels that his Static Program is now ready for distribution throughout One World. He is just waiting for the word from Your Highest of the Council to begin transmitting the program with the next Buddy transmission."

SPA: "Oh, my dear HOC! How *truly excellent!* Do tell Lord Ekene that I, SPA, the Highest, do hereby decree it to be done. That it is to commence on the next Buddy transmission of news and instructions."

HOC: "Oh, thank you, SPA, the Highest! Thank you indeed!"

SPA: "Yes, and do tell My Lord Ekene that with *him* the Council is well pleased, yes, very well pleased, indeed!"

* * *

Tafari is in a daze when the AI paramedics open the back of the Cloudambulance and deposit him on the grass, where he almost lost his life just a little while ago. The Cloudambulance takes off, and Tafari, the Overseer Groundskeeper and the gardeners are left there, not quite sure what to do next.

"I guess we had better get him inside," says the Groundskeeper to the two gardeners.

Turning to Tafari he says, "Do you think you can walk, my friend?"

Tafari gets up slowly and carefully and attempts to take a step. Everything seems to be in working order with his legs. "Uh, yes, I think I can."

"Good," says the Groundskeeper. "My hut is not very far from here," and looking at the other two he says, "Come on, let's get him out of here before someone sees him."

"Good idea," they both agree, and take Tafari to the Overseer Groundskeeper's hut.

When they arrive, Tafari finds himself in cozy quarters surrounded by soft cushions that are close to the cloth-covered, earthen ground. There are plants and flowers all over the hut, as well as bottles and jars of various herbal blends. The Overseer Groundskeeper helps Tafari over to a particularly inviting corner of the hut, and he offers Tafari one of his soothing herbal drinks. The others join him with the same herbal drink and they all begin to feel a sense of calm come over them. At this point the Groundskeeper takes out four djembe drums and offers one to each of the other men present. He begins to drum gently and slowly as the others follow his lead. The beating of the drums is having a peaceful effect on Tafari's soul, as if it is healing and transforming the ill effects of the static mind control programming that he was just so brutally subjected to.

After a while, the Groundskeeper ceases the drumming and begins to speak, "My friend, allow me to introduce myself to you," says the Groundskeeper as he smiles, looking at Tafari. "My name is Bem."

"And I am Nassor," says one of the gardeners.

The other gardener chimes in, "My name is Dumaka!"

The four men all smile at each other as they have broken a big taboo against the UC by speaking their names to one another. And for some unknown but glorious reason, they are all feeling something deep within their souls which they have never felt before. They are feeling fearlessly free!

* * *

Lord Ekene's servant arrives with the new Communications Overseer recruit. He is a young man with a cheerful disposition and friendly voice. "Hello, Overseer, welcome to your new assignment." Ekene says.

"Oh, thank you!" the young man beams with enthusiasm. "I am very much looking forward to being of service to you, My Lord!"

"Yes, yes, indeed. That's nice," says Ekene as he thinks to himself, *now his voice should be a great cover for the Static Program.*

"Let's get you started Communications Overseer, here is your script for tonight. Read it out loud to me . . . now."

"Oh yes, My Lord. Yes indeed!" The Overseer begins to read the words that will soon be transmitted to all three Continental Territories, through the Universal Translator. It will have an underlying subliminal message, static, and music played at an amped up 440 hz. The effects will be rolled out slowly as the Council does not want to raise any suspicions. For now, the people should experience nothing more than a mild irritation within themselves and with each other.

* * *

Word has gotten out amongst the Lords and Ladies that the Static Program on My Buddy transmissions is about to begin. Although the Masters are aware of Operation Pied Piper in general, they are only privy to their own part in the plan and not the operation as a whole. So, while the Masters are busy cranking out neurotoxins for seeds and food, the Lords are about to go into action with subliminal messages and toxic frequencies.

* * *

Lady Liling is walking around her garden, lovingly attending to her flowers. "How beautiful your fragrance is today little ones! It seems our goddess of compassion, Kwan Yin, has truly blessed you with her beauty!" She leans over to kiss their little buds and hears them giggling back to her.

We love you too, White Jasmine Lady. You are our favorite flower!

"Well, my oh my, Lady Liling sings back to them," when presently her Lord's Communication Device begins to pulsate in her pouch.

"I wonder who that could be?" she says to her flowers. Looking at her incoming message, it is from her High Overlord Contact. She accepts the message:

"Lady Liling," he begins, "I have some wonderful news for you!"

"Oh?" she says rather hesitantly.

"Why yes indeed, My Lady. It is regarding Operation Pied Piper and the Static Program. Everything is ready to go! You and High Lord Yakov will be hearing from High Lord Kenneth shortly. He will give you further instructions, and my guess is that he will want to get together with the two of you again, so be prepared for imminent departure."

"Yes, my HOC."

"Very well then. I shall sign off, and good luck with your assignment My Lady. This is truly a great day for us all!" The HOC disconnects, and Liling's heart sinks to the ground.

Not long after, she receives another incoming message. This time it is from Kookie.

"Ni Hao, my Sister," Kookie says.

"Hello *yourself*," answers Liling, trying not to sound too sad but knowing that this is going to be difficult for both of them. Since Kookie, Yakov and Liling are now being more closely watched by moles, they must be extra cautious about what they say on their Lord's Communication Devices, discussing only what the Council wants to hear.

"Well then, isn't it just wonderful that we finally have a plan of action to eliminate the slaves, one that sounds like the most promising plan yet!" says Kookie.

"Oh my, yes indeed it is, Brother! Yes indeed, it is!"

"So, we really need to get together, that is, you and Yakov and I to discuss our own part in this program and the fulfillment of Operation Pied Piper."

"Oh yes, Brother dear, we certainly must!"

Kookie fears Liling is overacting just a touch, which could cause suspicion with a mole. *Don't overdo it, woman!* He thinks to himself. "I want the three of us to get together as soon as possible. I have some other business to attend to first in preparation for our gathering, so let's say we meet at our usual California location in 48 hours."

"Sounds good to me, Brother."

"Okay, Sister, see you then!" They disconnect, and in spite of her ridiculous display of overacting, Liling actually does feel some kind of hope after talking to Kookie.

* * *

Lord Ekene is satisfied that the new Communications Overseer is going to work out well. The time is approaching for the unveiling of "Static" as it has been dubbed by some of the Lords. The pre-recorded, inaudible, subliminal message which he recorded himself is also ready to go. It will be transmitted simultaneously with the audible message which the Communications Overseer will read, as well as the background music of a strengthened 440hz. The underlying sound of static will also be transmitted outside of hearing range. While the people of One World are listening to the foolish chatter of the Overseer, they will also subliminally "hear" Lord Ekene's voice in a sinister whisper mixed in with the static, saying the following:

> *"YOU ARE STUPID . . . YOU ARE WORTHLESS . . . YOU ARE TRASH . . . YOU ARE USELESS . . . YOU ARE VERMIN . . . YOU ARE SCUM.*
> *YOU ARE STUPID . . . YOU ARE WORTHLESS . . . YOU ARE TRASH . . . YOU ARE USELESS . . . YOU ARE VERMIN . . . YOU ARE SCUM.*
> *HEAR ME . . . FEAR ME . . . HEAR ME . . . FEAR ME.*
> *TAKE YOUR LIFE, USELESS EATER . . . TAKE YOUR LIFE, USELESS EATER.*
> *DO IT! DO IT! DO IT TODAY! DO IT TODAY! DO IT! TODAY! DO IT! DO IT! DO IT!"*

This will be played over and over every day with each and every daily news and instructions transmission that goes out on My Buddy, all across One World, in English, Russian, and Chinese. Once the drugs have been added to the food and water and the chemical changes to the seedlings, the effects will be intensified. Operation Pied Piper will then be fully underway with a pandemic of mass, global suicide and homicide.

It is time for the Communications Overseer to transmit his message:

"Hello! Hello, Dear Ones! We are back! Yes indeed! No Ebola! No siree! Yes indeed! Yes indeed! No Ebola! No siree! And don't I have even more wonderful news for you Dear Hearts. Yes, indeed I do! Your Council, who loves you SOOO much has decided to lift the 'emergency only' usage of My Buddy. WOO HOO! WHOOP DEE DO! That's right My Dears, now you can message and speak to one another again on My Buddy! So do not delay! Send out your messages on My Buddy today! Speak to your loved ones, wherever they are! DO IT TODAY! DO IT TODAY! DO IT! DO IT! DO IT!"

People everywhere are having inexplicable feelings and varying degrees of irritation, sadness, anxiety, and confusion. All except one person, that is. In a little hut, an Overseer Groundskeeper and two gardeners suddenly jump up and run to the aid of Lord Ekene's former Communications Overseer who can't stop screaming.

"It's okay, Tafari! It's okay, my friend! We are here with you! We are here!" Bem, Nassor and Dumaka are desperately pleading.

The sudden change in Tafari from calm and peaceful to wild and frantic has them lost in hopeless bewilderment. *What could have possibly set him off like that,* they wonder while trying unsuccessfully to calm Tafari down. Bem decides to try one of his herbal remedies while the other two continue to offer comfort to their completely inconsolable friend.

"What can we do for you Tafari? Is there anything we can do?" asks Nassor.

"Make it stop! Make it stop!" Looking upwards, Tafari pleads, "If there is a higher being out there, please make it stop!"

The three men are all touched by Tafari's outcry to heaven. Dumaka looks at the other two and says to Tafari, "I do not know what it means to pray, but I do remember my grandmother used to do that when she did not know what else to do when someone was sick, or hurting, or just plain scared. Maybe we can try that."

The others nod in agreement and decide to give this thing called praying a try. Bem is just bringing over the herbal tea preparation and invites Tafari to drink it. With trembling hands, Tafari puts the cup to his lips, as Dumaka closes his eyes and begins:

"To the one who is our Overseer above; I do not know your name, but my name is Dumaka, and these are my friends, Nassor, Bem and Tafari. I am very sorry and I mean no disrespect when I call you the Overseer above. I am sure your name is much better than that. Please forgive me kind one, I just do not know what else to call you." Then Dumaka thinks about if for a moment and continues, *"Perhaps I can call you Kind One. I mean, you must be very kind to be willing to help us poor folks out."*

As Dumaka continues to pray he becomes aware of a softening in his heart, with a feeling of serenity coming over him. In fact, he notices that it is suddenly very quiet in the little hut and even Tafari has quieted down. Dumaka continues, *"Please help us, Kind One. Help us to help our friend Tafari. Help us all to understand what has happened to him and what is still happening to him even now. Oh, and one more thing Kind One, if it is not too much to ask of you. Please let us know what to call you. Please tell us sir, what is your name? Thank you."*

The others all repeat, "Thank you."

When Dumaka opens his eyes and looks up, he sees a strange and beautiful sight in the window. The window is covered from top to bottom with Monarch Butterflies blocking out the sun and darkening the space.

"You seem to be doing better," Bem says to Tafari, who is now in the same relaxed state that he was in before the transmission.

"Yes," says Tafari, "I do feel quite better. Thank you for the tea." Turning to Dumaka he says, "And thank *you* for those words you spoke.

I felt my heart getting lighter as you were saying them. What did you call it?"

"Praying," Nassor cuts in, smiling at everyone. "I remember my grandmother doing the same thing when I was little. But then the Security Guard Overseers came one day while my grandmother was praying, and they said that the Council told her she could not do that anymore. And since she refused to stop, they took her away in their van. It was the last time I ever saw her. So, I knew that it was a dangerous thing to do and never thought about it again."

Suddenly, Tafari stands up and looks at the others. "Oh my! Gracious!" he says, as a realization has just hit him.

"What! What is it Tafari?!" the others all gasp at his sudden change in demeanor.

"Words!" he says, "Words! That has been my function for so long. To speak words to the people. Words that I was told to say. Words which I had a feeling deep down were not true. Words that I thought were just silly and meaningless. But I have just learned something, my friends," he says, almost choking with a new kind of emotion that has been buried deep down inside of his soul.

"What have you learned, Tafari?" Dumaka says gently, seeing that his friend is struggling to finish his thought.

Looking at Dumaka, Tafari says, "I have learned that words are very powerful. As your words, my friend, have helped lift the darkness from my heart, I have just this moment learned that *Words of kindness are more powerful than words that are unkind.*

"What I have been telling people over My Buddy transmissions have *not* been words of kindness or words of the Kind *One*," he says with a smile, looking at Dumaka. The Monarchs on the window are taking this all in and they are smiling too.

Bem has been listening to everything with amazement and wants very much to hear what happened to Tafari that would cause him to jump out of a window. Although he is hesitant to ask, he decides to go for it, ever so gently. "Tafari, my friend, would it be too difficult for you to share with us what happened to you back at Lord Ekene's?"

"You know something? I don't rightly know," he says, "any more than I know what happened to me just now as I was listening to the transmission. Lord Ekene said he needed my help with something; that he was putting the finishing touches on a program he was working on. And all of a sudden, I, uh, well, I just lost it. Only much worse than I did just now. And I couldn't make it stop, and he– he– **WHOA!!**" Tafari shrieks suddenly, knocking everyone off their seats. Even the butterflies fluttered off the window for a moment.

"What is it! You scared the devil out of all of us, man!" they chide at once.

"Yes! I'm sorry. And that is what I suddenly remembered. It is exactly what Lord Ekene did to *me*!"

"Wait, *WHAT?*" all three gentlemen are confused.

"When I cried out to him in agony to help me, to make it stop, he did just the opposite!"

"WHAT? What do you mean?" asks Nassor.

"He told me that my only hope was to jump out of the open window. And then, then . . ." Tafari screams through the rafters with a release of thunderous rage, "*HE ORDERED ME TO JUMP! AND I DID! FOR NO REASON!*"

Tafari is seething, but something inside of him knows that he has been set free as he has recognized and spoken words of truth for the first time ever.

* * *

Upon hearing Tafari's hard-hitting words, the Monarchs on the window of the little hut take off in a flash. With no time to lose, they know what they have to do. Turning to the one called Angel, the other butterflies ask her, *where are you leading us, holy one?*

Angel replies, *we must make haste to Shang Hai to see the human creature White Jasmine. Much of our hope for human creatures rests on her shoulders.*

* * *

From the three Continental Territories of One World: Panamerica, Euroslavica and Sinopacifica, three terminals activate. The incoming message is from PA and it is accepted by ES and SPA. They each turn on their Universal Translator devices and speak in their respective languages, English, Russian and Chinese:

PA: "Greetings Brothers of the Council."

ES: "Greetings, my Brethren."

SPA: "Greetings, my esteemed and fellow Highest Ones."

PA: "I have some excellent news to share with you, my Brothers."

ES: "What is it PA?"

SPA: "Yes, yes! Do tell us!"

PA: "It is about the seedlings of Operation Pied Piper. And I also have news for you regarding the traitorous one with the illegal device."

ES and SPA: *"Yes?!"*

SPA: "Then you have heard from your mole, Brother PA! The one who said he had some information on the traitorous one. That is, the one whom it seems no one has been able to apprehend as of yet. The treacherous one with the unregistered device."

PA: "I am expecting to hear from him momentarily and shall get back to you just as soon as I have any news to report."

ES: "I shall look forward to hearing from you."

SPA: "And I, as well."

PA: "Meanwhile, Operation Pied Piper is moving forward. The toxic seeds have already been distributed to Center Markets throughout One World, and as of this moment, Howard Pharmaceuticals is getting ready to release the chemical compound for the water supply. They have also created, shall we say, a little additive for the tea cakes and juice that are so terribly popular amongst the slaves. It will be ready for distribution to the Center Coffeehouses throughout One World very shortly."

ES: "Such wonderful news, my Brother!"

SPA: "Yes, truly wonderful news!"

PA: "Yes, yes. And I shall now take my leave of you, until we speak again."

The transmission is terminated.

Chapter 2 – Seedlings

IT IS A COOL AND MISTY SPRING MORNING at Bear River Farm. The sun is rising, and soon the earth will warm up with the touch of its gentle rays. Little Eve Elli loves this time of day on the farm, when she can smell the fragrant earth and say good morning to her friends, the Monarchs. "There you are, Angel!" she laughs with delight as a Monarch comes over to kiss her cheek and settles in her hair. Holding out her hands so the other Monarchs know it is okay to fly over and join them, Eve Elli begins her daily routine in the garden.

When Mimi comes outside to say good morning to her sweetie pie, she is taken with what she see; her happy little Eve Elli skipping and dancing through the rows of newly planted vegetable seedlings with a trail of Monarch butterflies fluttering behind her. When she sees the Monarchs in Eve Elli's hair, Mimi is reminded of the dream that she had not too long ago where she and Elli were separated in a crowd, and how little Elli told her in the dream not to cry, that everything was going to be okay. Now that she is looking at the blessed child *Eve* Elli with the Monarchs in her hair and others all around her, Mimi believes in her heart that no matter what happens, somehow, someday, things really and truly *will* be okay.

"Good morning my little sunshine!" Mimi calls out to Eve Elli.

"Good morning, Gramma!" Eve Elli beams.

Mimi is sure she hears the Monarchs saying *good morning Gramma* as well. "What is my sweetie pie doing this morning?"

"We are making the seedlings grow big and tall Gramma!" Eve Elli says, stretching her arms out wide.

"Oh, and who are *WE* honey?"

"Angel and me," Eve Ellie proclaims, pointing to the Monarchs in her hair with little-girl pride, "and *AAAALLLLL* these other butterflies, Gramma!"

"I see. How do you and Angel make the seedlings grow big and tall, honey?"

"Like this," Eve Elli says. She gets down on her knees and strokes the little seedling. Mimi's heart is filled with pure joy when Eve Elli leans over, kisses the seedling ever so gently and says, "I love you, Baby Tomato." The Monarchs do the same, flying from one seedling to the other resting sweetly on them for a while. Mimi is sure that she can also hear the Monarchs whispering, *I love you Baby Tomatoes.*

When it is time for breakfast, Mimi and Eve Elli join the others in the main farmhouse where Lisa is cooking up something exquisite for everyone.

The Chrysalenes are chatting pleasantly while passing around Little Suzie of the Seashells, who is giggling with delight.

"Good morning, Phil, how are you and little Suzie doing today?" Mimi asks when she sees her friend.

"We are doing very well Mimi, and how are you and *your* family doing, my Sister?"

"Couldn't be better," Mimi replies as Ryan comes over to join them, giving her and Eve Elli a big hug. Eve Lydia and Adam Sam are not far behind, finishing their morning "loving" on the seedlings, too, as are the rest of the Chrysalenes.

When everyone is seated and ready to eat, Lisa says to the crowd, "Good morning one and all. I have an announcement to make this morning. Oh my, it is truly a wonderful day! I heard the most excellent news last night on My Buddy about the Ebola outbreak being all over!"

Everyone cheers around the table and applauds saying, "Amen, Sisters and Brothers! Amen!"

"And if that news wasn't good enough, this morning there was even *more* wonderful news. We are getting in brand new seeds that are healthy and very good for us, unlike the old ones that they said caused the Ebola outbreak. These seeds will help keep us safe from harm. We were told to discard and destroy whatever is left, including the seedlings that are already growing and plant the new healthy seeds instead. So, Kenny and I are going to the Center Market later today to pick up our new seeds."

The merriment dies down and silence comes over the Chrysalenes. They are listening to the cries of all the little seedlings out in the field; the baby tomato plants and all the others. Only moments ago, the Chrysalenes were loving on the growing sprouts, and now the seedlings hear they are about to be terminated. The Chrysalenes bow their heads, close their eyes and hold out their hands to the heavens.

Lisa, Kenny, Phil, Doc, Mimi and Ryan do not know the seedlings can feel their impending doom, and the friends are surprised to hear the Chrysalenes murmuring and whispering, "It's alright little Brother and Sister fruit of the earth, we will protect you."

* * *

Lisa is on her way to the Bear River Center Market. She is excited about getting the new seeds, especially since they now have all this extra farm help with the arrival of the Chrysalenes. The many helping hands will really make a difference in getting the seedlings planted and eventually harvesting the crops. Besides, there is something wonderful about the Chrysalenes' energy that Lisa just knows will make a huge difference in the growth, quality and abundant yield of the fruits and vegetables.

One thing that has her bewildered, though, is the reaction the Chrysalenes had to the message on My Buddy regarding the new seeds. However, they didn't elaborate further, and Lisa was so excited to get her new "healthier" seeds, as the Overseer referred to them on My

Buddy, that she just puts the Chrysalenes reaction in the back of her mind.

Arriving at the Center Food Market, Lisa walks straight to the gardening area to see what new seeds have arrived. There is a big sign that says, "New Seeds! Disease Free!" and a rack full of seeds for tomatoes, cucumbers, kale, romaine lettuce, carrots, zucchini, eggplant, bell peppers, and corn of all different colors. *That should get things started,* Lisa thinks to herself.

She gathers some other supplies and heads back to the farm. Returning to the cottage, Lisa walks in and sees that everyone has gone outside and the Chrysalenes are all tending to the seedlings in the field. Mimi and friends are following them around with great curiosity. They don't want to disturb the Chrysalenes from their work, but they are just too fascinated with these incredibly sacred, higher-level human beings.

Mimi finally interrupts her little grandchild very gently, trying not to disturb her.

"So, what are you doing Eve Elli?" Mimi asks. She is watching her precious grandchild get on her knees and whisper to the seedling, cupping it gently, kissing it and moving on to the next one.

"I am telling the babies to *be still and have no fear,* Gramma," Eve Elli says with a sweet little smile on her cherubic face.

"Oh, I see. Um, why should the, um, *babies* be afraid, sweetheart?"

"Because they do not want to die, Gramma."

Mimi stops and stares at Eve Elli. Then she stares at the other Chrysalenes and realizes they all seem to be doing the same thing; that is, they are offering comfort to the seedlings! *What is going on?!* Mimi thinks to herself. Then it hits her. It was the message from the Overseer on My Buddy when the Chrysalenes suddenly went quiet and started praying "We will protect you." The Overseer said the seedlings that are growing right now were responsible for the Ebola outbreak and that they would have to be destroyed; that new, healthy seeds are now being issued to all the farmers at the Center Markets.

"Good Lord!" Mimi says out loud as she turns to Eve Elli. "Honey? Do you think that the babies here will make us sick if we eat their food when it is ready?"

"Oh no, Gramma! These are very *good* babies! And they are very sad because they want to grow big and strong and give us so much love one day with their *nutritious!*" Eve Elli says with much compassion for the babies.

"I see! I think you mean *nutrition,* sweetie." Mimi says, flabbergasted, and chuckling at her three-year-old granddaughter. "May I ask you just one more question darling?" Mimi says with a beaming smile. "Then Gramma will shut up and leave you alone, so you can go on loving on the babies!"

"Hee hee! That's funny, Gramma!"

"Sure," Mimi says, clearing her throat and asking one last pain-in-the-cherub's-butt question. "So, how do the babies know all this is going to happen, and how do *you* know that *they* know . . ." Mimi pauses and realizes that she still has just one more question, "And how can you reassure them not to be afraid?"

Before either one of them can utter another word, Mimi is suddenly aware of a gentle chorus of laughter coming from behind and all around them. During her Q & A session with Eve Elli, several Chrysalenes as well as Kenny, Doc, Phil and Ryan have gathered around and are listening to their conversation.

"If I may, kind Mimi," says Eve Helena. "The seedlings know everything that is going on in our human world. They can sense the energy that we put out and then they talk to each other about it, as well. So, when the Overseer announced that they were to be destroyed because they were responsible for making us sick, that disturbed them greatly."

"Well, if they know all of that," says Mimi, "then how can you reassure them not to be afraid?"

"Because," replies Eve Helena with much sympathy for the seedlings, as well as for Mimi and her bewilderment, "Love is the most powerful force of the universe, and they trust the love that we are giving them."

Mimi looks at the gentle faces of all the Chrysalenes gathered around, as well as her little granddaughter, and somehow Mimi finds herself also believing in the power of love.

Ryan comes over to Mimi and takes her in his arms. He says, "And I believe in the power of love too, honey."

For the moment they are lost in their own little beautiful world, until they hear Lisa calling out from behind them.

"Hey everyone! I'm back! Got all these awesome, healthy new seeds with me! So, let's get started tearing up all these here other diseased seedlings and make way for the new ones! Yes indeed!"

Kenny turns to his Woman and says, "Lisa, there is something I have to explain to you."

"What? What's going on?" Lisa asks, noticing the solemn look on the faces all around her.

"It's about the seedlings, honey, the ones here which have already been planted," Kenny begins to explain to her.

"*So?*" Lisa says, very perplexed.

"So, according to the Chrysalenes, there is nothing wrong with them. And that is why they told the seedlings that they would protect them when we were all told on My Buddy to destroy them."

"Oh, my goodness!" Lisa exclaims, although she is still unsure of all this. "So, why were we told to do that, then? And why on Earth were we told to get these here new seeds that I just got at the Center Market?"

Chrysalene Adam Mark asks Lisa, "Dear lady, might I see those new seeds you just received?"

"Certainly," Lisa says, handing the entire bag of seeds over to him.

Adam Mark summons the other Chrysalenes to come over as he begins to hand out the seed packs to each of them. They all seem to know intuitively what to do, including Eve Elli, as they each take their pack of seeds and hold them up in the air and look up to the heavens. Then they hold the seeds to their chests, close their eyes and begin to whisper something inaudible. There are pauses with moments of silence followed by other whisperings, until they finally open their eyes and look at the other folks gathered around. Everyone, of course, is most anxious to hear what the Chrysalenes have to say. Adam Mark begins to speak for all of them.

"The seeds we are all holding are truly suffering, my good people. They are in pain and crying out for our help."

"Oh dear! Oh my goodness! Gracious! Good grief!" the others all shout out at once.

"Dear Lord!" cries Mimi, "Whatever is causing them to be in pain?!"

"Neurotoxins," Adam Mark says with sadness. "They have been infused with neurotoxins and it is causing them great suffering."

"Besides the physical pain they feel from the chemical agents, their emotional agony is even greater," says Eve Helena.

Eve Elli pipes in, "And it makes them all *very, very, very sad,* Gramma, because they cannot be *nutrition* . . . I mean *nutritious* anymore!"

Everyone feels grieved, and they also begin to burn with anger. "And they love us so much that they cannot stand the feeling of hurting people with their harvest," Adam Mark says.

Kenny, Lisa, Doc, Phil, Mimi and Ryan are suddenly reminded of the horror Vi experienced when she realized that she was the one who unknowingly administered the fatal Ebola injection to all those people, and they are all overcome with compassion for the broken souls of the new little seeds.

"But what can we do? How can anyone help them and help us *all?*" Lisa implores to all of the Chrysalenes.

Doc, who has been standing there quietly lost in thought suddenly says one word, *"Metatron."*

Mimi understands the implications of what Doc has just said. She takes her own hand-held device out of her pouch and holds it up to the Chrysalenes. "This, my friends, is the tool that was used to restructure your DNA. It is the reason why you are all here and not buried at the bottom of a Shelter hole. You're also safe because of a program called 369, and the courageous actions of a brave man, the Major, and the self-sacrificing love of a tender-hearted soul by the name of Kookie."

The Chrysalenes understand everything, and Eve Jasmine tenderly says to Mimi, "We have been holding the seeds to our hearts as you have explained all of this to us, good lady Mimi, and they are suddenly filled with hope. You and Doc have made their pain go down considerably already, and for that they are saying, *thank you, thank you, Ladies of Light!*"

Doc says, "I will send out pigeon #1 to Judy and tell her what is happening, that she is *not* to destroy the seedlings that are already growing and to send word to all the other farmers in her network to do the same. Also, that they are all to await further instructions regarding the new seeds."

Mimi says, "And we must also get word to the Major, Vi, Angie and Kookie about everything we have just learned here. We need to call upon them for an immediate Gathering!"

She then turns to Kenny. "We've just got to get two more pigeons out, one to send word immediately to the Major and Vi, and the other to go as fast as it can to Angie and Kookie. Do you think you can—"

"I'm right on it, Sister!" Kenny blurts out, as he wastes no time heading straight for the coop.

The Chrysalenes smile blissfully at each other and turn back to the little seedlings. Holding the packs of new seeds in one hand against their hearts, and cupping the seedlings tenderly with the other hand, they go back to loving on their Sisters and Brothers of the field. Mimi is deeply moved when she hears her precious Eve Elli saying to them, "It's okay little babies, you see? I *told you* my Gramma was gonna fix everything!"

* * *

Judy has just come back from the Center Market with her bag of new seeds. She has been puzzled like everyone else in her farming network over the order to destroy the old seedlings and plant the new ones instead. Since Judy does not like to listen to My Buddy on a regular basis, she is often out of the loop in regards to the latest news and instructions. Ordinarily, that suits her just fine, but this time it all seems just a bit strange. The reason given that the old seeds had something to do with the recent Ebola outbreak does not make any sense to her at all, nor to most of the other farmers for that matter.

Going out to the garden she notices another strange thing this morning; the Chrysalenes are all down on the ground gently petting the seedlings and whispering to them. In fact, Judy thinks to herself, *they seem to be, well, comforting the little guys. I wonder if that is because I am planning on removing them from the soil in a little while and throwing them out.*

"Hmph! Strange," she says out loud.

Judy goes into the greenhouse to plant the new seeds in their peat pots, preparing them to become the next seedlings. As she walks out to the garden to check on the Chrysalenes and find out just exactly what they *are* doing with the blighted seedlings, Judy sees an inbound pigeon coming in for a landing.

"Woo Hoo!" she exclaims, excited to see what message the bird has brought her today. She sees the tag on his leg, #1, and knows that it is from Bear River Farm. The message reads:

DO NOT DESTROY OLD SEEDLINGS – HOLD NEW SEEDS ASIDE – PASS THIS ON TO NETWORK – AWAIT FURTHER INSTRUCTIONS – BIG DEAL

"Well, my goodness!" exclaims Judy, talking to #1. I guess there's a whole lot more going on here than meets the eye. Well, better go and see if I can get some clarity from the Chrysalenes. What do *you* think, #1?"

The bird looks sideways at her with an inquisitive expression and extends his foot to her for their usual "handshake." Judy laughs and says, "I guess that's your way of saying *sure thing, lady!*"

Going out to the garden, Judy runs into Adam Tate who is bent over one of the zucchini seedlings. He stops what he is doing and looks up to greet Judy, "Hello Miss Judy, I am so happy to see you!"

"Hello, Adam Tate. I am so happy to see you too. I'm curious to know what you and the others are all doing with the seedlings. It almost seems to me as if you all have been comforting them or something."

"That we have, good lady, that we have."

"Why, whatever do you mean, sir?"

Adam Tate explains, "Well ma'am, until just a few moments ago the little zucchinis were very sad and frightened."

"Really? I mean, they *told* you that, or some such thing?"

"Yes ma'am. But now the little wakanjeja zucchini seedling is happy because she just heard that she is not going to die after all."

"Wait, *WHAT?*" yowls Judy. "Who told who *what?*"

"Oh, it's really very simple, ma'am. The wakanjeja, that is *sacred child,* zucchini seedling, heard from the wind, which carried the message from #1, that the seedlings are not to be destroyed. So now she is not afraid anymore and is most happy! And I am most happy *for* her!" he says smiling.

Gazing at the other Chrysalenes out in the garden Adam Tate says, "I can see that everyone else has heard the news, too. We shall now thank the Creator for the blessing of saving us all today." Bending over the little wakanjeja zucchini seedling, Adam Tate offers up a prayer in Lakota to the Great Spirit.

* * *

The Major is waiting outside his father's office suite to discuss the business at hand. Since his return to the main plant of Howard Pharmaceuticals, production has been cranking away day and night. There are many new things Master Howard, the biochemist has created over the years and has never gotten a chance to actually use. But now that Operation Pied Piper has been ordered and gone into effect, all of the Master's wildest and deadliest dreams are coming true.

The Major receives an incoming message on his Master's Communication Device from his father. Master Howard is ready to receive his son in his chambers.

"Come in, John," Master Howard says as the Major walks into his private office. "It seems we have both been busy these days and haven't really had a chance to get caught up, have we?"

"No father," the Major replies in a sullen tone.

"Well now John, I think you can muster a little more enthusiasm than that. I mean I do realize that the Ebola outbreak didn't exactly pan out the way we had hoped it would, but now we are onto something even bigger and better, are we not?"

"Yes father, we certainly are. Yes, indeed!"

"Now *there's* my boy! What have you been working on, then? I understand that you have been busy lately with your Overlord, Lord Kenneth. So, what have the two of you been up to?"

"Well father," the Major knows that he had better make this one look good, *really* good. "My Overlord and I have been working on the frequency thing, you know the static and the 440hz."

Actually, he and Kookie haven't even talked about that one yet, but it sounded like a good thing to say to Master Howard, and something that he and Kookie might even *have* to start working on, as the Major makes a mental *note-to-self*.

"Yes father," he continues, "We feel that Lord Ekene doesn't really have the frequency thing quite right yet, including the subliminal messaging. So that is something that Kookie and I are going to have to work on until we get it just right."

"Ah yes," says Master Howard, pleased that his son is taking some initiative in this matter. "And there is also something I need you to do for *me*, son."

"Of course, father. Whatever you need, just name it."

"Well John, we are currently putting the finishing touches on a little *additive* for the tea cakes and juices that are so popular at the Center Coffeehouses in all three Continental Territories across One World. That's what makes it so easy to, shall we say, add something to it and easily have the desired effect on the slaves. In fact, you could say that it will be a piece of cake! Ha Ha!"

The Major forces a grimaced grin. "Yes, ha ha."

"Okay, okay, no need to remind me. My sense of humor is not the greatest," Master Howard says, grimacing back at his son.

The Major is anxious to get out of there, so he quickly adds, "Well, so what is it that you need from *me* with the cake and juice additive, father?"

Master Howard says, "I know how good you are with transportation and all of your various gadgets, and AI driven Autovehicles. We really need to get this stuff distributed quickly and quietly. Since the cakes and juices are all made on the premises at the Center Coffeehouses, the people must never for one moment suspect that there is anything in any way wrong with what they are adding to them."

"I see," says the Major. "You want me to go through my other channels to get the additive into the food preparation areas, is that right father?"

"Yes son, that is exactly right. And I know you can do it, too."

"Yes father, I can. So, what exactly *is* this, um, additive that I will be making arrangements to have *smuggled* into bazillions of Coffeehouse kitchens all over One World?

Master Howard looks at his son with an evil-genius glare and says, "It is a brand-new neurotoxin, with a specific targeted area of the brain. The basic effects are a sudden rush of euphoria followed just moments later by a feeling of extreme hopelessness and despair alternating with anger. It is certainly most suited to Operation Pied Piper, and the Council has already told me how pleased they are. Yes, my son, you and I will definitely be going places with this one."

"Indeed, we will father, and I had better get going right away."

"Okay, John, stay in touch."

The Major leaves his father's office and dashes off to find Vi. Since the end of the Ebola outbreak Vi has been reassigned to the chemistry lab at Howard Pharmaceuticals. Now that the Major knows what she is specifically going to be working on, he knows that he will have to take her out of there. He finds Vi outside in the back area where the pigeon coop is visible from her office.

"Hey," Vi calls out to the Major when she sees him coming. "Over here!" she says pointing to a pigeon she is holding.

"Hey yourself, woman," the Major says when he reaches her, trying to keep his voice calm. "Let's get out of here for a little while. I need to talk to you."

"And I need to talk to you, as well," Vi says showing him the tag on the leg of the pigeon she is holding.

The Major says, "Number 13? Now who the devil is #13? We don't have a #13 in our group, and he suddenly realizes what is going on. A new pigeon means that multiple messages are going out at once, and that's serious.

"What does the message say Vi?" his tone has gone soft and worried.

"Here," she says, "Take a look."

GATHERING – LITTLE CUB – 24 HOURS – GRIZZLY

"So 'Grizzly Kenny' is calling for all of us to gather at Bear River Farm in 24 hours. This means it is urgent, and we had better start heading that way. I just have a few things to organize for my father first. But I will tell you all about it on our way to Bear River."

"Okay Major," Vi says, as she prepares a message for #13 and his return trip to Kenny.

* * *

Since Kookie's return from the Gathering of the Lords of the Council at the Great Dining Hall of the polar palace, none of his servants have actually seen him. In fact, no one has seen him except Angie. Kookie has kept himself shut in and isolated from the rest of the world, including his staff. The responsibility that he feels over Operation Pied Piper is weighing heavily on his soul and he knows that he must come up with a plan immediately. There is just no time to lose. He has set the Holographic Imager to show himself involved in all kinds of activities that the Council expects him to be doing, but the truth is he is spending much of his time just staring at the floor.

Angie has been spending much of *her* time in her suite with Metatron against her chest. She is reaching out to all the positive energy in the universe to give her some sort of answers for Kookie. She is trying desperately to help him figure out how to combat the horrid plan the Council and the UC are already in the process of unleashing on 94 percent of the global population. The 94 percent, of course, are the people of One World, which she and Kookie know the UC are now hell-bent on destroying.

Kookie turns on the console at his workstation. He is trying to make sense of what he sees in all three Continental Territories, watching people joyfully return to normal since the Ebola outbreak has been eradicated. The people are going to their Center Markets and getting the new "safe" seeds as they are being told. Thinking of the devastating effects that these new seeds will have on the people, Kookie feels overwhelmed.

What can I do, Father in Heaven, please tell me what can I do? Who will listen to me? Who will help me try to stop the worst plague that has ever been let loose on humanity?

There is only so much that Kookie can stand, so he leaves his workstation and goes down the hall to his private suite. Knowing that he needs to step back and detach for a while, Kookie takes out his tuba and turns on the program for the Tuba concerto in F Minor. The deep, gentle tone of the tuba soothes his soul, and he thinks about calling Angie in to sit with him for a while.

As Angie sits in her private suite with Kookie just down the hall, she can hear him playing. She feels his sadness coming through those deep sounds of the horn and holding Metatron against her chest, she begins to pray:

Dear Lord, please show Kookie a way out of this nightmare. And please, please let me know WHATEVER I can do to help him. I know there is much that we have not explored yet with Metatron, flowers, trees, and energy of all kinds. But most of all Lord, I think we have not yet learned how to use YOUR full power, the power of Love. Teach me oh Lord, please teach me, show me how to be your loving servant . . . to be more like the Chrysalenes.

Walking out to the veranda, Angie decides to go for a walk in the beautiful gardens, for some comfort. She is particularly drawn to the Lilacs and their sweet fragrance and decides to ask them what messages they hold for the world.

The Lilacs respond in her heart. *Sweet lady, we are here to help soothe your heart and calm your spirit. May we bring peace to your mind, letting go of all that is troubling you, knowing that as you relax and let go, all the answers that you seek will come to you, and your hope will be renewed.*

Suddenly, Angie sees a bird overhead flying straight for the pigeon coop; she runs excitedly to see who it is.

Kookie stops playing his tuba for the moment and stares at the floor in misery when he hears Angie's voice calling out to him from down the hallway.

"*Kookieeeee!*"

Good grief! he says to himself, hearing Angie's sudden change from somber to excitement. *What has she been smoking?*

"Bring it in here, honey," he calls out to her.

Angie is laughing as she walks in the door. "How did you know? You are amazing!"

"Huh? What do you mean?" Kookie sputters out, totally befuddled until he sees that Angie is holding a pigeon in her hands. He blurts out, "Oh my goodness!"

Proudly displaying the bird to Kookie she says, "This is #15. Apparently, Kenny and the gang had to use a few extra pigeons for this one!"

Holding out the message for Kookie to read, she also hands him a bunch of Lilacs. "Before you read the message, sweetie, why don't you smell those. Just take in a deep breath through your nose and inhale. Then let the air go slowly through your mouth and repeat it a couple of times."

"Okay," he says, inhaling the healing fragrance of the Lilacs. As he does, Kookie feels lighter in his soul as a weight seems to be lifting from his heart. Then he reads the message sent from Kenny:

GRIZZLY – CALLING UPON THE LORD – GATHERING – LITTLE CUB –24 HOURS

Suddenly Kookie's heart fills with hope. Giving Angie a big smile, he says to her, "Let's get packing, woman!"

"You're on, man!" she replies, as they both start laughing.

* * *

Master Commandant Alexei arrives at Kookie's Kabin in the woods located on the farther reaches of the grounds on Kookie's estate. The lush landscape of trees and foliage make it difficult to track anyone with the usual tracking system, making it a perfect hideout. He messages Nickolai, Kookie's Overseer Groundskeeper to let him know that he has arrived, and Nickolai answers that he is on his way.

When Nickolai arrives, he greets Alexei, "Privyet, Alexei."

"Da, privyet Nickolai, bratan," Alexei replies. "It seems that we have a lot to tell each other." They continue speaking in Russian:

"Yes, indeed we do." says Nickolai. "I have a feeling that perhaps I should go first."

"Very well then. Continue," says Alexei. "We are talking about the hand-held device the Council has us searching for everywhere and seems to evade us each time we almost catch up with the traitor."

"Yes, well, I think that now I understand *why* he keeps evading us."

"Just what are you talking about, Nickolai?"

"I am talking about the High Lord Kenneth, or Kookie as everyone around here calls him."

"What about him?" inquires Alexei, the obvious flying right over his head.

Nickolai can see that the Master Commandant is too weary to even think about what he is hearing, so he just blurts it out. "Master Commandant Alexei, the person we are looking for—the owner of the illegal hand-held device, the traitor, the treasonous one, and the one who you have been ordered to shoot on sight—is none other than the High Lord Kenneth himself: Kookie, *Sir!*

Alexei looks at Nikolai in total disbelief. "You can't be serious, bratan." Alexei scoffs at Nikolai.

"I'm afraid so, Master Commandant."

Sighing and shaking his head, Master Commandant Alexei says to his mole Nikolai, "I do not care to know *how* you know this for certain Nikolai, only that you *ARE* certain. You are absolutely sure that the High Lord Kenneth, Kookie, *your Lord*, is the traitor who we have been searching for. The one with the illegal device."

"Yes Master, I am certain."

"Very well then." After a brief pause, Alexei continues, "Now you listen to me, Nikolai. First, you must not breathe a word of this to *anyone!* And I do mean *anyone!* Next, I will have to speak to a few people on my own and decide how to proceed. This is a very difficult situation and could put us all in grave danger. So only a few of us are to know about it as we come up with a plan.

"A plan, sir?" asks Nikolai.

"*Da*, Nikolai, a plan. We must find out if there are others involved, who they are, and then decide how we are going to stop them. And make no mistake," Alexei adds with a seething anger welling up inside of him, "*WE **WILL** HAVE LORD KENNETH'S BLOOD!*"

Chapter 3 – Toxins

KENNY AND LISA ARE PREPARING FOR a large gathering. Everyone helps and scurries around with great excitement looking forward to the arrival of the Major, Vi, Kookie and Angie. Lisa has been baking bread and assorted pastries, making sure to include lots of chocolate chip cookies, Kookie's favorite. The Chrysalenes have created cozy living quarters, not only for themselves, but for all visitors coming to the farm.

Word has gotten around Bear River that the farm is blossoming with a promising harvest and a life-force from the Chrysalenes that seems to be spreading love and healing energy to the entire community. The new energy is especially welcome in this humble farming town that has nearly been abandoned since the Ebola outbreak.

The only one who seems to be somewhat leery of the goings on at the farm is the Center Overseer in the Bear River Center. Lisa, Kenny, Doc, Phil, Mimi and Ryan have been protective over the Chrysalenes getting too much "outside exposure." The friends certainly do not want to draw any attention to the UC regarding the fact that these are the same folks who survived the Ebola bioweapon and were marked for execution. So, the closer the Chrysalenes stay to the farm, and away from the bear River Center, the better.

Now that My Buddy has been restored as a communication device for the people, folks are happy to be able to message and speak to friends and family again. Of course, people are not aware of the tracking and other nefarious forces the UC is perpetrating through My Buddy; the Static Program being the most sinister force yet. The group at Bear River Farm knows more than most people about the activities of the UC, but nothing can prepare them for what they are soon to learn from the Major.

Doc is working in the front yard, so she is the first to see the Major and Vi when they pull up in his Autocar.

"Hey there! Hello, hello!" she waves and calls out to the two of them.

"Hey, yourself!" shouts Vi, jumping out of the Autocar, happy to see Doc.

"Come on out to the back and let everyone know you are here," Doc says as the three of them head toward the garden.

Everyone is excited to see the Major and Vi, and the friends shower the two with greetings, including little Suzie of the Seashells. She stands up on wobbly legs, toddles a few steps, flops down on the ground and crawls over to Vi.

"Well look at you, young lady!" Vi squeals with delight. "Taking your first few steps!" Suzie giggles and tries to toddle again, only to flop down and repeat the process.

"It's so good to see you both," says Mimi. "There is much to talk about and a lot that we have to do."

"Yes," says the Major. "And I am assuming that you have also invited Kookie and Angie?"

"Of course," says Mimi. "They should be here momentarily." No sooner does Mimi say those words when Angie arrives skipping merrily toward the group, with Kookie right behind her.

"Hi everyone! Hope we are on time!" she says.

"You sure are," says Lisa giving her friends a cheerful grin. "Just in time for a meal with our new farm family!"

Kookie is happy to hear such heartwarming words. He is especially relieved to be able to put his cares aside for the moment and just be in the wonderful company of these loving people, and eat all the chocolate chip cookies that he can stuff in his face!

Lisa and several others start bringing plates of food out from the cottage to the large outdoor tables. When everything is set out before them, the community of friends at Bear River Farm take their seats and bow their heads to observe a moment of silence.

Phil begins to chant softly, "Thank you Great Spirit for bringing us here, all together on your sacred land. We also thank the seedlings for the harvest that they will bring, and the Chrysalenes for the love that they give to us all."

With that, everyone digs into the feast of fruits, vegetables, nuts and seeds, soup, breads and all the sweet pastries imaginable. Water has been drawn straight from the well and tastes as delicious as the food.

While everyone is enjoying the food and fellowship, Kookie has a sudden moment of sadness drinking down the cool, clean water. He knows that it is going to take more than just his brain power alone to keep that water clean, sparkling, and pure. It is going to take a miracle.

* * *

Lady Liling is walking through her garden, thinking about leaving early in the morning for her trip to California. She is worried about what part the Council expects her, Kookie and Yakov to play in Operation Pied Piper, and how the three of them are going to implement their true plan while hiding it from the UC.

She is also thinking back to the last gathering the Lords and Ladies of the High Council had, not too long ago at the Great Dining Hall of the polar palace. While it seemed that the majority of the Lords and Ladies present were cheering enthusiastically for Operation Pied Piper to go into effect, not everyone appeared to be happy. Kookie, Yakov and Liling each made a mental note of which Lords and Ladies seemed *not* to be cheering very much, if at all. After that meeting when the three of them met again in Kookie's hot tub, they discussed who the less sympathetic ones to the Council seemed to be and made a list.

Liling knows that it is now time to track down those whom the three of them feel they can trust to help with Operation Monarch.

One such person is an old friend of theirs. Going back to the summer when Kookie blew his tuba mouthpiece furiously at the Major, there was one girl who tried to comfort Kookie before he let it rip. She asked him if he was okay, but he didn't answer. Lady Liling saw that same woman at the Great Dining Hall and remembered that her name was Neely. Neely was *not* one of those who was cheering over Operation Pied Piper.

Well, regardless of whatever the Council is expecting of us, we have our own agenda to fulfill. And that includes gathering and organizing a team of our own, like-minded Lords and Ladies, Liling thinks to herself.

One of Liling's house servants, Bi (pronounced Bee), comes out to the garden to let her know that dinner is ready. "Will you be taking your dinner out here My Lady or will you be eating in the dining room?" Bi politely inquires of her.

"I think I would like to have my dinner out here this evening. Thank you for asking." Lady Liling says, speaking most kindly to her servant.

The woman retreats into the kitchen to arrange for Liling's dinner to be served in the garden, when suddenly there is a flutter of butterflies overhead. Liling is astounded as they come right over, gently fluttering all around her. Feeling the Monarchs' energy with her powerful intuitive skills, she can sense they are trying to tell her something. She closes her eyes, places her hands over her chest and asks them if they have a message for her. Liling hears the following, in her heart:

Human creature, I am Angel. We have come here to give you an urgent message.

With her eyes closed, Liling bows her head and raises her hands up to the Monarchs saying, "What is your message, sweet Angel of the sky?"

Toxins, human creature. Many toxins. Toxic earth, toxic food, toxic water, toxic sounds, but worst of all, toxic air. The air that comes out of the mouths of a few, fearful human creatures is very, very toxic. It is forming toxic words, telling other human creatures to fly out of windows. Only, they cannot fly as we do; they do not have wings. If they leap from a window, they will die. If the toxic words from the mouths of fearful human creatures does not stop, then flying out of windows will not stop either.

Although Liling already knows that this has been coming since Lord Ekene's announcement at the Great Dining Hall, it does not prepare her emotionally for hearing that is has now come to pass. She falls to her knees, weeping and praying:

"Here me Kuan Yin, goddess of compassion, mercy and kindness. I beseech you with all of my heart to show me the way—the way to stop this madness of the fearful ones, the way to bring your sacred spirit back into the hearts of people everywhere. Teach us kind Mother. I pray that you be with us; with Kookie, Yakov and me, and guide us to your way, the way of love."

A voice answers and Liling hears it in her heart. It is whispering to her softly saying:

Fear not, for I Am with you; do not be dismayed, for I Am your God. I will strengthen you and help you; I will uphold you with my righteous right hand.[2]

The Monarchs also hear the voice and begin to dance with great joy and Liling's sorrowful tears turn into tears of gratitude. Reaching up to the sky all she can say is, "Thank you . . . thank you . . . thank you . . .

* * *

Dinner is beginning to wind down at the Bear River Farm Gathering. The mood is turning somber because they must turn to the serious matters at hand and what has brought them all together. Mimi can sense that the time is ready for them to begin. She stands up slowly to address everyone.

---

[2] Isaiah 41:10

"Thank you, Lisa, for a wonderful meal, and to all of our friends gathered here. I would like to begin by saying that if it weren't for the Major and Kookie, the Chrysalenes gathered here and the ones at Judy's farm would not be alive today, not to mention myself. And for that," she turns to the two men, "you both have our deepest gratitude and love."

All eyes are on Kookie, Angie, the Major and Vi with an outpouring of love radiating to them from every heart present.

Mimi continues, "There is a matter of great urgency which we need to discuss and why the four of you have been called here. One thing in particular is something that we have only learned recently." Holding up a packet of seeds, Mimi says, "These are the new seeds which have replaced the old ones. They are the seeds that farmers everywhere have been ordered to plant, supposedly because the old ones caused the Ebola outbreak, and the new ones are alleged to be healthy and disease free. But when these seeds came to us the other day, through the Chrysalenes they have told us quite another story."

Kookie, Angie, the Major and Vi are all listening, fully enraptured.

"Yes," Mimi says with sadness in her voice. "They told us that they are in terrible physical pain from the toxic chemicals that have been infused into them and emotional pain because they know that once harvested, their fruit will cause untold suffering to others."

The four who are hearing this for the first time are flabbergasted and saddened to hear about the physical and emotional pain of the seeds.

"Oh my! Good heavens! What can we do?" are the reactions heard around the table.

"Well," says Mimi, "that is why we have brought you all here." Turning to Doc, Mimi asks, "Doc, would you like to continue?"

"Sure Mimi," Doc says. She stands to address Kookie and the Major. "What you two have done so far is nothing short of a miracle. And a good part of that has to do with Metatron and the 369-Program. So, here are my thoughts. If there is some way that you can maybe use 369, or something, to do to the chemically treated seeds what you did to the live Ebola bioweapon, well, then . . .”

“*WHOA!*” Kookie and the Major jump out of their seats and shout a bunch of head-slapping, *DOH* comments.

Kookie says, “Oh, of course! Why didn’t I think of that?”

“Yeah genius!” the Major snips at him, “Having a brain fart perhaps?”

Everyone starts to laugh and Mimi and Doc smile at each other. Mimi says to Doc, “I guess they must have figured the rest of it out!”

“Ya’ *think?*” says Doc, tongue in cheek.

Angie is overflowing with gratitude watching Kookie truly happy and hopeful for the first time since she has known him.

The Major turns to Vi and says, “This might be an answer to the problem that I am having about following my father’s dreadful orders regarding distribution of the neurotoxins to the Center Coffeehouses.”

“Yes, it does!” Vi responds with enthusiasm.

“*Neurotoxins?* At the *Coffeehouses?*” voices quip around the table.

Everyone quiets down again as the Major reveals his news. “As part of Operation Pied Piper, Howard Pharmaceuticals has created two neurotoxic chemical cocktails. One is to be added to the tea cakes and the other is for the juices. Basically, one will be targeting the adult and youth population while the other will be targeting primarily—” he pauses for a moment before saying his next words, “young children, and . . . babies.”

Hanging his head down in shame and fighting back tears that are stuck in his throat, Vi takes his hands in hers and says, “It’s all right Major, just remember who you truly are.”

“And just who am I, Vi? Truly,” asks the Major in a sullen voice, still staring at the ground.

For the moment, Kookie has joined him in a floor-staring contest.

"You, Master John, and you too, Lord Kenneth, are both—" Vi stands and holds her hands up to the heavens, "*Most* righteous Men,"

Rising to her feet, Angie says, "Amen, Sister!"

Everyone else, one by one, stands up, holds their hands out to Kookie and the Major and says, *"AMEN, BROTHERS!"*

Vi and Angie put their arms around their respective men, both of whom are hanging their heads down and staring at the floor. Giving the two men a moment to process their thoughts, the group leaves them alone and begins to clean up the tables.

When everything has been cleared away, Mimi picks up Eve Elli and places her on the center table. "And now," Mimi says with much grandmother-pride, "My granddaughter, Eve Elli, has her own announcement to make. Go for it, sweetie!"

"Hi everybody!" she giggles. "The Chrysalenes have something special for everyone. We will now sing our songs for you!" Eve Elli starts them off, and then the sweetest, most gentle voices come out of their mouths, singing in tones that can only be described as a choir of angels. There are no words, only sweet harmonies, as each Chrysalene voice joins in, blends with the others, and flows with sounds of beauty and love. Mimi, Ryan, Doc, Phil, Kenny, Lisa, Kookie, Angie, the Major, Vi, and even little Suzie of the Seashells listen in complete adoration. The pure, cleansing air emanating from the mouths of the Chrysalenes brings a peaceful healing to all.

Kookie in particular is enthralled and feels that he simply must join in. He excuses himself and moments later returns with his tuba.

"*Oh Kookie!*" Angie beams.

"Oh *Lord!*" the Major snorts, rolling his eyes and shaking his head.

Kookie adds his tuba tones to the angelic voices of heaven.

Later, as the revelry calms down for the evening, the Chrysalenes retire to their dwellings, and the others go inside Lisa and Kenny's cottage. Phil asks Eve Jasmine to take Suzie for a little while so he can join the group inside. Lisa gets busy preparing a few flasks of coffee and a fresh plate of fruit and pastries. They all know that there are serious decisions to be made, plans to be laid out, and strategies to devise before the night is over. The first thing that everyone wants to know is what Kookie can do with Metatron and how fast he can do it.

"First," Kookie explains to everyone, "I will need some samples of the neurotoxins, either in their pure form or the organisms containing the biochemical toxins that have been implanted in the seeds."

Lisa says, "I can give you all of the packets of seeds that I brought back with me from the Center Market the other day."

Kookie nods and Lisa retrieves the bag of seed packets.

"Next, I will need a sample of the neurotoxins that are going to be infused into the Coffeehouse tea cakes and juices."

The Major tells him, "I will be at our Silver Beach plant tomorrow and can get a sample for you then."

"Works for me," says Kookie. "Once I have the actual biological material in some form, I can program 369 to, you know, do its thing."

"Really? Is it that simple?" asks the Major in astonishment.

Kookie looks at the cciling and sighs, to which the Major replies. "Yes, yes of course it is!"

Angie and Vi are enjoying themselves watching the two men engage in their youthful banter.

Mimi asks the Major, "So what were you saying earlier about the distribution problem with your father?"

"Ah yes! Well, I have been sent by Master Howard to Silver Beach to arrange for distribution of the neurotoxins throughout all three Continental Territories of One World. A whole shipment is expected to be released tomorrow from our Silver Beach plant. However, I can create a postponement for a day or so while Kookie *does his thing*, hopefully, to come up with a 369-Program that will neutralize the toxins before distribution."

Everyone is intrigued and hopeful as the Major continues, "If Kookie can genetically alter the toxins that will be sent out to the Center Coffeehouses, then no one from the UC, especially the Council will suspect, at least for the time being that what they are putting into their tea cakes and juice is completely harmless. I will then be able to set in motion the same sort of distribution process that we normally do when we don't want the Centers to know what they are working with. And no one will be the wiser."

As the Major speaks, he begins to hang his head down again, going quiet and staring at the floor.

Vi interrupts him. "Major, one day I really hope you will let go of the guilt you are carrying for the things you had no control over in the past. Just remember that you now have the freedom to be the righteous man that we all know you truly are."

Sighing deeply the Major looks at her, gives her a faint smile and says softly, "Okay. Thank you, Violet."

Phil is next to speak. "I will help Doc spread the word to the farmers about *not* destroying the old seeds or the seedlings that are already planted and growing."

Kenny chimes in, "I'm sure it will be safer to use the pigeons for anything to do with Operation Monarch instead of the open channels of communication with My Buddy. I can also breed more of the homing pigeons; whatever we need."

Kookie takes his turn to address the group. "Tomorrow I am meeting with Yakov and Liling at our secret gathering place. I will bring them up to date on everything we have discussed here and see what ideas they have come up with. Also, there is one thing the three of us talked about before we left the Gathering of the High Lords of the Council at the polar palace."

"What was that?" asks Angie.

"We watched the expressions on the faces of the Lords and Ladies at the Great Dining Hall and the three of us talked about it afterwards in confidence. There definitely appeared to be some who were not so enthused about the idea of Operation Pied Piper and who seemed to be more in sympathy with our own feelings. We made a list of those whom we might need to get in touch with afterwards. I am sure Yakov and Liling are probably thinking the same thing at this point; that we need to reach out to those who might be willing to join us. Only it will have to be done with great caution, as I'm sure you all can imagine."

Ryan has been listening to the conversation quietly yet intently, this whole time. He speaks up. "I love the gardening that we are doing here, but," he looks at Mimi and continues, "I think there is also another way that Mimi and I can both be of service to our people, if you would be willing, my darling."

"Um, wow. What do you have in mind, sweetie?" she asks him.

"Well, since we, or I should say, *you,* did such a great job at the part we played at Howard Pharmaceuticals in Silver Beach the last time we were there, I, um, that is to say . . ."

Mimi smiles, knowing where her wonderful Man is going with all of this. "Since they already know us and think we are, like actual servants of the plant, and they know that we are connected with the Major, and my awesome Woman Mimi here put her self-cloaking talents to great use, well, um, I think we would make some, you know, that is, some great, ass-kicking moles!"

"*AMEN!*" the whole table thunders, bursting into a round of applause. Mimi is beside herself with laughter and says to Ryan, "I guess that settles it then, honey. Assuming of course that the Major is okay with it," she says glancing at him.

"You know I can't ask the two of you to risk your lives that way."

Ryan walks over to the Major and looks him square in the eye (something he does not do with people often). "Sir, as you and Kookie have pledged your lives to us, and have risked your lives for us, and have been doing your best to help us, all people, everywhere, throughout One World, you both have taught me what it means to be a righteous man. And sir, (Ryan is now staring at the floor) I wish to become a righteous man like you and Kookie."

The Major is deeply touched in his heart. He looks around at everyone else, also deeply moved and then puts his hands on Ryan's shoulders, "My good man, you *are* a most righteous man, *sir.*"

Mimi moves over to them, smiling and with tears of gratitude. The Major warmly says to them both, "We will leave for Silver Beach in the morning."

* * *

Having received his orders from Master Commandant Alexei, Nikolai, the Overseer Groundskeeper of Kookie's Kastle, and mole for the Council, is out on the estate grounds doing his gardening. He has heard that Lord Kenneth is away on business for a few days, which is giving him some time to consider what the Commandant has said to him; that taking Kookie down is going to be a delicate business. And if a mistake is made, Nikolai knows that it could cost them all dearly.

Nikolai understands just how smart Kookie is, having worked for him many, many years now. He was planted there by the Council when he was quite young, as one of PA, ES and SPA's sleeper agents. Unbeknownst to the Lords and Ladies of the Council, each and every one of them has a sleeper agent arranged by PA, ES and SPA living amongst them. The Council and their associates just do not trust anyone. They are as fearful as they are greedy.

Nikolai is trimming the hedges of Angie's veranda when suddenly he notices something that has been sitting right there in front of him ever since Kookie showed up not too long ago with this young woman.

He puts his gardening tools down and takes a closer look. He opens the door of the pigeon coop and looks inside. Then Nikolai sees it, and the seeds of a plan begin to formulate in his brain as to how he is going to take Kookie down. Nikolai holds the two pigeons in his hands, looking at the little leg bands with the markings #3 and #4.

Smiling to himself he thinks, *homing pigeons, eh? Ha ha, you sly devil, you! Well, two can play at this game!*

Chapter 4 – Voices

YAKOV RECEIVED KOOKIE'S MESSAGE to join him and Lady Liling at their usual secret gathering place. There was something urgent in Kookie's tone, more so than Yakov would expect. Something in Yakov's gut tells him to arrive early and do some snooping around, so he arrives the night before they all meet.

Their secret gathering place is actually the same Kabin where Alexei and Nikolai met the other day, in the heavily wooded area on the grounds of Kookie's large estate. Kookie does not know that anyone other than the three of them and a select handful of his staff including Nikolai, is aware of his private Kabin and he certainly does not know that anyone was there recently.

Kookie's Kabin has six bedrooms and all the comforts of a luxurious home, so Yakov knows it will take some time for him to check things out. He lights a fire in the cozy living room, which offers him comfort as well as light. Yakov feels serene as he settles down with a few provisions. He goes to Kookie's favorite ultra-plush overstuffed chair in front of the hearth to snuggle in, eat, relax, and meditate before combing his way through the Kabin.

During his meditation, Yakov is so at ease that he is beginning to think he might be making a fuss over nothing. He falls asleep and begins to dream . . .

He is walking through a field of corn. The corn is large, lush, golden, and very sweet. Yakov breaks off an ear and chomps into it. He continues walking through the sunny cornfield until he comes to a hut. Upon entering the hut, he sees a hole in the ground with a ladder descending into it. Suddenly the sky outside of the hut darkens and Yakov is aware of a red glow coming from the bottom of the dark hole. He is instantly gripped with a fear of going down there, but cannot stop himself from doing so. When he is on the last few rungs of the ladder, he hears a low, growling voice coming toward him. Through the grunts and growls of the deep voice he is able to make out two words:

"DO IT! . . . DO IT! . . . DO IT!"

Yakov wants to dash back up the ladder but he cannot; he is frozen and helpless as the angry voice slowly approaches.

"DO IT! . . . DO IT! . . . DO IT! . . ."

Yakov cries out, "REVEAL YOURSELF, OH HORRID BEAST!!" and the growling turns to snarling, and to groaning, and then to sinister laughter. Like a flash of violent lightening, a red-eyed beast jumps into Yakov's face, letting out a blood-curdling scream.

Yakov wakes up with a jolt that nearly knocks him out of the overstuffed chair. He is shaking, out of breath and his heart is pounding.

Talking out loud to himself in Russian he yells: *"WHAT THE *&%$ WAS THAT!?"*

Yakov decides that he must indeed check out the house room by room as soon as his heart rate calms down. It has gotten dark outside while Yakov was sleeping, and he feels it would be better not to turn on all the lights in the Kabin and risk his presence to be known.

He uses the light from his Lord's Communication Device to do his search. Everything seems to be okay, and nothing is out of order. He knows that the servants come in to clean the place and keep it stocked with provisions on a regular basis, so the Kabin is always ready to receive Kookie, Yakov and Liling. After doing a thorough search, he fixes himself a light snack. As he starts to throw out his trash in the kitchen trash bin, he notices a candy wrapper from the gourmet chocolates Kookie keeps stocked in both the Kabin and his Kastle. He reaches down into the bin and pulls out the wrapper.

I guess one of the servants decided to munch on this Yakov thinks to himself. *Can't say that I blame him or her . . . wait, what's this?*

Yakov notices something stuck under the candy wrapper that is most definitely *not* chocolate. Touching it and smelling it, he detects a small piece of dried out . . . *bacon?*

Hm, he thinks to himself, *now what the devil is bacon doing here? In fact, it doesn't even look like regular bacon, more like the kind we get from those out-in-the-field dehydrated packages of stuff . . . What the? Where is that dumpster outside?*

Yakov steps outside to the dumpster shed using the door at the back of the pantry. In the starlight the little shed reminds him of the hut that he just dreamed about, causing him to feel a bit uneasy. Turning on the light of his Lord's Communication Device, Yakov opens the door to the dumpster shed. He removes the round lid from the dumpster bin, which also reminds him of the dream and going down into the dark hut hole, disturbing him a little more. He peers down into the darkness of the black, plastic-lined bin, and sees what looks like recent food trash amidst a red metallic container. The shiny red container flashes at him when the light of his device hits it, and he sees familiar Slavic writing on the side.

Good grief! Okay, Yakov thinks to himself as he bends over all the way down into the bin to dig out the container. He takes it out of the shed to get a better look at it and instantly recognizes what it is before reading the label.

As a High Lord Commandant of a commando unit, Yakov has seen plenty of these boxes. It is a dehydrated meal box for commandos on duty. There is still a little bit of food left in it, including a couple of small, chopped pieces of bacon.

Yakov's jaw drops while holding the edible remains inside a red Slavic commando food ration box, completely unable to wrap his brain around what he has stumbled upon. He takes the box back into the Kabin and places it in a storage bag thinking *I will deal with this one in the morning. My brain cannot handle any more for one night!*

Yakov gets into bed, although by no means does he fall asleep.

* * *

The next morning, Kookie and Angie pull up to the Kastle. As they are about to enter using his private entrance it occurs to him that Angie has never come in by the front entryway. This means that she has never heard his front door greetings.

"There is something I would like to show you. It's at the front entrance to the Kastle," Kookie says.

"Okay," Angie responds with curiosity, realizing that she has not yet been to that part of the Kastle.

When they get to the front entryway, Kookie says, "Okay, now ring the doorbell."

"The what?"

"The doorbell," he says, pointing it out to her.

"Yes, Kookie I can see where it is. I just didn't know that a castle has a doorbell."

"This one does," he says smiling.

"Okay," Angie smirks and rings the thing. First, she hears a moment of celestial music which is followed by a soft voice saying, *Step inside, the Lord will see you today.*

"Oh for heaven's sake!" she says laughing.

Kookie presses a button on his Lord's Communication Device and says, "Okay, ring it again," so, she does.

This time there is the crackling sound of something burning followed by a deep voice saying, "Take off your sandals, for the place where you are standing is holy ground.[3] The Lord is awaiting your arrival."

"Oh, for crying out loud!" Angie howls.

---

[3] Exodus 3:5 NIV

Then Kookie presses the button again and grinning says, "I think you will like this one."

More angelic music followed by a soft female voice says, "Step inside and follow the light to the end of the tunnel. The Lord is waiting for you."

Laughing out loud, Angie says to him, "Well just how many of those *doorbell greetings* do you have?"

Still grinning Kookie says, "How many would you like, my dear?"

Busting out laughing Angie manages to say, "Oh, you silly man!"

High Lord Kookie taps the tips of his fingers together, beaming with an ear-to-ear grin. He is well pleased with himself.

"Can we go inside now?" Angie asks Kookie. They both enter the Kastle, getting ready for the day ahead.

* * *

Liling is just arriving at the Kabin. She is full of hope and anxious to meet her High Lord Brothers, Kookie and Yakov. Upon entering the Kabin she smells the rich, fragrant aroma of roast turkey with roasted vegetables and roasted potatoes, usual fair for the Lords. The UC are the only meat eaters in One World while the rest of the people are all vegan. Yakov is quite the chef and enjoys preparing his own food whenever he has the time, or when the occasion calls for it. And today, the time and the occasion are both calling for it.

They greet each other in a mixture of their own languages.

"Hello Yakov. My, that does smell wonderful! Is our host here yet?" asks Liling.

"Hi there Liling! Thank you! Kookie isn't here yet, but he should be momentarily."

They hear voices outside and know that Kookie has arrived. But who is the other voice, they wonder?

Kookie walks in with Angie and says "Hey there everyone! Mmm! Yummy! That smells great, Yakov! May I introduce to you my recruit? Her name is Angie. Angie, this is Liling and Yakov."

"Hello Angie. Recruit?" Liling says with a giggle, glancing at Kookie.

"Hello Angie, that's some *recruit Bratan*'!" Yakov says, raising his eyebrows at Kookie.

"Yes, she is," says Kookie, smiling and tapping the tips of his fingers together.

"Bratan?" Angie ask Kookie

"Ah yes, my dear. That's Russian for Bro'," he replies.

"My *dear?*" Yakov inquires. "Is that a new English word for recruit?"

They all chuckle.

The four of them sit down to eat, and Angie is blown away at the combined language she is listening to around the table. It is as if they are speaking one language together and yet it is all three languages, and all at the same time. For her benefit, Kookie, Yakov and Liling are using more hand gestures than they normally would and exaggerating some of their words and facial expressions, and to Angie's surprise, she is able to follow the thread of the conversation. Then an amusing thought occurs to her as she speaks up to the Lords and Lady.

"You three are really amazing," she says, "and I thank you so much for allowing me to be a part of your company."

They all look at her with much affection replying in unison, "You are welcome, pazhalusta,[4]and bu keqi."[5]

"I just wanted to say that I am completely amazed listening to all of you speaking together in a blend of all three languages."

They all chuckle thinking about how their uni-language of Russian, Chinese and English evolved over their years together. Since they were

---

[4] *Russian for "You're welcome."*
[5] *Chinese for "You're welcome."*

children, Kookie, Yakov and Liling always wanted to use their own special language with each other, never wanting to use the Universal Translator that all Lords and Ladies are given. It is a sign of great respect among all the Lords and Ladies to speak to each other "naturally" as they refer to it, rather than relying completely on the Universal Translator.

"So, I have been sitting here listening to you all and come up with a new word for what I am hearing."

"Oh?" They all look inquisitively at her.

"Yes," Angie says "the word is *Slavachinglish.*"

They all laugh out loud. "Well, that's better than some of the things *we* have called it over the years!" says Yakov.

As they finish their meal, all four of them know that the discussion to follow will take on a more serious tone. Kookie is the first one to break the ice. "Okay," he says. "May I have your Lord's Communication Devices, please?" Yakov and Liling dutifully take out their devices and place them on the table.

"As you know," Kookie says to them, "We are all quite safe here in the Kabin from the mole implants in our bodies, since we are surrounded by all the trees and heavy foliage. However, now that our work is about to get, shall we say, riskier and more dangerous, we cannot afford any more exposure of this sort."

He picks up the devices including his own, one at a time. Next, he takes out his Metatron device and proceeds to block the incoming and outgoing mole transmitter signals from all three of them. He adds, "And with your permission, I feel it is best to destroy the moles that are in our bodies, as well."

"Oh yes, Kookie! Please do!" says Liling.

"Can't wait to get rid of the thing!" says Yakov.

"Good grief!" says Angie, hearing about this for the first time.

Kookie has them stand up one at a time and scans their bodies with Metatron. At first there is a red flashing light. Then he activates the 369-Program, scanning them again and the red flashing light turns to a slow pulsating green. Next, he turns it on himself and does the same thing. "Well, my friends we are now free." They all let out a grateful sigh, until Yakov realizes that it is time to bring out *his* news.

"Well," Yakov sighs, "we are not exactly free just yet."

Looking bewildered Liling says, "Why? What do you mean, Yakov?" Yakov leaves the table to retrieve the storage bag from last night.

* * *

Across One World in all three Continental Territories, three terminals activate. The incoming message is from ES and it is acknowledged and accepted by PA and SPA.

ES: Esteemed Brethren and fellow High Ones, it is with most urgent news that I am calling upon you today.

PA: What is it ES?

SPA: Yes, fellow High One. What seems to be the trouble?

ES: Only moments ago I learned that there has been a breach in our security system.

SPA: Dear oh dear, esteemed Brother!

PA: Oh my, Brother! However did *that* happen?

SPA: What exactly has happened?

PA: Yes. Do tell!

ES: We are not exactly sure yet. Something about three moles.

SPA: What about them ES?

ES: Well, my Brethren, they seem to have been terminated!

PA: Oh my! How simply shocking!

SPA: Yes, yes! I daresay. Simply shocking!

PA: Does anyone know *who* the moles were and *where* they were terminated?

ES: They were AI moles, and the location is somewhere in Panamerica, but our technical team has so far been unable to determine where.

SPA: Dear oh dear, Brethren. AI moles. How *terribly* dreadful is that? Had they been slave moles, you know, those Overseer slaves that we use sometimes, that would have been alright, useless eaters that they are. But AIs! Now *that* is just a *terrible waste!* Quite unacceptable!

PA: Quite! Well, we ought to put our Lords on it right away then.

ES: Oh yes, in fact, perhaps that very bright, ambitious young Lord of *your* Continental Territory Brother SPA, would be the right one to lead up a team for an investigation. You know, young Lord Ekene.

SPA: Why yes, I do believe he is the right choice to take care of things. A very good idea, Brother ES.

PA: Truly.

SPA: Very well then, I shall get in touch with his HOC right way.

ES: Oh yes Brethren. This cannot be tolerated. Imagine, someone destroying three perfectly good AI moles! Such insubordination shall not be tolerated!

PA: No, it shall not be tolerated!

ES: Very well then, it is done. Signing off for now.

The three Highest of the Council, PA, ES and SPA disconnect. They are indignant and determined to track down the "killer" of the three Artificial Intelligence moles.

* * *

Yakov opens the storage bag and reveals the contents to the other three. "What is that?" asks Liling. "And where did it come from?"

"It is a Slavic meal box, typically issued to commandos out on an assignment. There is some leftover food in it which looks to be no more than about 24-48 hours old, considering that it does not smell bad yet and it still looks somewhat fresh," says Yakov.

"So, where did it come from?" asks Kookie.

Yakov looks at him with a worried expression on his face. "From your dumpster right behind the kitchen pantry, my Brother," he says pointing to the kitchen. "I also found a piece of bacon stuck to the bottom of this chocolate candy wrapper, right here in your kitchen trash bin, Kookie."

They all stare at each other in silence.

Finally, Yakov says, "It looks as if we still have a mole problem. "

"So it does," says Kookie, lost in thought staring at the meal box.

Angie has an idea. "That is a metallic wrapping on the box, is it not?" she asks Yakov.

"Yes, it is," he replies.

"May I have it please?" she asks him.

Yakov hands Angie the Slavic meal box and she immediately places it against her chest.

Liling asks Yakov if she can have the candy wrapper and sits down directly in front of Angie. They both close their eyes. Angie begins to feel the energy coming from the box, and Liling feels the energy coming from the candy wrapper.

"Wings," Liling says. "But not flying."

"Angry, very angry!" Angie says. "I'm hearing . . . angry words."

"Sad, very sad." Liling continues. "A voice is saying, *NO. I will not hurt them!*"

"They killed him! They killed him!" Angie cries out.

"I will not harm them, no, I will not harm them," Liling whispers sadly.

"They killed . . . D– D– Dimitri!" says Angie.

"I am #3 . . . I am #4 . . . Love you, Angie! He . . . Will . . . *not hurt you!*" says Liling.

Both women open their eyes and see the two men staring wide-eyed at them.

"Good job, ladies," says Kookie, and to Yakov asks, "Who is Dimitri?

Yakov responds, "Who's #3 and #4?"

"Dimitri was my second-in-command, a Master and very pro-Council. From what Angie just said, I guess he is no longer among us. He has a brother, Alexei, also a Master Commandant, and also very pro-Council."

Yakov takes out his Lord's Communications Device and opens up a bio-assessment program. "May I have that box please, Angie?"

Yakov enters Alexei's ID information along with a scan of the box into the bio-assessment program. The two match and Yakov is able to positively identify the box as being recently used by Master Commandant Alexei.

"It is him. It is Alexei. He was here, Kookie, not 24 hours ago!"

Kookie closes his eyes, "How can that be? And what about #3 and #4?" Looking at Angie while speaking to Yakov and Liling he says, "They are our homing pigeons."

Then it hits all four of them at once, as Kookie says the words that they are all thinking: "I have a mole in my Kastle, and he or she is apparently Slavic."

"And he or she has been touching our birds!" says Angie, greatly annoyed.

"So, I guess one of the tasks before us it to figure out who the mole is," says Kookie.

"Yes," agrees Liling, "And the other task before us is to gather our forces. I brought the list of those who seemed to be like-minded Lords and Ladies from our last Gathering at the Great Dining Hall."

"Good work, Liling! Thank you, Sister!" Kookie and Yakov both chime in together.

"And *I* want to know who's been messing with my birds!" Angie snarls.

"Well," says Kookie, "I guess we'll just have to find out who that nasty bird meddler is now, won't we!"

Everyone is grateful for a chuckle.

Yakov and Liling look at each other for a moment before turning to Kookie and blurting out, "PIGEONS?"

* * *

The Major, Vi, Mimi and Ryan have just arrived at the Howard Pharmaceuticals plant in Silver Beach. On the way over they discussed their plans and are clear about what each one of them must do.

"Are you sure that you will all be okay once I leave here?" the Major asks nervously.

"Yes, yes, we'll be fine," Vi says.

"We're okay," Ryan agrees.

"We got this covered," Mimi insists.

"Okay then," the Major sighs, as he takes them all into the plant.

Once inside the main lobby they are greeted by the Security Overseer. "Hello Master John, sir. How goes everything with you?"

"Fine my man, just fine," the Major responds to him cordially.

"Sure glad that whole business with Ebola is over and done with Master, yes indeed!"

"Yes, my man, it is good to be over with the Ebola *business*. I need you to take these three folks over to the dwelling units. They will be serving us here for a little while. So be sure to get them situated in a couple of dwellings. This man and this woman served here not too long ago, but I needed them at our main headquarters. You are to give them a dwelling together. And this other woman will be needing a garden unit since she is doing some work for me with these birds that she has brought with her."

"Oh my, yes! Yes, indeed, Master," the Security Overseer is smiling at the pigeons. "I will be sure to get *everyone* situated, just right!"

"Good," the Major replies, and turning to Vi, Ryan and Mimi he says, "Why don't you folks go with this good man, let him get you all settled in and then come and meet me back at my office."

"Yes, Master John," they all say together, trying not to appear too familiar with the Major in front of the Security Overseer.

They are taken to the dwellings, and for a moment Mimi is emotionally taken back to the last time she was here. She knew that it was not going to be easy coming back to this place; the place where she almost saw her precious Elli and family killed right in front of her. But she is also determined to "follow the course" as the Indian Paintbrush have continuously reminded her. She is carrying all her precious flowers with her now since they are about to descend into an underworld of espionage.

* * *

"After we finish going over the list, I would like all of us to go back to my Kastle. We can feed some misinformation to the mole and give the impression that we are doing the Council's bidding," suggests Kookie, "And I would really like the two of you to snoop around."

"Sounds like an excellent idea, Kookie. Besides, I would love to meet #3 and #4," Liling says with much affection.

"And I would *love* to get my hands on, I mean *meet,* the person who left this chocolate candy wrapper!" says Yakov.

"Something I don't understand here," Angie says to Yakov. "If you can uncover the identity of Alexei with your, what's it called, bio-assessment program, then why can't you do the same with the candy wrapper?"

"I will show you," Yakov says, scanning the candy wrapper and showing Angie the screen.

"Whoa!" she says, in amazement. "It's just pulsating green, like . . ."

"Like the mole himself does not even exist at all," Yakov says. "And that is the power bestowed upon a very special kind of mole."

"Very special?" asks Angie.

"Yes, one who has been planted in the house of a Lord by the evil and corrupt forces of the Council itself."

"OH KOOKIE!" Angie cries, looking at him. *"That's just terrible!"*

But before Angie can think another fearful thought a voice in her head says, *fear no evil, for I Am with you.*

Then the thought comes to her. 'Self-cloaking! WHOA!"

"WHAT?" they all shout out at Angie.

Looking directly at Kookie, Angie smiles and says, "I think you will like this one, my dear!"

They all raise their eyebrows in anticipation of what Angie is about to tell them, and Kookie is grinning and tapping his fingertips together.

* * *

Two communication devices are pulsating. The incoming message is accepted by the other one.

"Any word yet, Nikolai?"

"Yes, Master Alexei. The Lord and his companion have returned, but they did not stay for very long. When I asked around, one of the Lord's personal servants said that Lord Kenneth told him he had some business to attend to and would return shortly."

"Did you arrange things, Nikolai? The things we discussed?"

"Yes, Master Commandant. Everything is all set and ready to go."

"Excellent. Let me know as soon as . . . you know . . . anything happens."

"I certainly shall."

Master Commandant Alexei and Nikolai the Overseer Groundskeeper of Kookie's Kastle, disconnect.

* * *

"Come on in!" the Major says to the Security Overseer who is knocking on the door of his office.

"I have shown all of these new servants to their dwellings, Master. And here they are, all ready to serve you and Howard Pharmaceuticals."

"Thank you, my good man, thank you. You may leave now."

As the Security Overseer returns to his front lobby duty, Vi, Mimi and Ryan step into the Major's private office and exhale. The Major looks at them with caution in his eyes, looking back and forth between them and the security camera in one of the corners hanging from the ceiling. They simply nod at him, remembering the drill that they all went through with him on the way over. Using his most Masterly, Master John voice, the Major says to them, "Well now, my good people. Welcome to the Howard Pharmaceutical plant at Silver Beach, Oregon."

"Thank you, Master John. Thank you for the opportunity to serve you and Howard Pharmaceuticals. It is a privilege to serve you, Master," they each say in turn.

All four of them are playing their parts well.

"Thank you," he says with a nod, a trace of a smile, and at Vi a sparkle in his eye. "Your help is most needed in packaging and shipping. As you know, we ship our products to all three Continental Territories all over One World. Right now, we are short-handed at a time when we have lots of shipping to do, so I will need you all to work as quickly as you can. You will be a part of our shipping team. We will be shipping flavor enhancing additives to our warehouses everywhere, with the ultimate destination of the Center Coffeehouses across the globe!"

Their pre-arranged dialogue continues:

"Wow! I am so excited to be a part of something so big and so important!" says Vi.

"Me too!" says Mimi.

"Yup!" says Ryan.

"And I will be coming by periodically to make sure that everything is in order, especially in the quality control department."

"Oh, my yes! Yes, indeed!" exclaims Vi.

"Yes, indeed!!" chirps Mimi.

"Indeed! Indeed!" squawks Ryan.

As the Major is listening to all the chirping and squawking, he finds it difficult to keep a straight face. He covers his mouth with his two hands until he is able to say to his dearest friends, the chirping trio, "Okay, let's go down to the shipping department, then."

* * *

"Let me explain it to you," says Angie. "It is something that our friend Vi taught us, and it has helped us avoid quite a bit of trouble so far. It is called self-cloaking, and before we leave here, I would like to teach the three of you how we do it."

"Self-cloaking," says Liling. "That sounds familiar. Like something I once learned from a Tai Chi Master. From what I understand it has been used by many cultures, many teachings and various practices down through the ages."

"I wouldn't be surprised about that," says Angie, "And that is really great because it means that you and I can both teach the men."

"Agreed!" says Liling enthusiastically. "So let us discuss the list and then we can practice self-cloaking."

All nod in agreement and Liling proceeds with her plan. "As I'm sure you both recall, my Brothers, during the Gathering at the Great Dining Hall, when Lord Ekene revealed his plans for Operation Pied Piper, most of the Lords and Ladies cheered and chanted wildly."

The painful memory of this causes Liling to be still for a moment and the three of them to bow their heads. Angie has much compassion for them and can only imagine what it must feel like to be raised in such a way, with so much fear of and disdain for one's fellow humans.

Liling continues, "But there were also those present whom we all noticed were not cheering so enthusiastically, if at all. And it gave us enough hope at the time to remember who those Lords and Ladies were, and to write their names down afterwards. And so," she produces the hand-written list from her pouch, in a loving gesture as if were a sacred scroll, "here it is."

Liling passes the list around for Kookie and Yakov to refresh their memories and for Angie to look at as well. Angie sees there are exactly 36 names on the list and doing her 369 observation she says to everyone, "Well then, it seems we have another example of the power of 369."

"What are you talking about?" asks Kookie who is intrigued by what Angie is driving at.

"Thirty-six, plus the three of you here. That could be seen as a kind of 3-6-9, yes?"

Kookie thinks about it for a moment and smiling to himself, he says, "Yes, I do see the possibilities." Glancing at the three of them he says, "We need to get in touch with every single one of our peers, in the true sense of the word, and form a secret alliance. Each one of us must pick and choose who we are going to contact and set about doing that immediately. Then we must call for a gathering of our allies. With our combined knowledge, connections, technology, and most of all, love for humanity, we can form a strong and effective Alliance."

"The Alliance should also include our connections to the Masters within the UC who are also sympathetic and are creating the deadly toxins of Pied Piper," says Yakov.

"Yes," says Liling, smiling at Angie, "Let us also recognize and honor the most important factor of all, my dear family, the power of love, which is where we are all coming from, as opposed to the weakness of fear."

Angie is touched by Liling's kindness and a sense of love and belonging that she inspires. Angie's heart opens wide with joy as she says to Kookie, Yakov, and especially Liling, "Amen!"

"Amen!" they all repeat.

"And now, dear Angie," Liling says, "Let us teach the menfolk here how to self-cloak!"

* * *

"Groundskeeper!" Kookie's personal servant is calling out, looking for Nikolai.

"Groundskeeper!" he says, waving his arms in the air when he sees Nikolai and catches up with him on Angie's veranda.

"Personal servant, have you seen the Lord and his companion yet?" Nikolai asks as the man approaches.

"Yes, indeed sir, yes I have," says the personal servant. "That is what I have come to tell you since you wanted me to let you know just as soon as they got back."

"Yes, yes, thank you," Nikolai says as he picks up #4.

"Oh, and perhaps you should also like to know that they are not alone," says the personal servant, with a joyful expression. "It seems that they are in the company of High Lord Yakov and High Lady Liling. I guess that means we will be having a feast and some gaiety this evening as we generally do when the three of them get together! I had better get everything ready!" he says disappearing into the house, heading toward the kitchen.

Nikolai's expression darkens as he puts #4 back in the coop. Looking at both of the pigeons he says to them with a sinister sneer, "And I must also get things ready. That will be four for tonight instead of two. What do you think #4?"

Both #3 and #4 look at Nikolai. They lift their hearts to the heavens and other winged creatures who can hear them:

NEVER! they say.

Chapter 5 – Juice

"MAKE YOURSELVES RIGHT AT HOME," Kookie says to his guests Yakov and Liling when they enter his private residential wing. They each go to their usual suites when visiting Kookie's Kastle, normally under much happier circumstances.

Angie of course, runs to her veranda. She cannot wait to see #3 and #4, and hold her babies. "There you are my little sweetie pies!" she exclaims, gently taking each one out of the coop, nuzzling and kissing them. "Did some naughty, boo boo bother my babies?" she asks them, upset at the idea of #3 and #4 being touched by some vile human.

Number four puts her little foot out to touch Angie's hand, letting her know that they are both fine. But #4 is also worried about the evil human among them, and the pigeons know that they must find a way of warning their dear human loved ones about him.

Kookie brings Yakov and Liling out to Angie's veranda to meet the birds. Liling in particular is anxious to meet them, and they both are fascinated to learn more about homing and how the pigeons are used for communication.

"So, *these* are the little darlings called #3 and #4!" Liling exclaims. "I am so happy to make your acquaintance," she says to them both as Angie holds #4 up to Liling.

"Put your hand out to her, Liling, like you are going to shake her hand."

"Okay," she giggles, and #4 proceeds to do what all the pigeons have been trained by Kenny to do. She extends her foot to meet Liling's hands, and they "shake" on it.

This impresses Liling and Yakov immeasurably, and both start laughing with delight.

"Will she shake my hand, too?" ask Yakov.

"Well," says Angie, "just hold out your hand to her and say *hello.*"

"Can I say it in Russian?" Yakov asks with a chuckle.

Kookie replies, "Well, let's see, bro!"

"Privyet, #4," Yakov says extending his hand to the bird. And much to his great delight, he too gets a "handshake."

"Of course, we mustn't leave #3 out of this," Angie says. "He is the male partner of #4."

They repeat the whole process with #3. Then Angie shows them both the leg-bands and explains how the messages are attached and how the actual homing process works.

"You know," explains Kookie, "In the past, in times of war, soldiers used homing pigeons for communication. It was apparently quite effective. I do believe we should present this idea to our Alliance once we get everyone altogether. The others agree that this sounds like a great idea.

Yakov asks, "Kookie, is there a way that I can see your staff? Perhaps you can take me around and let me do some snooping. We really must find out who the mole is. Besides, it will give me the opportunity to practice this self-cloaking thing that we have just learned."

"Okay," says Kookie.

"And I would like to acquaint myself more with #3 and #4," says Liling.

They all agree to meet up later and see what Yakov has been able to uncover.

What none of them are aware of is that Nikolai has planted a device inside the coop and has been listening to every word that has been said, watching from the garden nearby. He takes out a small pouch that Alexei left with him and has been concealed in his pocket. Then Nikolai heads for the kitchen.

"Kookie, how many of your house servants are Slavic?" Yakov asks.

"Hm, well, let's see," Kookie says to Yakov, going through his staff in his head. Meanwhile, Yakov starts to practice self-cloaking. As they are going through the corridors, they pass a few servants. Kookie makes sure to say hello or acknowledge each one of them, and, of course, they all respond, yet not one of them says anything to Yakov.

This is good stuff! Yakov thinks to himself. Then he has an idea and says to Kookie, "Say, why don't *you* try this. I will *un*-cloak, *you* self-cloak. I will say hello and you don't say anything. Let's see what happens."

"That's a great idea," says Kookie.

They go outside to walk through Kookie's favorite garden, where he is always seen and always strikes up a friendly chat with whomever he runs into. Lo and behold, the results are the same. One after another, each person acknowledges Yakov and doesn't even seem to notice that Kookie is standing there right next to him.

"Well, my Brother? I think these ladies are onto something! And I'm *sure* it will come in handy at some point!" says Yakov.

"I'm sure you're right," says Kookie, tapping his fingertips together. And no one seems to notice his finger tapping either, including the next person they run into.

"Good day to you sir," Yakov says to the man in his very best English, as the man simply bows his head without saying anything and keeps walking.

"Oh yes," says Kookie. "You were asking me how many Slavic people I have here on the estate? Well, that man you just spoke to was one of them. I do believe there are six more. I guess most are local folks."

Yakov stops. "Are you saying that man I just said hello to was Slavic? A *Russian* Slav?"

"Well, yes. I believe so, why?"

"He looks familiar to me, Kookie. I just know that I have seen him somewhere before, but I can't seem to place it. What is the man's name?"

"Oh, no" says Kookie. "He has been here for many, many years. He is my Overseer Groundskeeper. I'm sure Nikolai is just fine."

"Hmm" says Yakov. "Perhaps we should go to the servants' quarters and begin our little investigation. I will do the self-cloaking, you do the talking, and let's see what we come up with."

"Okay, bro'."

Nikolai has reached the kitchen. He sees a few of the cooks at various stages of preparation for the evening meal for Kookie and his companions.

He goes to the Overseer Server, and taking a Center Coffeehouse juice container out of his pouch he says, "Excuse me, but I was asked to give this to My Lord Kenneth and his companions this evening. It is a gift from the local Center Coffeehouse. They are very pleased with all the people who are now flooding back in there and just wanted to say thank you for all that the UC has done to end the recent Ebola outbreak. It is one of their most popular drinks, you know.

"Well, my oh my, isn't that nice!" says the Overseer Server. I will see to it that they each get a glass."

"Good man," says Nikolai. "Yes, very good man, indeed!"

And with that, Nikolai heads out to do some gardening. Going past Angie's veranda, he notices that she is not there. He goes over to the pigeon coop and checks on his device. It is still there, and so are #3 and #4.

"Oh now, don't you two look at me like that, filthy birds that you are! Hmph!"

As he tends to the flower beds nearby, he continues talking to them. "Now, now, no need to fuss," as the pigeons are indeed getting agitated. "It will all be over before any of them know it. Commandant Alexei is very smart and well connected, you know. He knows a mole at Howard Pharmaceuticals who just happens to be working on the new toxins for Pied Piper. Yes Indeed! And when the Commandant approached him with a little favor, why he just didn't mind at all. Said it would be *no trouble at all* to fix a container of juice that is, how shall we say, mixed with the neurotoxin concentrate. It is strong enough to be fatal if swallowed, without *greatly* diluting the concentrate before adding it to the juice. And that is the stuff that is currently being mass produced and distributed to Center Coffeehouses all over One World. Oh no, my smelly little buddies, #3 and #4. Oh no indeed!"

Nikolai hears Angie returning to her suite, so he waves good-bye to the pigeons whispering, "Oh and don't you two worry about yourselves, either. You will both make great pigeon moles for us! Yes indeed! Ha ha!"

It is just about time for dinner. Angie and Liling have been practicing their highly advanced intuitive skills together and deciding how they are going to contact the various Lords and Ladies within their own Continental Territories. They realize that even though there are 36 who do seem to be unsympathetic with the Council, they may not all be that way or be willing to take the risk of becoming a part of their Alliance. They realize they may just have to gather their forces a bit more slowly than they would like in order to be safe and secure.

The group has gathered around the dinner table, ready to indulge in another exquisite meal for the day.

"Well Ladies," says Kookie, "Yakov and I have done quite a bit of investigating today, and we have not come up with very much. What have you two come up with?"

"Oh, Liling and I are having lots of fun exploring our gifts of, you know, being able to see and hear things."

"Yes, you two certainly are gifted in that way," Kookie says, happily tapping his fingertips together. "So have you come up with any other great suggestions?"

"Actually," says Liling, "We have been talking about the need to proceed with caution when we approach our peers in regard to moving forward with the Alliance."

"Yes," says Yakov, "Kookie and I have been talking about that too. We will have to approach them with caution. But I know for certain that there are others who feel as we all do. And I believe that once we get the ball rolling, they will come out and join us."

As Kookie, Yakov, Angie and Liling are talking and about to enjoy the first course of their meal, Angie sees something out of the corner of her eye. There is a large dining room window overlooking a flower garden, and Angie sees something coming towards the window. Before she can say anything, Liling notices it too. The two of them jump up from their seats and are at the window just in time to see a few butterflies landing on it.

"I know them!" Liling cries out.

"So do I!" Angie says excited to see them.

Together they both say, "*ANGEL!*"

The men are only a few moments behind them, and a swarm of many, many more Monarchs are now filling the sky.

"Angel wants to come inside! Oh, please open the window and let her come in!" Angie implores Kookie.

The two men find a way to crack open the large window and nine of the monarchs come racing inside. The rest remain outside.

As one of them comes forward to the women Liling says to her, "What is it, Angel? Why have you come to us? And with such great urgency?"

Angel and the other eight Monarchs gradually move towards the dining room table, beckoning the human creatures to follow them.

"What's happening, Angel?" Angie whispers to her softly.

The Monarchs flutter over to a flask on the table. There is a note with it no one has noticed, which Kookie now opens. "It is from the folks at the local Center Coffeehouse," he says, "Thanking us for ridding the world of the recent Ebola outbreak."

Turning to the others, he says. "It is one of their juices. Not the one targeted for the neurotoxin, but . . . hm, I wonder."

He reaches for the flask to pick it up, but Angel and the Monarchs start fluttering around the flask so frantically that Kookie cannot even touch it.

"Whoa!" says Kookie.

"Good grief!" says Yakov.

But the women are not at all surprised and just wait to see what the Monarchs are trying to tell them. Angel and the other eight butterflies calm down and perch themselves on the edge of the flask. One of the Monarchs slowly flutters down into the flask, barely touching the liquid inside. When he comes out, he makes an agonizing screeching sound and goes into convulsions. Moments later, the Monarch is dead.

The others remain perched on the edge of the flask, completely still. When the humans look at the window, they see thousands of butterflies also perched motionless on the outside of the window, looking in.

Angie says sadly, "They are mourning the loss of their friend."

Tenderly touching the crumpled body of the butterfly who has perished, Angie continues grievously, "He did that for us, so we would be warned of the danger."

The other Monarchs flutter down to where the body of their friend is lying on the table, and together they lift him up and carry him out of the window. The others on the window start to fly away and Angel comes over to Kookie, Yakov, Angie and Liling and flutters over their heads for a moment.

The two women tell the men what Angel is saying:

Do not be sad, human creatures. We love you, and so do the other winged creatures. There is hope . . .

Angel leaves along with the rest of the butterflies.

Angie and Liling both look at each other and exclaim, "The pigeons!"

"They called out to Angel!" says Angie, and turning to Kookie, she says, "We owe #3 and #4 our lives."

* * *

Nikolai is not far off. He is waiting to hear the sounds of mass screaming and agonizing suffering, but neither is forthcoming. He is sure that their dinner is over by now, *so what went wrong,* he thinks to himself.

From the garden area near Angie's veranda, he sees Kookie, Angie, Yakov and Liling emerge with some drinks in their hands. *Ah! I guess they were saving it for dessert. Even better,* Nikolai thinks to himself with an evil grin appearing on his face, *because now I get the pleasure of watching it happen!*

The four friends bring out a partially filled flask which appears to contain juice and looks like the drinks they are holding in their glasses. Setting everything down on the patio table in front of them, they begin to talk, but Nikolai cannot hear what they are saying. At one point, Kookie picks up the flask, shakes the liquid in it and puts it back down on the table, and then he continues to drain his glass. After a little while, they finish their drinks and continue talking. When they are done with their conversation, they simply get up and leave.

Nikolai watches in confusion and irritation. *What went wrong?* he wonders.

He goes over to the table where the empty glasses and the semi-filled flask are still sitting. There is some juice left in the glasses which obviously do not contain any poison, so Nikolai picks one up and finishes it. He wonders if it is the same *type* of juice as the one he left with the Overseer Server, which would explain what happened.

AHA! Nikolai says to himself. *It guess the fool Server must have given them the wrong juice! Lord Kenneth does have several of them in his pantry. I suppose the Server put the new one away and gave them an older one.*

Well, he continues with a contemptuous snort. *He's bound to drink it sooner or later. Too bad I couldn't have gotten all four of them at one shot though.*

Nikolai picks up the flask and fills his glass with some more juice. *Mmm that really does taste good. No wonder they are targeting babies and children with this stuff.*

* * *

After dinner, Kookie and company realize they must do something with the poisoned juice and they go to discuss it on Angie's veranda. The four of them come up with the idea of using the poisoned stuff as a matrix for the DNA restructuring 369-Program.

"It's all very simple," Kookie explains to them. "We use the good juice to basically tell Metatron that this is how the other one is supposed to be structured. It's the same idea we're using to neutralize the neurotoxins that Howard Pharmaceuticals is sending out to the Center Coffeehouses.

"I don't know who did this," Kookie says picking up the flask and swirling the liquid around before putting it back down, "but we can use this as a prototype to create the antitoxin."

The group follows Kookie into his workstation to get Metatron, and to have a quick peek into their favorite room of his Kastle.

"Here it is," says Kookie, picking up Metatron. "Now let's go back out there and take care of that juice."

In that moment, they hear horrid screaming.

"What's that?" yells Yakov.

"IT'S COMING FROM MY VERANDA" Angie cries out.

The screaming becomes violent and jerky, as if the person screaming is going into convulsions.

"OH GOD!" shrieks Kookie. *"WE LEFT THE POISONED JUICE IN THE FLASK ON THE TABLE!"*

The four of them tear down the hallway to Angie's suite. The screaming becomes louder and more horrific as they approach the veranda. They arrive just in time to see Nikolai screaming and writhing on the ground with bruises and lacerations all over his body. There is broken glass everywhere. Nikolai is shaking and convulsing badly, desperately trying to get something out of his pocket. He is finally successful, and when the others see the gun in his hand, they shriek and jump back. Staring straight into Kookie's eyes Nikolai puts the barrel of his gun into his own mouth . . . and pulls the trigger.

Kookie, Angie, Yakov and Liling are overcome with shock and horror as they look down at the torn-up body of Kookie's Overseer Groundskeeper.

"I guess we now know who the mole is," Yakov says softly, "Or at least, who he *was*. But we must be sure."

"How are you going to do *that?*" Angie questions him.

Yakov approaches Nikolai's body and removes the communication device from his pocket. Holding it against his own, he presses a few buttons. Kookie looks over Yakov's shoulder and the two of them see the last person Nikolai was communicating with. Kookie is even more saddened when he sees the confirmation. The Overseer Groundskeeper Nikolai was someone he knew for many years and trusted.

Kookie takes the device from Yakov and holds it up so Angie can see it. "The last communication Nikolai had was this morning with Alexei."

Angie says, "Well, like you said, Kookie. At least he left us with a sample of the neurotoxin, so you can get on it right away."

"Yes, yes I can. I must notify the Major immediately and let him know that we can have the program to him by tonight."

"We can?" asks Liling. "But how?"

Kookie smiles as Angie walks over to the pigeon coop. She takes out #3, strokes his feathers and kisses the top of his head. "This is how," she says to Liling, and #3 winks at Angie saying, *I'm on it, Sister!*

* * *

Vi, Mimi and Ryan are finishing up for the day at the Howard Pharmaceutical plant at Silver Beach. The Major is going to be there with them until the next morning and then he will have to report to his father at the main headquarters. Everything is moving forward at lightning speed in all their facilities throughout One World since the new "additive," as it is being referred to, is about to be rolled out everywhere. The Center Coffeehouses have all been notified that they are receiving a new product that will not only make the tea cakes and juice taste better but will also be healthier and soothing; a welcome relief people need after all the stress and loss from the Ebola outbreak.

My Buddy's news and instructions are being piped through the Howard Pharmaceutical factory just as the servants are finishing up for the day, leaving everyone feeling inexplicably miserable, confused, and irritated:

Hello, Dear Ones! Hello, hello! My, what a wonderful day it is! Truly it is! Yes, indeed! There is some wonderful news today, coming your way.

As always, your most devoted Council has your health and happiness at heart. They have prepared something for you that is truly wonderful and exciting. Yes, indeed! They know how much you all love their wonderful Coffeehouses at the most excellent Centers, all of which they provide for you, their Dear Ones. They also know how much you love their tea cakes and juice! Well, me oh my, didn't they just come out with a wonderful brand-new sweet little something for you all to enjoy! Yes, indeed! Yes, Yes! As if those tea cakes aren't yummy enough. There is now an extra yummy thing that will be added to them making them even yummier and healthier than ever! Oh, my yes! Yes, indeed, Dear Ones. Can you imagine those wonderful tea cakes even more wonderful than ever? Ha Ha! Why yes indeed! And as if that is not even enough, you know how all the little ones just love the juice. Well! Now they will have that same yummy extra something added to the juice, too! Woo hoo, little ones! Enjoy, enjoy!

So, your instructions my Dear Ones, are to have a good relaxing time and enjoy your evening activities at your local Center Coffeehouse and make sure to have lots and lots of those yummy tea cakes, and especially juice for the little ones.

Vi turns to Mimi and Ryan, "If that isn't the grizzliest thing ever! Yuck!" she says.

"Let's go back to the dwelling complex," Ryan says, "And get ready for our *own* evening activities."

"Amen to that!" says Mimi, as they all head for their units.

The Overseer at the Dwelling Complex watches all the servants as they return to their private units. They are allotted a certain amount of time to eat their meals and then listen to the evening programing on My Buddy. For those who want to, they may go down to the local Center and use their food points at the Market or the Coffeehouse. However, they must return to the dwelling complex by 9 p.m., or they will receive a warning. Once they have been warned three times, they are dismissed from Howard Pharmaceuticals, which is how some folks come to be homeless. It is those people who end up sleeping in the Freshen-Up areas of the Centers.

For Vi, Mimi and Ryan the Coffeehouse is a way of getting the people's news. And until Kookie comes up with a 369-Program for the teacake and juice antitoxin, the best they can do is engage in Coffeehouse conversation and see what information, or people's news, they can ascertain. That is the plan, as they each get their evening meals and then prepare to head on over to the Coffeehouse, until Vi comes pounding on Mimi and Ryan's door.

Mimi answers. "What's going on, Vi?"

Breathless and excited, Vi hands a little piece of paper to Mimi, "This!" she says, "#3 was waiting for me when I walked in!" Mimi reads the small, scrolled up note:

RED – 369 – RESET – 13935/777 – GREEN

"Kookie has worked out the program!" Mimi says.

Vi nods, "Yes! And I have got to get this to the Major immediately! So, you and Ryan go on over to the Coffeehouse and I will meet you both later."

"Okay Vi! Be careful!"

"No problem!" Vi smiles, as she takes the note back from Mimi and proceeds to self-cloak.

The Major left the office early and went to his beachfront apartment. It is part of the residential unit for the Overseers of Howard Pharmaceuticals, with a few empty suites that are kept available for visiting Lords and Masters. A servant enters and asks if he is ready for dinner and, if so, how many will there be this evening.

"Just myself for this evening my good man," the Major says, realizing that he misses Vi. However, they both knew that they would have to spend less time together and stay in living quarters much farther apart than they normally would, in order to keep their covert activities, including the pigeons, well concealed. For one thing, how would he explain the presence of carrier pigeons to anyone on his fancy beachfront property?

Looking out of his living room window, the Major is watching the sunset over the ocean. Thoughts of the mass Coffeehouse distribution project that his father has charged him with are disrupting the peaceful scene for him.

Father in Heaven, he says to the setting sun, *the neurotoxins are all ready to go. I can only delay the shipment for so long, until Kookie sends me the 369-code. Please dear Lord, do not let me send this horrid poison out to an unsuspecting world. Although I do know that there are other things we can do to counter balance the effects of the neurotoxins, it will not be easy.*

The Major lowers his head to the sun and as usual, asks for forgiveness.

Then he hears a voice calling out behind him, "Your dinner is ready, Master. Will you be taking it out here, or would you like to dine indoors this evening?"

The Major turns and starts to tell his servant that he will take it inside, when all of a sudden he says, "I will take it, oh . . . uh, just leave it out here, my good man. In fact, I'm feeling rather hungry this evening. Would you kindly fix me an extra serving?"

"Sure thing, Master, I will be back with it shortly."

"That's alright my good man, kindly leave it on the dining room table and I will fetch it myself in just a little while. I wish not to be disturbed anymore this evening."

"As you wish," he says and disappears back to the kitchen.

Vi steps out from the shadows of the patio where they have been smiling at each other during the Major's whole exchange with his servant. He goes over and puts his arms around her.

"I've got it!" Vi says with a great big smile on her face.

"Got what, Violet?" the Major says affectionately, having forgotten everything else for the moment.

Giggling, Vi says, "Um, well, does #3 ring a bell?"

"Number 3? Wait! *WHAT?! OH, YES . . . #3!*"

Vi laughs handing him the scroll.

Reading the message, the Major erupts into shouts of joy. *"WHOA! KOOKIE! YOU DID IT, BRO'!"*

"Yes, he did, *INDEED!"* Vi is still laughing.

"Yes, indeed!" says the Major, "And you did it too, dear Violet."

"And you as well," she says. "So, um, what was that about an extra portion of dinner?"

"You just have a seat right here, my dear. I will go get it from the kitchen!"

* * *

Mimi and Ryan enter the Silver Beach Center Coffeehouse. It is bustling with activity which is quite the contrast from the last time they were in a Coffeehouse. Mimi looks for a table while Ryan gets the coffee. She is looking for a more secluded spot, if possible, where they can talk with Vi once she gets there. Mimi spots a table in the corner and heads for it, trying to catch people's conversations along the way.

Definitely the best way to get any REAL news she thinks to herself as she hears such comments as:

"So thankful to the UC for getting rid of that terrible Ebola!"

"Yes, yes indeed!"

"What about that new flavoring for our teacakes and juice! Isn't *that* exciting?"

"Sure is!"

"Can't wait to give it to my little Henry. He really loves that juice, and they said it is even healthier than the old stuff!"

"Oh indeed, that *is* wonderful!"

"With the added flavoring I'm sure he'll just *guzzle* it all down!"

As Mimi takes her seat, she can hear two men at the nearby table:

"Those new seeds from the UC are just amazing, Morris. Only just planted them not too long ago and already the seedlings are ready for the fields; even bigger and stronger looking than the old ones."

"Is that so?"

"Yep! Sure is. In fact, I was gonna let the old ones stay anyway, but they looked so much inferior to the new ones, and they are supposedly not healthy, so I just tore 'em up like the Council says we ought."

"Was wonderin' about that one myself. I guess I better go back and do the same."

Mimi feels sick from what she hears. When Ryan comes over with the coffee, she is grateful not to have to listen to such talk anymore. Keeping their voices low Mimi says to Ryan, "I sure hope Vi gets here soon. Can't wait to hear what the Major has to say about the message from #3."

"Yes. Wouldn't that be awesome, honey, if he can get things rolling with the 369-Program for the *you-know-what's* right away?"

"It sure would, sweetie, and knowing Kookie and the Major, I'm sure he will," Mimi says with confidence.

* * *

A little while later Vi enters the Coffeehouse. Mimi and Ryan see her and wave. Getting her coffee and joining the other two, Vi can't wait to give them her news, and they are both very anxious to hear what the Major had to say.

Smiling over the little table, hunched over and talking just above a whisper, Vi says, "He's at it right now, as we speak."

"WHAT?" says Mimi, a touch too loud.

"Shhh!"

"Oh, uh, yes. *What?"*

"It's a very simple program," Vi explains, keeping her voice as low as she can, grateful for the background din of all the other folks chattering away.

"The Major says that he has another excuse for going back into the shipping area this evening, where we got all those boxes ready to go today. With Metatron and Kookie's new code, he should be able to restructure the DNA of everything tonight. Then we will both leave in the morning for his father's main plant."

"Oh?" says Mimi somewhat surprised. "I thought our plan was to stay here together until the Major returned?"

"Well," says Vi, with a girlish grin on her face, "I guess he, that is, we . . ."

"Well, my oh my, woman!" Mimi says laughing.

"Oh, oh . . . no!" Vi says, trying unsuccessfully to conceal her grin, "It's nothing like that!"

"Yeah, right!" says Mimi.

"No really," she chuckles, "He says he, you know, *thinks* better when I'm around."

"*Yyyyyup!*" says Ryan.

"You go, girl!" Mimi laughs and winks. "We *do* want the Major to have his best *thinking cap* on now, don't we!"

"Oh, stop it you two!" the three of them chuckle together.

* * *

There is an incoming message on a terminal in Johannesburg. The screen is activated, the message is accepted and the Universal Translator is turned on:

"Greetings, Lord Ekene. Thank you for accepting my message."

"Yes, what can I do for you?" Lord Ekene asks.

"There is a storm brewing, My Lord. May I say that I have analyzed their plan and a very real and dangerous threat exists for all of the UC."

"Yes, the Lords of the Council are aware of a threat, but not that it is as dangerous as you are suggesting. Do you have some information for me?"

"Yes, My Lord Ekene, I believe that I do. But I must speak to you in private, sir."

"Very well, Master Commandant Alexei. I will meet you at your present location."

"Thank you, My Lord. And one more thing sir, *do* be careful. I don't know what happened; they are very clever. But I fear they may have taken out my number one mole."

"Indeed, Alexei!"

"Yes, My Lord. Indeed!"

Chapter 6 – Resistance

EARLY IN THE MORNING IN JOHANNESBURG, the Overseer Groundskeeper, and gardeners of Lord Ekene's estate are beginning to rise and prepare for their day. They tend to the estate's expansive grounds, including the many flowers, herbs, and fruit and vegetable gardens. Lord Ekene prefers to eat the fruits and vegetables that are grown under his own watchful eye, and he also prefers his gardener's herbal medicinal products over anything put out by Howard Pharmaceuticals. This keeps his servants fairly busy all the time, between growing, harvesting and processing all the food and herbs.

As a result, the Overseer Groundskeeper, Bem, as well as all the gardeners on the property have become expert at food, flower and herbal medicine. So, when Lord Ekene's Communications Overseer Tafari is left abandoned by his Lord to die on the ground from a broken body and spirit, Bem and the others know what to do.

As they begin their day's service, Bem first checks in on Tafari, who is just waking up in the other room.

"Good morning, Tafari, how are you feeling today?"

"I'm not sure. Seems I had a bad dream last night."

"Ah!" says Bem, "Do not speak another word just yet, my friend. Our gardener, Dumaka, is an expert in such matters. Let me call him in along with Nassor."

As Bem goes to fetch his gardeners Dumaka and Nassor, Tafari remembers the details of the dream and becomes agitated. Tafari is especially afraid of Lord Ekene, who does not know that Tafari survived the fall from the Lord's window. Bem returns with the gardeners, and they all sit down respectfully on the floor in front of Tafari's bedroll.

Dumaka begins. "Bem has told us that you had a bad dream last night. Won't you please tell us about it my friend so we can help you figure out what your dream has to say."

Tafari sits up and feels reassured by the other men's presence. They have been taking care of him and nursing him back to health since his fall, so he trusts them and finds them comforting.

"Okay," Tafari begins:

I was swimming in a lake in the jungle. It was very warm and inviting and the trees hung over my head as the loving arms of a mother holding her child. As I got to the deepest part of the lake, the middle, I realized that I was not alone. Other people started to show up out of nowhere and they were also swimming along quite happily. Then the people turned into young children as they continued to swim around. And suddenly everything started to darken, like a storm was coming, only there was not a cloud in the sky. I found this to be very frightening since the sky was darkening for no reason, no reason at all. But the children did not even seem to notice that shadows were forming all around them, and they just kept on swimming, seeming quite content."

Tafari stops as he is becoming agitated.

"It is okay, my friend," all three men reassure him. "We are here with you now and you are quite safe."

Taking a deep breath, Tafari calms and continues: *"Then the lake started to get very cold and murky. It was like trying to swim in cold mud. The children became distressed, but they could not figure out what to do. So, I tried telling them to follow me to the edge of the lake where they could get out. But they couldn't hear me, or something."*

Now Tafari is weeping, *"They were so lost, so scared, and they started to cry. Then all of a sudden, from the center of the lake, a frozen statue rose up out of the mud. The eyes of the statue were closed, and the arms folded over its chest. And little by little it started to come to life, opening its mouth and drawing a breath. And for the first time the children became scared. I called to them again to follow me to the edge of the lake but now they were too frightened to move. So, they stopped moving and the lake became colder and colder, until one by one they froze to death. I looked up at the statue and it had turned into Lord Ekene. He was laughing. . . laughing at the frozen bodies of dead children as they lay floating on the surface of the lake."*

Tafari buries his face in his hands, sobbing heavily. While he was sharing his dream with them, Bem made an herbal tea concoction. He offers it to Tafari. "Here my friend, drink this. It is very soothing." Turning to Dumaka and Nassor, Bem says, "So what do you think?"

"I think it is as we have suspected all along," says Dumaka. "Only it is not just Ekene's intent to harm *us* in some way. He is apparently focused even more on doing great harm to our children."

"It also seems," Nassor says, "that they are kept in the dark and blinded to the truth, right up until the very end."

"Until they can no longer *be* helped," agrees Dumaka.

"My Brothers," says Bem to Nassor and Dumaka, "We have all seen the terrible power Lord Ekene wielded over our Brother Tafari here. Whatever it is and however he is doing it, we must not let him do this to our children!"

"No! No! We must *NOT let him harm our children!*"

The gardeners cry out. In their old language of long ago, which has been all but lost to them, there are a few songs that remains in their hearts and memories. The men begin to sing out one of those songs in Zulu, their true native language:

Asikatali! – We are the children of Africa!
Asikatali, nomas'ya bozh, sizimiseli Nkululeko
Asikatali, nomas'ya bozh, sizimiseli Nkululeko
Unzima lomtwalo, ufuna madoda
Unzima lomtwalo, ufuna madoda
We do not care if we go to prison,
It is for freedom that we gladly go.
A heavy load, a heavy load,

And it will take some real men.

* * *

Lord Ekene has just arrived at Master Commandant Alexei's secret location. It is a small coastal retreat in California, not very far from Kookie's estate. Since the disappearance of his mole, Alexei is overcome with anxiety about what happened to Nikolai and what kind of danger he himself is now facing.

Speaking through Ekene's Universal Translator which the Lord's sometimes wear as a pendant necklace, Alexei greets Lord Ekene. "Come in, come in My Lord! I am so grateful you are here! I have been very worried since the disappearance of my mole."

"Yes, yes I understand. We are all, how shall I say, *concerned,* these days. So, what information do you have for me?" says Lord Ekene, looking out of the beachfront window. He is watching the waves crash against the shore and feeling for something under his vest.

"I know who the owner of the illegal device is My Lord. The one we have been searching for. And it is the same person who sabotaged the Ebola bioweapon."

At this Lord Ekene turns around and looks straight at Alexei. *"Really?"* he says. "Are you sure Commandant?"

"Yes, yes! I am absolutely certain! And what's more, he is not working alone. There are others helping him; although, I do not have their names, not as of yet, My Lord. However, I believe my mole discovered their identity, and I also believe he was about to give me all of that information, when he was. . . that is. . . I am unable to contact him now, sir."

"Well then, so who is it?"

With great fear in his eyes at what might happen to him when he reveals what he knows to Lord Ekene, Alexei finally says, "It is the High Lord Kenneth, My Lord!"

Lord Ekene stares at him in disbelief. "Wow! Well, I guess I should not be surprised. I have wondered myself at times about High Lord Kenneth's true fealty and where it lies. Thanks for the tip, Master Commandant. I shall take matters into my own hands *immediately*."

Alexei breathes a sigh of relief when he hears those words from Ekene. "Thank you, My Lord, thank you."

"Oh no, Master Commandant. It is *I* who must thank *you*," Lord Ekene says with a smile, and reaching under his vest he pulls out an automatic weapon.

"Spasiba[6], Alexei," Lord Ekene says to him in Russian, still smiling, as he opens fire. Alexei hits the ground. Staring down at the dead body through Ekene's cold-blooded eyes, speaking in the flat tone of a killer, he says, one last time, "Spasiba, Alexei!"

Leaving the property, Lord Ekene messages a local contact: *Clean-up required*. Getting into his Cloudcar he says to the AI driver, "Take me to High Lord Kenneth's Estate."

* * *

After the incident with Nikolai at the Kastle, Kookie, Yakov, Liling and Angie know they have no time to lose. They must reach out to all the Lords and Ladies whom they feel are like minded and organize their Alliance immediately. They spend much of the day sending messages to all 36 Lords and Ladies on their list. Since all the Lords and Ladies know that they are under surveillance and cannot communicate freely through their Lord's Communication Devices, they are simply told that they are

---

[6] *Russian for "Thank you."*

needed at the Kastle immediately to discuss ways in which they can be helpful in implementing Operation Pied Piper.

Kookie, Yakov and Liling also tell the 36 that, "We shall also have a picnic and spend a lovely day in my gardens!" With an invitation for an immediate picnic together, the Lords and Ladies know something peculiar is afoot and waste no time making their way to Kookie's Kastle. The guests soon arrive in their Cloudtransporters from every corner of One World.

Angie has gone out for a walk on the lush acreage of Kookie's estate, which she finds soothing, especially after witnessing Nikolai's grisly death. She has decided to take #3 and #4 along with her, one perched on each of her shoulders, talking to her little companions as they roam the grounds and beautiful gardens together.

"Isn't it just beautiful here? Look at all these flowers! You know, one day I would really love to learn what messages they all have for us. Just think of all the good we can do if we could help heal the world with the love from our friends the flowers."

You bet! #3 and #4 seem to say as they coo with delight.

Angie and the pigeons make their way around to the front of the estate just as the last Cloudvehicle arrives, and what a sight it is.

"Wow!" Angie says. "Thirty-six magnificent Cloudtransporters all parked in one space! Sheeeeesh!"

Turning to her pigeon pals on her shoulders she adds, "Well, I guess it's about time to go inside. Gotta get ready for the *picnic on the beach.*"

As they start cooing at her she says, "Oh now don't you worry, you're both coming too. Let's go and pack up your coop with some chow for the two of you," Angie says as they all go inside.

Angie did not count the Cloudtransporters parked out front, though. If she had, she would have seen that there were not 36 of them but 37.

The Lords and Ladies of the Council are all gathered in Kookie's living room. They are enjoying themselves with pastries and good conversation, waiting for their host to announce the true purpose of their gathering. When Kookie feels that the time is right, he addresses the group, and they all turn on their Universal Translators.

"Welcome, welcome Brothers and Sisters to my Kastle. What a wonderful day it is for a gathering! Truly is it!" Kookie continues looking around at the expectant and somewhat uncertain looks from some of his guests. "In fact, it is such a lovely day that I say we have a picnic at my nearby beach Kabana."

"Ah!" a few voices from the crowd murmur their consent.

"So why don't you all get back into your Cloudvehicles and you can just follow me over there."

"Sure thing, Kookie! Right Brother! Okay then!" some voices are heard saying, and they all start heading out. Yakov and Liling go with Kookie, Angie and the birds, and a floating caravan is on its way to Kookie's Beach Kabana.

What none of them notice however, is that one of the Cloudtransporters is trailing behind, *far* behind and out of sight.

Once they get to the Kabana, Kookie hands out beach blankets for everyone and they all help with the set up. Before he brings out any food, Kookie knows that this is the time to make his announcement.

"Brothers and Sisters," he begins, "I can now tell you the true purpose of our gathering."

He has their full attention, and they are each quite anxious to hear what this is all about.

"As you know, most places including our homes are under 24-hour surveillance."

Everyone looks at each other, nods, and sighs.

"So, we cannot have a private gathering of any kind in most indoor places without being prepared. That is why I have brought you all out here. It will be much more difficult for anyone to track us to this location, and if they don't suspect anything, then they will most likely not bother. That is why Yakov, Liling, and I made it sound like we were getting together for Operation Pied Piper. Well, my friends, we *are* in fact here to talk about Operation Pied Piper, but not in a supportive way."

There are smiles of relief among all the faces of the Lords and Ladies. Some pat each other on the back while others hold hands, and they all turn to Kookie with either a nod of agreement, big thumbs-up, or both. All 36 Lords and Ladies are intrigued to hear what Kookie, Yakov and Liling have in mind.

As the two High Lords and the High Lady are laying out their plans, nobody sees what is going on above their heads on a beach cliff directly overlooking their gathering. Two automatic firearms are being loaded with two fully loaded magazines.

"I am happy to report to you all," says Kookie, "That I have found a way of neutralizing the neurotoxins that are on their way to the Center Coffeehouses throughout One World, and as we speak, that operation is being put into effect."

Everyone stands up and starts to cheer, "Bravo! Bless you! Thank you, Brother!"

With the crowd standing, they become easy targets for Lord Ekene looking down on them from the cliff. He picks up his weapons, one in each hand, and aims.

Suddenly Angie looks up and shrieks, *"KOOKIE! WHERE ARE THE BIRDS?!"*

Flying overhead, #3 and #4 drop a number two in both of Lord Ekene's eyes, blinding him with bird poo just as he pulls both triggers of his guns. The ammo is discharged into the air, and #3 and #4 flap their wings all over his head so he loses his footing.

At the sound of the gunshots everyone stops and looks up to see Lord Ekene falling over the edge of the beach cliff, screaming on his way down. He smashes into the jagged rocks below, splitting his head wide open and spilling his brains out on the rocks.

Kookie rushes toward the lifeless body lying on the rocks and shouts, "Someone please call a Cloudambulance!"

Yakov pulls out his Lord's Communication Device and immediately calls while the others are all stunned into silence. Kookie looks at what is left of the face on this man and recognizes Lord Ekene. Lying nearby on the rocks are two discharged automatic weapons, and Kookie begins to put two and two together, except he can't figure out how Lord Ekene ended up going over the cliff.

Angie sees #3 and #4 flying straight toward her, only #4 is faltering. "Oh no!" Angie cries out when they both land on her shoulders, noticing that #4 is bleeding.

Moments later the Cloudambulance shows up and Angie shouts out to the Overseer Paramedic getting out of the vehicle. "Over here! Quick! She's bleeding!" and all eyes turn towards her.

When Kookie hears "Bleeding!" from Angie, he flies into a panic and races back to her.

"Angie is okay!" Liling shouts to Kookie, "It is #4!"

Liling has already heard the pigeons cry and intuits what has happened to them. She says to the crowd, "These pigeons have just saved our lives! They saw the man on the cliff up there about to open fire on us, and they were able to throw him off balance, so he tumbled over the edge!"

"But who would want to kill *us*?" Lady Neely says.

"Yes," says Lord Jackson, "Who *is* that man?!"

"It is, or rather it was, Lord Ekene," says Kookie sadly.

Without giving Ekene another thought they all turn away from their would-be executioner and turn instead to the two heroes who just saved their lives.

Now, 39 Lords and Ladies, and Angie, care about only one thing—saving the life of a little pigeon, #4.

* * *

News has gotten back to Johannesburg that Lord Ekene died courageously while single-handedly stopping a group of insurrectionists from attempting to interfere with the distribution of food to the people. Such is the story that is being put out by the Council. He is to be honored with a full hero's funeral, attended by the UC. His son, Emeka who is only five years old, will eventually take his father's place in all affairs involving the Lords of the Council. Since the servants of the estate are not invited to the official funeral, a "day of respect" has been declared for Lord Ekene. All are expected to cease usual activities, gather amongst themselves, and talk about their good memories of the departed loved one.

When Tafari, Bem, Nassor and Dumaka hear about the passing of Ekene they have no problem at all in organizing a gathering. In fact, word has gotten out among the people of Johannesburg about what happened to Tafari, so numerous gatherings are being organized in Ekene's "honor," Indeed!

This satisfies PA, ES and SPA, for the time being.

"There will not be enough room in my little hut," says Bem, "for all those who will want to attend our gathering."

"How about using one of the gardens?" Tafari says.

"From what I am hearing, our small gardens will not be large enough either," says Bem.

"Hmm, it's too bad we can't use that large open field just behind the main residence of Lord Ekene's estate. I'm not so sure they will understand or appreciate the kinds of memories that *we* will be talking about, eh?" Tafari snickers.

"No, I don't suppose so," chuckles Bem. But considering the idea for a moment he says, "You know, maybe that *will* work out."

"Whatever are you talking about?" asks Tafari with surprise.

"As you know it is generally forbidden for the UC and the people to mix with each other, and the Council did say that we should be gathering "amongst ourselves" for this special occasion."

"So?"

"So, we ask permission to do a large gathering right under their noses, as we expect there to be many sad people all over Johannesburg who will want to honor our fallen "hero," especially as he died (supposedly) protecting our food supply--"

Tafari cuts him off. You are *brilliant!*' he says laughing.

"Yes, well, thank you!" he says with a smile. "Once it is all arranged, we tell each person to bring a candle that we will light when we have shared all of our *'wonderful'* memories of Lord Ekene."

"You mean, so those who might be watching from a distance will be thinking of it as some kind of memorial to Ekene?"

"They can if they like. But *I* was thinking about lighting a flame inside all our hearts together as the flame of freedom, proclaiming a new life for us all."

The two men nod and smile at each other.

* * *

On the day of rest and remembrance, Lord Ekene's family is pleased by the thought of the people using the back field for a Memorial Gathering, and many are arriving with candles. It is somber and quiet on the estate, and everyone seems to be doing exactly what the day is calling for; resting. A few small groups are gathering indoors, and the Overseers are basically taking the day off while all the UC "official folks" have gone off to the "official funeral." Though Lord Ekene's young son is part of the official UC people, he is considered too young to go to a funeral. So Emeka is staying at home with one of the servants.

When people start to arrive in the back field, the estate is quiet and deserted. It does not take long before the grassy area becomes full of people. In fact, it has become packed. Everyone sits down on the blankets they have brought, with small baskets containing their provisions for the day, and a candle. Bem stands up in the middle of the crowd and begins to speak:

"Welcome good people of Johannesburg, welcome one and all. We have gathered here today to share our memories with each other of the one who has fallen; our late Lord Ekene."

As Bem is speaking all eyes and ears in the back field are upon him, focusing intently on the message that he is about to deliver. There is another pair of eyes focused on him, too, but they are not close enough to hear anything. So, partly out of boredom being in an empty house with nothing much to do by himself, but mostly out of curiosity of the colorful crowd in the back, little Lord Emeka makes sure that his servant is occupied with other matters and not really watching him when he sneaks out of the house.

"We have been asked to gather, my Brothers and Sisters, to share memories. And to share his own personal story, there is one here whom I am about to introduce to you. You will most likely recognize his voice because up until recently he gave you the daily news and instructions on My Buddy."

A sudden gasp swells through the crowd when Tafari stands up before them. Whisperings and murmurings can be heard sweeping across all those who are gathered:

"It is true! He is alive! Oh my! Praise be!!"

Tafari begins, "Good people, I have come here to tell you what happened to me, and I will begin by saying that I must apologize to you deeply. I was misled."

Little Lord Emeka is standing far back from the crowd and still cannot hear what anyone is saying out there in the back field. He is afraid to get any closer to this large Memorial Gathering of strangers, but curiosity gets the better of him. Gradually he moves closer toward the crowd.

Meanwhile, Tafari recounts the grisly details of how Lord Ekene used psychological torture to send him jumping out of his office window, and what little he really knows about how it was all accomplished. But he does know that listening to My Buddy set him off again very badly and that he believes somehow there is a danger in this. He recommends no one listen to My Buddy anymore, and to try to get their news instead from each other at the Coffeehouses.

In their hearts, the people know that Tafari is speaking the truth, because that is where the truth resides; in the hearts of all people.

Tafari sits down and Bem addresses the crowd again. "And now I would like to ask you to sing a song with me. It is one that some of you might remember, although many of you will not. It is a song about love and freedom, and it is in our own language from long ago. As we sing the song, I ask that we light our candles, lighting the flame of love and freedom in our hearts."

As Bem begins to sing, the others who remember join in. The Light is passed around from one candle to another and from one heart to another. Before long everyone is singing the song of long ago, in their forgotten Zulu tongue:

Siyahamba kukhanyeni kwenkos

We are marching in the light of Love (Truth, God, the World)

Moving in closer to the crowd and almost there now, little Lord Emeka is listening to the singing. It is joyously uplifting, and he has lost all fear. Listening to the words, he is beginning to repeat them and sing along with the people, *his* people, and the people whom he belongs to. Emeka watches them pass the Light from one to the other as they light each other's candles, and suddenly he feels in his heart what it is that they are all feeling; what his father Lord Ekene never felt - love.

Little Lord Emeka stands at the edge of the crowd singing along with everyone else, when suddenly Bem sees him. Bem stops dead still in his tracks and goes quiet. When the people see Bem's sudden reaction they all turn to see what he is looking at, and they instantly recognize the child.

Everyone goes quiet and still.

* * *

In a small village just outside of Lord Ekene's estate, a group of Chrysalenes are tending to the seedlings out in the field. They are loving on the baby vegetable plants with their joyous singing and tender caressing. Laughing and singing to each other and to the seedlings, one of the Chrysalenes looks up when she notices a flutter of Monarch Butterflies coming their way.

"Oh look, my good friends!" Eve Zula chants to her eleven fellow helpers in the field. "It is Angel! What message does she have for us today, I wonder?"

Adam Makena puts his hands out to receive Angel, who settles lightly into his palms. The others gather around as the Monarch Angel speaks to their one heart in her language of love:

"Your time has come, Chrysalene creatures. The child is ready and waiting. It is time for the Chrysalenes to rise. Go now, beautiful Chrysalene creatures, go to the child, go to his people. They are all waiting."

* * *

Little Lord Emeka stands at the edge of the field looking at everyone staring at him, feeling a little bit scared with so many eyes upon him.

All the "what-if's" Bem and Tafari can imagine start rolling in their heads at the thought of being caught by the UC. The people are sitting there not knowing *what* to think, feel, or say, when suddenly, off in the distance they all hear voices:

Siyahamba kukhanyeni kwenkos, Siyahamba kukhanyeni kwenkos

Twelve Chrysalenes, led by Eve Zula and Adam Makena come into full view to everyone, singing Siyahamba and radiating their love and light outwards to all present. The loving energy of the Chrysalenes enters the hearts of all the people, taking away their fear.

Little Lord Emeka runs over to Eve Zula and lifts up his arms. They all laugh and their singing continues as Eve Zula lifts the little Lord into the air and begins to dance with him through the crowd of people. Everyone stands and they all begin to dance and sing, making a most joyful noise, the likes of which they have never experienced in their lives.

Little Lord Emeka is passed around the people who joyously give him their love and laughter.

High up above, Angel looks down upon them and says:

And the Truth will set you Free[7], human creatures!

---

[7] *John 8:32 NIV*

PART 2
HUMAN
CREATURES

Chapter 7 – Connecting

ANGIE IS HOLDING #4, TENDERLY cupped in her hands. She knows the AI paramedics must work on her pigeon friend, so she will have to let go of her for a little while.

"Please make her better, please, oh please!" Angie cries as the Overseer Paramedic takes #4 and brings her inside the Cloudambulance.

The Lords and Ladies all gather around Angie, trying their best to offer her comfort.

Kookie is holding her too. "It's okay, my woman. I'm sure they will fix her up just fine."

Through her sobs, Angie looks up for a moment at Kookie. "Your what?"

"Uh, oh! Uh, my, that is . . ." but he cannot find any other words. Angie stops crying as she looks at Kookie and smiles. He is at a total loss for words, and finally says to Angie nervously, "I sure do wish I had my tuba here right now!"

Angie smiles at him sweetly and says, "I will hold you to that later, my man!"

He gazes into her eyes and says softly, "Ok."

The Overseer Paramedic finally emerges from the Cloudambulance holding #4. "Well," he says bringing the pigeon over to Angie, "she's a little shaken up but physically she is on the mend."

Tears of joy overcome Angie and melt the hearts of everyone there as they all hug each other. The Lords and Ladies also take turns touching, petting, and some of them, kissing #4 and #3, thanking them both for saving their lives.

Kookie turns to the crowd and says, "I don't feel that it is safe for us to stay here right now, and if you all don't mind, let's move one more time. I have a Kabin in a heavily wooded area on my property where we can continue."

They all agree, return to their Cloudtransporters, and follow Kookie over to his Kabin. Once they are all safely inside, Yakov lights a fire in the living room hearth and the others gather round seated on whatever they can find, the overstuffed sofas or even the plush carpeting on the floor. Yakov eyeballs the overstuffed chair, but he knows that is Kookie's favorite spot, even though he "borrowed" it when he was there by himself the other day. Looking around for a vacant spot on the carpet, Yakov notices someone else rather inviting sitting there.

Although there is no room next to her, he says, "Pardon me, please" and politely squishes his butt between the lovely Lady Neely and the not-so-lovely Lord Jackson sitting next to her. Jackson catches a bit of an attitude when he sees all the open space on the carpet nearby and was rather hoping to be sitting next to the lovely Lady Neely himself.

Kookie sits down in his chair and continues the discussion. "At the beach Kabana we have all just witnessed the serious division that exists among us. A long time ago in our Panamerican history there was a president who said these great words:

> *"A house divided against itself cannot stand.[8] I believe this government cannot endure, permanently half slave and half free. I do not expect the Union to be dissolved – I do not expect the house to fall – but I do expect it will cease to be divided."[9]*

The crowd seems touched by these words, and Kookie continues, "As we move forward together my friends, I would like us all to think of those words, and what is at stake here. *A HOUSE DIVIDED*

---

[8] *Mark 3:25 NIV*
[9] *Excerpt from Abraham Lincoln's 1858 acceptance speech as candidate for president.*

AGAINST ITSELF CANNOT STAND! And our house is teetering on the brink. The Council knows this as they desperately try to maintain their power and control. But they cannot because ultimately their house *WILL* fall, and it is already on the way down.

"But, my friends, when a house has become evil and corrupt then the only place for it to go *is* down. And therein lies our hope. As long as we keep a foundation of love under our feet, we can rebuild a much better world, one brick at a time, for each and every human being of the three Continental Territories of One World. We are the Lords and Ladies, with technology and various forms of communication at our disposal. I propose that we decide here today how each one of us is going to contribute our own expertise and knowledge for the greater good. And as we gather our forces of love we will stand by and watch as their house falls. But we will also be there to catch what remains of her and usher in a much greater humanity with a higher collective human soul than the world has ever known."

Kookie looks at Angie who is sitting on the carpet with #3 on her shoulder and #4 cradled in her hands against her chest. Angie's big, soft brown eyes and radiant smile are sharing a higher love with Kookie than he has ever known.

As he looks around at everyone else, he sees the faces of love and purpose filling the hearts of his fellow Lords and Ladies. This fills his own heart with hope.

* * *

Judy has just returned from the Center Market. While she was there, she spent a little time at the Coffeehouse hoping to get some news. Judy stopped listening to My Buddy a long time ago when she felt that the news and instructions being transmitted were just infantile and somehow not quite right. And Doc sent her a message the other day through #1 telling Judy to be absolutely certain NOT to listen to My Buddy at all.

There are a fair number of people hanging out at the Coffeehouse these days, and Judy has been watching as their attitudes and moods have been steadily deteriorating. Today it occurred to her to snoop around a little and ask a few questions. What she discovered is disturbing her so much that upon returning home she decides to find her friend Adam Tate and share it with him. Judy finds Adam Tate out in the field tending to the crops and goes over to him immediately.

"Hi there Adam Tate!"

"Well, hello, my friend Judy. How may I serve you today, dear lady?" he says with a warm smile.

"Oh, Adam Tate!" Judy says with worry in her voice. "I just don't know what's happening here. But I fear the worst."

He sits down on the soft earth and beckons Judy to do the same. "Do you feel the love from our Mother Earth?"

"Yes," Judy says gloomily.

"She is our Great Mother, and she has so much deep love for us, her children of the earth."

Judy is beginning to smile a little.

"So, tell me Judy, what is it that is troubling you today?"

"I just came back from the Center Coffeehouse and what I learned there has me very concerned." Judy sighs and then continues, "For the past few days, the Coffeehouse has been unable to transmit My Buddy's message on the public address system, and do you know *why*? I mean this is their whole reason for living, isn't it? I mean what in the world could possibly cause them to shut down all public transmissions of that thing?"

Adam Tate is listening to her with much compassion as Judy continues. "I also found out that after listening to that awful stuff piped through to the Coffeehouse a few days ago, a fight broke out. It wasn't any ordinary, everyday, run of the mill fight either, not that there are *ever* any "ordinary fights" at a Center Coffeehouse. Folks were just sitting there calmly, talking, enjoying themselves like always, but as soon as My Buddy came on their attitude changed instantly, getting irritable and upset, and for no apparent reason. I mean all the Communications Overseer on My Buddy was talking about was the usual stuff and nonsense. But when he came to the last few words at the end and he said, *'eat your fruits and veggies. DO IT! DO IT!'* the whole place just went up and crazy!"

Adam Tate has been listening to everything Judy is sharing; she goes on to describe specific acts of aggression that occurred, including one death.

"And *then,* the next day, most of the very same people came back AND WERE *FINE!* It was almost as if they had no memory of what had happened other than to report feeling a bit foggy headed. Now I ask you Adam Tate, as only a very polite, unassuming, older woman can, *WHAT THE CRAP WAS THAT?"*

Adam Tate laughs. "Dear oh dear, Miss Judy! May I offer you some comfort?"

"I was hoping you would say that," Judy replies.

Adam Tate holds his hands out to Judy. As she takes his hands, Judy begins to feel an instant warmth going through her as if she hadn't a care in the world. And yet, her feelings for others are actually increased at the same time. *How can that be?* "How can it be, my friend that I am feeling all the pain and suffering of the world and yet I am also feeling an ecstatic passion for those who are suffering? Is this what *you* feel? The Chrysalenes?"

"Why yes, Judy. That is exactly what we feel. When there is human joy, we feel a heightened degree of joy and pleasure for all. But when there is suffering of any kind, we feel ecstatic. We feel the presence of the Divine entering and transforming the soul which can then rise to the highest heights of human consciousness."

"But does that always happen?" asks Judy.

"For us it does," says Adam Tate, "And we can transfer it to others whose hearts are open to it and who desire it, as you did just now, sweet lady."

"Yes! Yes! You have done that for me! Oh, my goodness! Oh, thank you sir! Thank you!"

"And once you become a part of the Light, Judy, all things are possible, *all* things! And that is truly cause for great joy!"

"Oh yes, Adam Tate, yes, it is! Thank you! I must let you get back to the crops now. It looks as if we will be having out first harvest soon." Judy smiles and leaves the beautiful Chrysalene to continue loving on the forthcoming fruits and vegetables. Inspired by his words, Judy goes to the pigeon coop. She writes a message for both birds and attaches one to each of their leg bands. The messages are going to Bear River Farm and they read:

#10 – I AM SENDING YOU MY LOVE TODAY.

#9 – ALONE WE CAN DO NOTHING, BUT TOGETHER WE CAN SUCCEED AT THE GOOD WE ARE SEEKING.

As she sends them into the air, Judy watches as #9 and #10 go in two separate directions.

Well, I'll be darned, Judy thinks. *I guess even the pigeons know where they are most needed.* Judy chuckles at the thought and goes back to her kitchen. Time to prepare for the Chrysalenes' evening meal.

* * *

The Lords and Ladies at Kookie's Kabin have decided that if each one has a Metatron device and a pair of pigeons, they can effectively coordinate their efforts against Operation Pied Piper.

Kookie is preparing #3 with a message to Kenny requesting 36 pairs of male and female pigeons, 72 total if he has that many to send, and to let Kenny know that he will be sending a Cloudtransporter to pick them all up. Meanwhile, he and a few of the Lords who are exceptionally good with electronics are going into high production with the creation of Metatron devices, expecting everyone to be "fully armed" shortly. Before they break for dinner, Kookie has one last message for the group:

"I will train each one of you on your device and download the 369-Program. Tomorrow morning, I will let Angie train you with the pigeons!"

This elicits cheers from everyone and #3 and #4 seem happy to oblige.

"The most important things we can all do right now with Metatron is to block the harmful subliminal messages being transmitted through My Buddy. And with the pigeons, our number one challenge is to get the word out to everyone to use their old seeds for the fruit and vegetable crops, not the so-called new and healthy ones. As we go along there will be other messages that need to be transmitted under the radar, and the pigeons will be the perfect ones to do that. Besides, after what these two here did to Lord Ekene, they sure do make great Airmen in their own Pigeons Airforce Unit!"

"Yes!" says Lord Jackson to Lady Neely in a flirtatious voice, leaning over Yakov and winking at the lovely Lady. "Bombs away, babe!" Lady Neely giggles and Yakov wants to puke.

Everyone returns to Kookie's Kastle for what promises to be a wonderful dinner. Angie goes out to her veranda first to get #3 and #4 settled in their coop for the evening. And when she gets there, she is pleasantly surprised to be greeted by #9. When she sees the message that Judy sent, Angie is reminded of Kookie's "House Divided" reference and knows that she must share it with Kookie as well as the other Lords and Ladies just as soon as she can. As Angie is about to leave her suite and go to dinner, there is a knock on her door. She answers and sees Kookie standing there. He is dressed in black from head to toe, wearing a red rose on his lapel. *Wow!* she thinks to herself. *Isn't he the bomb tonight!*

"Before we go to dinner Angie, there is something I wanted to talk to you about."

"Oh? Okay. What is it?"

"Well," Kookie gets anxious and starts to fidget. "It's about this afternoon," he says, looking intensely at the floor.

"Yes?" She has no idea where he is going with this.

"Well, that is, I know it was a hard thing for all of us, what we experienced with Ekene's death, I mean.

"Yes," she nods in agreement.

"And, um, well, what I'm trying to say is, uh . . ." Kookie is fidgeting as he pulls his tuba mouthpiece out of his pocket, trying to find the right words.

"Yes?"

Taking a deep breath Kookie says, "When I saw his body lying there all broken up and then I heard your voice saying something about bleeding, well, I just went into a panic."

"Yes! I could see that." Angie is still waiting to hear where Kookie is going with this.

"And I came rushing back and saw that you were okay, and . . .and . . ."

"OO*KAY?*" Angie's curiosity is fully piqued.

Finally, Kookie musters up all his courage as he looks Angie straight in the eye and says, "And when I called you *my woman,* I meant it!"

Angie breaks out into a smile as Kookie says the rest of it. "Angie, will you be My Woman, My Lady, and one day when we have fixed this world and we are legally allowed to marry each other, will you be my wife?"

With tears in her eyes and a tender smile Angie replies, "This afternoon when I called you My Man, I meant it too. Yes, Kookie. I will be your Woman."

Kookie relaxes into a wide, joyous grin and takes Angie by the hand. He kisses her tenderly, first on her forehead and then on her lips.

As the Lords and Ladies are filing into the dining room and waiting for their host to arrive, they are startled by a sudden and thunderous sound of amplified human flatulence coming from down the hall as Kookie is happily tooting on his tuba mouthpiece. With everyone seated and in a light-hearted mood, thanks to the pre-dinner entertainment provided by their host, Kookie and Angie make their appearance. They enter the dining room, arm in arm, smiling lovingly at each other. Making their way to Kookie's seat at the head of the table, he picks up the water glass and taps it with a knife.

"My Lords and My Ladies," he says in a formal tone, "First I would like to thank you all for coming here today and being a part of this very special occasion. And now, I will tell you just what that occasion is."

The guests throw curious glances at each other, knowing that none of them can speak openly in the dining room about the plan they arranged covertly at the Kabin. What special occasion could Kookie be referring to?

Putting his arm around Angie, Kookie continues, "In the tradition of the people of One World, Angie and I would like to share with you something very special. He brings her over to the front of the table where everyone can see them. They turn to face each other and then, taking the rose out of his lapel, Kookie holds it out to Angie as they say:

"My dearest Angie, I offer myself to you completely."

"My dearest Kookie; I offer myself to you completely."

"To be the best Man I can be,"

"To be the best Woman I can be,"

"With all the love that is in my heart, for you only,"

"With all the love that is in my heart, for you only,"

"In the sight of our Father in Heaven, this I promise,"

"In the sight of our Lord, this I promise,"

"To be your lover and best friend,"

"To be your lover and best friend,"

"Today, tomorrow and for all of eternity."

"Today, tomorrow and for all of eternity."

"Bless you Angie, my beloved Woman."

"Bless you Kookie, my beloved Man."

Kookie gives Angie the Red Rose, takes her in his arms and kisses her.

Everyone breaks out into applause, and some into tears, and they all begin to cheer, "Bravo, Kookie and Angie! Bravo!" The servers are standing around in stunned amazement, happy at what they are witnessing.

Kookie says to the Overseer Server, "Please set another place here next to mine for My Lady."

"Yes, My Lord," the server says cheerfully, "Right away!"

The feeling in Kookie's dining room that evening can best be described as love fulfilled, hope for the future, and faith in a promise made by all in attendance; the promise of *"Freedom for the people, and for all of One World." Thy will be done, Amen.*

* * *

The Servers bring out dessert. It is a colorful mixture of toppings and fillings for every kind of chocolate, cake, cookie, and candy imaginable as well as those which are delightfully *un*imaginable. There isn't a servant in the kitchen, or anywhere else in the Kastle for that matter, who is not fully aware of Kookie's passion for chocolate. In the kitchen, the staff is even a little competitive with each other in cooking up something exotic in the realm of chocolate, especially when there is a dining room full of guests. For this occasion, the servers are carrying the decorative and scrumptious platters around the dining room table in a procession. To their delight they are receiving much *ooo-ing* and *ahh-ing* from the Lords and Ladies who are enjoying the fanciful confectionary parade.

Kookie is joyfully tapping the tips of his fingers together watching the pleasure fill his dining room when he suddenly has a brilliant idea. Motioning to one of his servers he whispers something into her ear and she scurries off. Moments later the woman returns carrying Kookie's tuba. Kookie stands up holding his tuba out for everyone to admire and they all let out a collective, "*AHHH!!*" as well as a round of applause. Kookie takes out the mouthpiece, with which he had entertained them prior to the meal, and connects it to his tuba, ready to entertain them again at the end of the meal.

Seeing the servers head back to the kitchen, Kookie calls out to them, "Please," motioning to the extra chairs in the back. "Do stay and joins us, if you like."

The Lords and Ladies all express amazement, nodding to each other and nodding to the servers who gladly take a seat and join in on the festivities. And the hearts of the people and the UC in Kookie's dining room are uplifted and united in this moment of love. Kookie takes his Lord's Communication Device out of his pocket, dims the lights and opens the program with the orchestral arrangement for the Tuba Concerto in F Minor.

I knew this would come in handy someday, Kookie thinks to himself smiling, and he begins to play along with the orchestra.

The romantic tones of Kookie's tuba swell to the beautiful orchestration of the concerto and Angie is in lover's heaven. The feeling is gently flowing around the table opening the hearts of would-be lovers and new friends. Yakov has managed to get a seat right next to Neely this time without "butting-in," much to Jackson's chagrin, who is seated across the table and eyeing them with envy.

Yakov notices the floral arrangement on the table and casually reaches out to grab whatever he can with finesse, trying to be very cool, that is, without making a mess. His hand comes back with a little stem of Baby's Breath. He has already caught Neely's attention with his floral maneuvering and glances at her with affection in his eyes. Just as debonair, casual, and ultra-cool as he can be, Yakov takes the little bundle of Baby's Breath that he is holding in his hand and passes it under the table to Neely's hand. He says to her in English, "Sweet flowers for sweet Lady," with a sweet smile on his face.

Neely takes the flowers from his hand and with the back of her fingers gently strokes Yakov's hand, sending him straight to the moon.

Kookie continues to enchant everyone with the haunting blend of his tuba and the love for his Woman. Jackson, however, is feeling sullen and sorry for himself, and not at all enchanted. Then, a tray of double chocolate chip brownies is placed in front of him, causing Jackson to look up and behind him. He sees a pair of beautiful, baby-blue doe eyes peering down into his brown eyes, and his heart melts.

"I thought you might like to try these, My Lord," she says with an embarrassed giggle. "I made them."

"Oh! Uh, really? Wow! Well don't they look scrumptious though!" Jackson says with enthusiasm as he pops a brownie into his mouth.

The music is over, and everyone is quietly enjoying the mood and the moment just as Jackson is swallowing the last bit of his second brownie. Turning around, giving Baby-Blue-Doe-Eyes a beaming smile, and forgetting all prohibitions between their strata he says to her, "Thank you so much, sweetheart. That is *incredibly delicious!* My name is Jackson. What is *your* name?"

Everyone hears the question, and a deafening silence fills the room. All eyes are on Jackson, except for Baby-Blue-Doe-Eyes, who is looking across the table at Kookie. He smiles at his server with a wink and a nod of consent. She then turns her attention to Jackson and says affectionately, "Hi Jackson, my name is Rita."

"Hi Rita," Jackson says warmly, "May I get a chair for you and bring it over here?"

Rita nods, and Jackson has now crash-landed on the moon, next to his buddy Yakov.

Just then, Angie remembers the message from Judy and stands up to make an announcement. "Good people, I have something to share with you." Everyone goes quiet as Angie continues. "It is a message I received a little while ago from a dear friend. And I think you will all appreciate it." Angie reads the message from #9:

"ALONE WE CAN DO NOTHING, BUT TOGETHER WE CAN SUCCEED AT THE GOOD WE ARE SEEKING."

Everyone nods and smiles, and with a happy sigh, they resume their after-dinner conversations. Every Lord, Lady and servant in the room is fully aware of what they have just witnessed. Taboos have been broken: Kookie and Angie have taken the vows of the people together, the servants of High Lord Kookie's kitchen have become a welcomed part of the festivities, and a new friendship has begun between a man of the UC and a woman who is a mere person of the populace. These taboos have been broken among the highest level of society. And in their hearts, they all know that the days of the Council are numbered, and the light of a new world is dawning.

* * *

Across One World, three terminals are activated. The incoming message is from ES and it is accepted by PA and SPA.

ES: Greetings my Brethren.

PA: Greetings fellow Highest Ones.

SPA: Greetings fellow Brethren.

ES: Something has come to my attention which we need to discuss and act upon fellow Highest Ones.

PA: What is it ES.

SPA: Yes, do tell.

ES: I have just received word from my deepest inside sources, that Our High Lord Kenneth and a few others have broken several of our prohibitions.

PA: Do tell, ES!!

SPA: Dear me!!

PA: Whatever has our High Lord Kenneth done?!

ES: He has taken a slave woman, in the vows of the slaves.

SPA: *NO!*

PA: *GRACIOUS!*

SPA: *It is an outrage! Truly! Insubordination!*

PA: Dear, oh dear! You don't suppose that we will have to terminate him then, do you?

ES: Well, my Brethren, it would truly be the best thing you see, because he took vows with this slave woman in the company of other Lords.

PA and SPA: *NO! NO! GRACIOUS ME! NO!*

ES: And it is now feared that he is encouraging the others to do the same!

PA: Well, well, well. The ungrateful wretch! After all we did for him!

SPA: And all we gave to him!

PA and SPA: *WRETCH! WRETCH! WRETCH!*

ES: Yes, yes, I know all that. But unfortunately, it won't be so easy to dispose of him now, not without raising the wrath of the others. Besides which, there is this strange phenomenon that appears to be occurring around High Lord Kenneth and his associates.

PA: Whatever do you mean, brother?

SPA: ES is right, PA. I have noticed it myself. There are rumors that my own Ekene was trying to take care of High Lord Kenneth and his associates, for reasons unknown to us, when Ekene was killed instead in the process.

PA: Gracious! Then we must find the ones who are helping him!

ES: That is exactly right, PA. But until we do, this sort of insubordination can possibly be dangerous to us.

There is a silence as all three of them consider the consequences of having a full out assault on Kookie backfire on them.

PA: I suggest that we retire to discuss the matter with our advisors; in particular, the HOC's of the Lords and Ladies. They are the ones who know their proteges the best.

SPA: And I say we do not waste too much time with it all. The smart little ingrate is undoubtedly hatching a plan of his own while we are sitting here waiting for him to make his next move.

ES: Now, now, Brother. We *will* take him down. You can be sure of that!

SPA: And that dreadful slave woman of his!

PA: Oh, for sure! Another useless eater!

SPA: Vermin!

Another pause, as the three of them consider what they just said.

ES: The *woman?*

PA: The woman.

SPA: Yes, the WOMAN!!

ES: We can capture her alive and use her as bait!

PA: Excellent, ES, excellent!

SPA: Magnificent! Let's do it!

ES: First we must find out who she is, you know, what her name is, and all that.

With a demonic growl in his voice PA says:

AAANNNGIEEE!!!

Chapter 8 – Wakanjeja

EVE ELLI IS THE FIRST ONE to see #10 coming in for a landing. "Ooo, look everybody!" she exclaims cheerfully, "It's a pigeon! Hi pigeon!"

She hears the birds calling out to her spirit, *Hello, sacred child!*

"Hee Hee Hee!" Eve Elli is laughing, squealing and dancing around with delight. "Hello *yourself!*" she says to #10.

Kenny is working in the garden near the coop and sees #10's arrival. "Well, hello there," he says, "Let's see what kind of message Judy has for us."

I AM SENDING YOU MY LOVE TODAY – LAUGHS ALOT!

Kenny is uplifted and thanks #10 for her service.

Don't mention it! she says in return.

Then he sees another pigeon arriving. It is #3 with a note attached from Big Kahuna:

NEED WINGS – 72 IN ALL – BIG KAHUNA

Whoa! Kenny laughs to himself. *Sounds like Kookie's Pigeon Brigade is ready for action!* Seeing Eve Elli he says to her, "Would you help me out, honey?"

"Sure Kenny!" she says, skipping over to him.

"I need to gather a few folks together so we can talk about the pigeons," replies Kenny.

"Oh boy! That sounds like fun! Can I go to the Pigeon Gathering too, and talk about the pigeons with the grown-ups?"

"Sure thing," he says chuckling to himself. "Let's go find Phil and whatever Chrysalenes are not too busy and have them meet us over here at the coop."

"Okay, Kenny," Eve Elli says, skipping off to find everyone.

One by one, Phil and the Chrysalenes are rounded up and begin to congregate at the pigeon coop. Eve Jasmine joins them along with her little companion Suzie of the Seashells. Eve Elli is happy to see Suzie toddle over to the coop as she takes her by the hand to help her walk.

"Wow, Suzie! You are such a big girl now!" Eve Elli says.

By now the Chrysalenes have gathered at the coop, and Phil is just coming in from the fields walking along with Kenny.

"Well," Kenny says to everyone. "I have some great news for you all. I just got this message from Kookie as well as a message from Judy." He reads the messages to the group and looks up to the sky saying, "Thank you, Judy, for sending us your loving message."

Addressing the group, Kenny continues, "We are going to be training our new little baby pigeons, very soon."

"WHOA!" Everyone exclaims all at once.

Doc asks "Have the eggs hatched?"

"Almost!" Kenny says with excitement in his face. "And that is what I have gathered you altogether to talk about. As soon as these little guys, oh, um, excuse me . . ." he catches himself looking at Eve Elli and Suzie, "and little *gals* hatch, we will be all focused on getting them prepared to go out into the field. There is no time to lose, so it will be Pigeon Boot Camp for all of you who would like to volunteer for this."

Eve Elli is on her feet in two seconds, "Ooo me! Me! I just LOVE the pigeons!"

Little Suzie of the Seashells gets excited at whatever it is that Eve Elli is excited about. Her eyes go wide and she starts bouncing up and down. "OO! OO! OO!" she says.

Everyone has a good laugh and Phil says, "Well Kenny, it looks like you've just got your first two recruits!"

The Chrysalenes head over to the coop where the hens are sitting on their eggs. Eve Elli is just fascinated with the whole process, and she begins to ask questions. "Where are the baby pigeons?"

"Well," says Adam Bill, "Right now they are still in their eggs. And the mothers are sitting on their eggs, keeping them nice and warm until they are ready to come out."

"Oh!" Eve Elli seems quite pleased. "That sounds very comfy for the babies in there!"

"Why yes, it is *very* comfy for the babies in there!" says Eve Jasmine sweetly.

"Well, if it's so comfy for them, when will the babies come *out* of the eggs?"

Doc has just come out of the kitchen and is walking towards the coop as she hears the last part of the conversation. Calling out to her and quickening her pace, Doc says. "Eve Elli! The babies will come out when they are too big to be comfy in the eggs anymore!"

Putting her index finger on her chin, Eve Elli says pensively, "Hm, now that makes sense!"

Everyone chuckles and little Suzie wants in on this too. So, she puts her index finger on her chin and furrows her little brow, and everyone just laughs out loud.

Doc picks her up and gives her a hug. "Well," she says, "I can see two young ladies who are going to be quite the leaders around here one day, that is, if you aren't already!"

Phil comes over to Doc and Suzie and the three of them share a big bear hug together.

Kenny counts the new pigeons that have been trained recently and are waiting in reserve. He realizes that he now has 80 of them ready for deployment, which he announces to the group. "Hey! Guess what everyone? We actually have enough birds in this unit that are ready to go to Kookie's Kastle right now."

"Woo hoo! Fantastic!" chant the folks in turn followed by, "Yippee!" from Eve Elli, and "YEEYEE!" from Suzie, fluttering her little hands with excitement.

"I had better send #3 back to Kookie with the news and have him arrange transport for 36 males and 36 females!"

That night as Eve Lydia and Adam Sam are tucking Eve Elli into bed, they say their prayers together for all the people of the world; their Brothers and Sisters of the UC, children everywhere, and last but not least for Mimi and Ryan.

"Please Lord, take care of my Gramma. She is so very brave. Please tell her not to be afraid and that Eve Elli loves her *very, very* much."

As Eve Lydia and Adam Sam say good night to their little girl, Eve Elli suddenly sees something in the window and becomes excited. "Oh Mama! Look!" she cries, jumping out of bed and running over to the window.

"What is it, sweetheart?" Eve Lydia asks her, but when she looks at the window, her mama sees it for herself.

"Angel! Angel!" Eve Elli shouts for joy. "Look Mama, look Papa, Angel is back!"

Hello, little human creature, the Monarch beams into Eve Elli's spirit.

"Hi Angel! Hi! Hi! Oh, your friends are here too!" Eve Elli says while opening the window and gently greeting the Monarchs with her light touch.

Eve Lydia and Adam Sam hold each other as they witness the exchange between their daughter and a flutter of Monarchs.

Yes, sacred little human creature, we have come to bring you news.

"Oh! Okay!" says Eve Elli as she reaches out to them, and they all come forward to kiss her face and nestle in her hair.

There is another sacred young human creature, a little boy who is very sad. He has lost his papa not too long ago, and although he has some loving, new human creature friends, he is being kept away from them. So, he truly feels very sad and lonely.

"Oh no!" says Eve Elli, "That makes me sad, too," as tears begin to form in her eyes.

Yes, sacred little human creature, you must cry for him, and pray for him and reach out to him with all of your heart.

"O – o – okay," whimpers Eve Elli, crying for the sad little boy who lost his papa.

You must call out to him in his lonely world, and we will be sure that he hears your voice in his heart. . . and your words in his own language.

"Okay Angel," Eve Elli, whispers softly. "What is his name?"

Emeka.

It is 7 p.m. and Eve Elli goes back to her bed. She gets down on her knees and begins to pray for the little boy who Angel called Emeka.

The Monarchs flutter high up into the evening sky, with the colors of the setting sun shining a golden light on their brilliant wings.

Angel looks down upon Eve Elli and says, *Bless you, Wakanjeja. Bless you.*

* * *

It is 4 a.m. in Johannesburg, and all is quiet on the estate of the late Lord Ekene. Everyone is sleeping peacefully, except for little Lord Emeka who is tossing and turning in the midst of a nightmare:

Little Emeka is running through the jungle. Branches of trees hit him in the face and tear into his skin as creatures of the night are suddenly screaming at him from the attacking branches. There is a deep rhythmic booming that sounds like something is chasing close behind him. Far off in the distance he can hear the high-pitched voice of an animal screaming wildly, sounding like a child who is being tortured.

Emeka is terrified as he keeps on running. He does not know where he is running to, but he knows that if he stops the evil force will catch up with him and make him scream too. He does not dare to turn around, but he is suddenly aware of what is pursuing him: a red-eyed monster. The monster is laughing at him and speaking to him, "Your father is here with us little boy, and soon you will be too! IT IS HIS SOUL THAT YOU HEAR SCREAMING! HAHAHAHAHA!"

"NO! NO! NO!" Emeka cries out; when all of a sudden, he hears another voice in the darkness.

"Emeka . . . Emeka . . ." the voice of a little girl is calling to him softly. He hears her words in his heart saying, "Don't cry Emeka. Everything is gonna be okay. Eve Elli loves you. Eve Elli is here with you. Angel is here with you. #9 and #10 are here with you. Everybody loves you. Everything is gonna be okay. Don't be afraid Emeka. You are safe here with us . . ."

The jungle begins to part as the sky turns clear and a light shines out in the darkness before him. Then he sees a most beautiful Angel appear before him, with golden wings of orange, white, black, and brown.

The Angel says to Emeka, "Sacred young human creature, do not be afraid of the monsters. They cannot hurt you, and with your forgiveness, they cannot hurt your father. Little Eve Elli loves you. Your new friends all love you, and we love you too. Wake up now sacred young human creature, and may your heart be at peace."

Little Lord Emeka slowly opens his eyes, and although he knows that the bad dream is over, in his heart he feels that the true nightmare is just beginning.

* * *

It is early in the morning and Bem is getting his day started. There is much to do now with all the new seeds that have arrived from the local Johannesburg plant of Howard Pharmaceuticals. After the funeral of Lord Ekene and day of rest for the servants, much has been happening on the estate. Since the arrival of the Chrysalenes, much of the fear and anger has been dissipating, day by day. Even the Overseers have been kinder to everyone, and more and more people have been calling each other by their first names. In fact, no one even knew the names of the people with whom they have been serving for most, if not all, of their lives. It is like discovering new friends in the same old people for the very first time.

From the UC's perspective, however, their uncertainty and anxiety has gotten worse. And no one really knows what has happened to Lord Ekene and how he died. Most of the Lords and Ladies of the Continental Territory of Sinopacifica are worried that something may have mysteriously gone wrong with Operation Pied Piper. Since My Buddy's subliminal program has come out, they are suddenly seeing an increase in depression, fear and anxiety within the UC and several suicides have been reported amongst them as well.

Fearing that there might be a link between the self-destructive behaviors of the UC and the subliminal portion of Operation Pied Piper, the Lords and Ladies of Sinopacifica have decided to temporarily suspend all transmissions of My Buddy.

However, the UC is hopeful once again with the arrival of the tainted seedlings. And of course, their own tables are filled as usual with food from healthy, untainted plants. But no one except the private servants of the UC know about this and they are absolutely prohibited from speaking about it.

This morning, Tafari comes into Bem's hut with Dumaka and Nassor. "Shall we break bread together my friend?" Tafari says to Bem.

"Certainly! And what a lovely morning it is, my Brothers!" replies Bem.

After finishing their meal together, Dumaka turns to the four of them and says, "Today we have been told to go down to the Center Market and pick up our new seeds. I should also like to stop into the

Coffeehouse while we are there. It has been a while since we have enjoyed ourselves in such a pleasant way, has it not?"

"Oh yes, that is a wonderful idea," says Nassor.

The four men load up their autobikes and plan on lingering at the Center Coffeehouse after picking up their new seeds.

As they are preparing to leave, Lord Emeka comes out of the house to greet them. "Hello, my friends," the five-year-old says a bit timidly.

"Well, hello there My Lord! What a pleasant day it is and how nice to see you!" says Tafari. "Is there something we can do for you?"

"Where are you going?" Lord Emeka asks the four men.

"Well," says Bem, "as a matter of fact, we are going to the Center Market to get some new seeds."

"Oh, um, may I um, come with you?"

The men are rather astounded by his request, and they also know that coming with them will not go down well with the Lady of the house, as well as anyone else from the UC who happens to hear about it. Yet, something in their hearts is telling them to find out what is going on.

Bem gets down on his knees and puts his hands on Lord Emeka's shoulders. "What is it, My Lord? Is there something troubling you?"

Looking a bit sullen, Emeka says, "I need to find Eve Zula and Adam Makena. Don't they live at the Center?"

"Oh my!" Bem says, and they all breathe a little bit easier. "Why no, they do not. They live in a small village nearby. We can get them over here for you though if you like. Might I inquire as to why there is an urgency for you to see them?"

Lord Emeka pouts a little and squirms, but then he comes out with it. "I had a bad dream, and I just want to talk to them."

They all gasp, and Dumaka says, "Oh my goodness! Now *that is* serious My Lord!"

Emeka continues to fidget and furrow his brow.

"Did you know," Dumaka, continues, "That I just happen to be very good at understanding and explaining dreams?"

Emeka wrinkles his nose and lets out a "Hmph."

"Why yes, My Lord. As a matter of fact, I am."

Thinking of a way to help little Lord Emeka without risking the consequences of taking him to Eve Zula or Adam Makena, Dumaka says to him, "Why don't we just go for a walk in the garden right here by our huts, and you can tell me all about it."

"Hmm, okay," he agrees.

The men feel much safer with this idea.

Bem turns to the others and says, "I guess we can put off our plans until this afternoon then," to which they all agree.

"So, tell me about your dream My Lord," Dumaka says to Emeka as they are walking through a vegetable garden.

"It was very scary," Lord Emeka says, and he begins to recount being chased and threatened by a monster. "But worst of all," he says and begins to cry, "The monster said that my papa was the one I heard screaming!"

They all stop walking; Dumaka gets down on his knees and he puts his arms around Emeka. "It is alright for you to cry and be scared, My Lord, but you must always remember one thing."

Sniffling into Dumakas' shoulder, Lord Emeka says, "What's that?"

"You must remember *why* these bad creatures come into our lives and why they say and do bad things and try so very hard to frighten us."

"Why?" snivels Emeka, feeling curious.

"Because they are the ones who are truly terrified of *us,* and that is why they make such a loud noise and try to frighten us. The truth is, they cannot really hurt us if we are not afraid of them."

"An Angel came to me afterwards and said something just like that," Lord Emeka says, a little bit more relaxed now.

"There! You see? Now why don't we take you back to your house so you will not make your family worried about where you have gone off to?"

"Well, okay," Emeka says with a smile appearing on his face.

Bem, Dumaka, Tafari and Nassor walk Emeka back to the front entryway of the Big House.

"You have a good day now," they all say to him, and little Lord Emeka gives each one of them another big hug. Smiling happily, he turns to go into the house.

Bem says to the other three, "Okay, Brothers, that was nice. But there is much too much to do here now, and I am thinking perhaps we had better wait until sundown to go to the Market. Besides, if Lord Emeka's dream is some kind of omen, then perhaps we can get some news later at the Coffeehouse. You know, later on there will be more people."

They all agree that it sounds like a good plan and get their day started in the gardens.

* * *

Kookie knew he would not be able to speak freely to the Lords and Ladies anywhere else on the grounds of his Kastle other than the Kabin, so before they all left the Kabin on the previous day, he made arrangements to meet most of them back there for their Pigeon training, the next morning. The others will be working with him at his workstation with the Holographic Imager going, deleting their presence in the room, of course. They will be taking 36 ordinary Lord's Communication Devices and turning them into Metatron Devices, also programmed with 369.

"Well, my friends," he says to everyone as they all gather in the dining room for breakfast. "I hope you all had a good night's rest, and you are enjoying yourselves here," he says like a gracious host.

"Oh yes, Kookie, we most certainly are! Isn't it just lovely here though! Oh Yes, yes indeed it is," they all chatter around the room in response.

For a moment Kookie looks at them and thinks to himself, *Hey! Don't overdo this foolishness, you guys!"* as he finds himself saying to them, "Oh yes, my yes indeed it *is* lovely here!" It is not so much the language they are all using though, that would cause suspicion. A dead giveaway to anyone observing the room that this scene is a contrived bunch of hooey, and something is not quite right, is the fact that Kookie is *not* tapping the tips of his fingers together.

After breakfast Kookie gives them the pre-arranged cue, "Okay everyone, how about going for a nice walk through the gardens this morning?"

"Oh my, yes! Why isn't that a simply marvelous idea! Oh yes, indeed it is, simply marvelous!" the crowd chatters away.

Yakov leaves the dining room hand in hand with Neely, Jackson leaves arm in arm with Rita, and the rest are making a few new intimate acquaintances amongst themselves. Angie looks at Kookie and giggles, "It was the tuba last night, honey!" Kookie looks at her and smiles, and then starts tapping the tips of his fingers together.

As 39 HOC's, including Kookie's, are covertly watching the scene unfold from various locations around One World, they all relax and figure everything is normal when Kookie begins to finger-tap.

"Well," I guess I shall go for a lovely walk around the lovely gardens, too, on this lovely day. Is that alright my *lovely* darling?" Angie says to her Man, trying not to laugh.

Kookie looks at her affectionately, "Yes dear," he says.

Kookie and his techie crew go to his workstation where the first thing he does is get the Holographic Imager all set up. Angie heads on over to the veranda to check up on #4 and see if #3 has gotten back yet. She sees the two of them snuggled happily together.

"Yay! You're back!" Angie exclaims and approaches the coop. Seeing the message attached to #3 she takes it off and reads it:

72 WINGS READY FOR TRANSPORT – GRIZZLY

"Woo Hoo! Yes! Oh, I love you guys! Wait until I tell Kookie!" She kisses the birds and takes off down the hallway for his workstation.

* * *

Kenny and his crew are busy placing bands on the legs of 72 pigeons who are about to be transported to Kookie's Kastle. They have also prepared 36 makeshift cages where they will put one male and one female into each cage. The pigeons are already bonding with each other in couple fashion, and Kenny feels confident that he is matching up the ones who are already "betrothed" to one another.

"Well, my friends," he says to the birds as he is about to pair them off for their cages, "if I guessed wrong, then you all can fix that at the other end, before your new people take you with them."

Eve Elli is seated on the floor next to the first cage that has been filled with two pigeons, all ready to go. Little miss Suzie of the Seashells is of course seated right next to her, as the two young ladies are about to get down to business.

Kenny, Doc and Phil are watching Eve Elli and Suzie, very curious and anxious to see what they are going to do. Eve Jasmine, Eve Lydia, Adam Sam and the other Chrysalenes already know, of course.

Phil finally asks Eve Elli, "So what is it that you two young ladies are going to do with the pigeons, if I may ask?"

"We bless the pigeons," Eve Elli says affectionately, as she takes the two birds out of their cage. She closes her eyes and holds the pigeons to her chest, feeling the warmth of their love. Then she opens her eyes and holds them up to the heavens saying, "Bless these pigeons, Lord, so they can help *everybody!*" And with that she holds the birds against her chest again, breathing her love into them, and kissing them both on the head.

Suzie puts out her hands and Eve Elli holds the pigeons out in front of her. Suzie leans forward and with a kissing noise touches her mouth to the top of their heads, *"mwah!"*

Everyone drops whatever they are holding, and they all form a circle around the two little girls. They bow their heads and say, "Amen."

Shortly afterwards the small Cloudtransporter arrives, and Kenny begins to load the spherical shaped transporter that stands about as tall as he is. One by one he places 36 travel cages containing two blessed birds each, into the shipping container. With one last blessing from the Chrysalenes and everyone else, Kenny sends the Unit of little Airmen on their way to join in and do their part for the cause of freedom and love.

* * *

Bem, Tafari, Dumaka and Nassor have finished their gardening for the day. The sun has gone down, and they know that they still have to get the seeds from the Center Market. But most of all they are very much looking forward to getting some tea cakes and news from the Coffeehouse.

"Okay Brothers," says Bem, "Let's go get those seeds at the Center Market."

Nassor says, "And some good pastries and conversation at the Coffeehouse!" They all agree to that one enthusiastically.

Arriving at the Center Market, the gardeners of the late Lord Ekene's estate get their seeds quickly and then head straight for the Coffeehouse. Seeing some friends, they are invited over to sit and chat with them.

"Hello Brother! Anything new since Lord Ekene's funeral?" a young man asks Bem.

"Not really my friend, except, well . . . "

"What is it?" they all look at Bem.

"Everyone seems to be so friendly all of a sudden, and even *happy!*" They all agree that this is true and that it is indeed very strange.

"You mean like the way those holy people came and Lord Emeka and everyone all got so happy?" another man asks.

"Yes," says Tafari. "In fact, I believe that I have never been happier in my life."

"Now that IS strange" Dumaka says, "And I think I have to agree with you on that one."

"Here, here," the rest of them say and it seems that this strange phenomenon of *happiness* has been affecting many people since the day of Lord Emeka's funeral and the arrival of the Holy Ones.

"Oh, there is one very important thing, however, which we are just hearing about," the first young man says. "There is a rumor going around that we are to continue using our old seeds and seedlings, and *not* the new ones. Something about toxins. And also, something to do with Lord Ekene's death."

The six men talk for quite a while and learn about many rumors that have been flying around lately regarding toxins and subliminal messages from My Buddy, and unexplained disappearances and UC suicides. As it starts getting near 9 p.m., they all promise to return and keep each other informed.

On the way back to their huts, Bem, Tafari, Nassor and Dumaka arrive at the estate. They are just coming down the lane and about to turn off to their garden dwellings when suddenly, they hear a most blood curdling, terrifying, high pitched, scream coming from Lord Ekene's Big House. The men stop dead in their tracks and look up just as another scream comes from the house; and another and another. In a flash, they start racing to the house as fast as they can. They arrive just in time to hear glass shattering, and to see three people jumping out of windows to their death.

The entire estate of the late Lord Ekene hears the screaming, and within minutes all the servants are out of their huts and at the Big House. Cloudambulances are arriving on the scene and pandemonium has broken out as all are witness to an inexplicable, horrific scene of mass suicide. More people are leaping from windows, and the AI paramedics are trying to get something set up to break their falls, but to no avail. The unfolding scene is progressing so quickly that no one is able to stop it let alone understand why it is happening.

* * *

The Cloudtransporter has just left Bear River Farm and is on its way to Kookie's Kastle. It is 12 noon and time for lunch at the farm, and Eve Elli and Suzie have worked up quite an appetite with all of their loving on the pigeons. The Chrysalenes come in from the fields and help bring the food out to the tables.

As everyone settles down and takes a seat, Kenny begins with a big announcement. "My dear friends, today marks a momentous occasion. Just a little while ago we sent out our first 72 pigeons to Kookie's Kastle. These birds are going to Lords and Ladies all around One World, and as such they are our newest and smallest recruits to Operation Monarch!"

Kenny's announcement receives a round of applause and expressions of awe and gratitude. "Thank you one and all for working so hard to make this happen, especially Eve Elli and little Suzie of the Seashells, without whose kisses the pigeons just would not be fully prepared!"

Everyone laughs out loud, followed by more applause.

"And now, my Brothers and Sisters, would one of the Chrysalenes kindly lead us in prayer?

Adam Mark rises and begins, "Father in Heaven, thank you so much for the food that we are about to receive, and for bringing us all here together . . ."

While Adam Mark continues to pray, Eve Elli is suddenly hearing another voice. It starts out as a quiet voice inside of her head. At first, she cannot quite make out the words, but within moments the voice from a frightened heart grows loud enough for her to hear.

Help me! Help me! Where are you? Oh, please help me!

Eve Elli closes her eyes and holds her hands up to the heavens as she speaks to Emeka's heart, "Do not be afraid my friend Emeka! Help is coming! Help is on the way!"

Everyone hears Eve Elli and they all grow quiet. The Chrysalenes close their eyes to see and hear what Eve Elli is experiencing. They see little Lord Emeka huddled in a corner of his bedroom with the sounds of screaming and glass breaking nearby. Then they see Eve Elli reaching out to Eve Zula and Adam Makena. She can see that they are already on their way to the Big House with the other 10 Chrysalenes of their village.

"Don't cry Emeka, it's okay. They are on their way. They will be there *very* soon! Do not be afraid!"

A tearful child's heart answers his little angel, "Thank you, Eve Elli. I will not be afraid as long as you are with me."

"I Am here with you. Do not cry Emeka. Everything is gonna be okay."

Chapter 9 – Whisperings

WHEN THE LAST BODY HAS FALLEN, 23 broken human souls are lying on the ground, having all jumped out of the same three windows. The servants below are crying out in anguish at the loss of their dear friends.

A man yells out, "Look! The open windows! That is Lord Ekene's office!"

The Overseer Paramedic says to the man, "Can you take us to the office?"

"Yes, yes! Just follow me!" says the man.

Tafari has fallen to his knees, rocking back and forth with his face buried in his hands. Bem, Dumaka and Nassor already understand what must be going on inside their friend as they sit down beside him in silence. They will stay by his side bringing him whatever he needs to be comfortable. And when he is ready to speak, they will be there to listen.

The rest of the crowd has broken up into groups, with some doing a room-by-room search to see if anyone is left inside while the rest all head for Ekene's office. When they arrive at his office, they see the three open windows and a shattered room with broken glass and furniture. . . blood is everywhere. There are the remains of Coffeehouse tea cakes and juice, scattered and spilled, with two audio recordings left running on a continuous loop.

They catch the words on one recording as the transmission from My Buddy. The second recording is the subliminal message that plays underneath the one that everyone actually hears. It is the voice of the late Lord Ekene calling them all human trash, telling them that there is no hope except through that open window. Each human standing in the room, which does not include the AI paramedics, becomes agitated. Recognizing the issue, the Overseer Paramedic quickly moves over and shuts down both recordings. Everyone begins to calm down immediately.

In silence the group begins to consider what really happened here tonight.

The Overseer Paramedic looks at everyone and softly says, "Come on good people, let's just leave this sorrowful place."

The small crowd couldn't agree more.

They all get back to the Cloudambulances outside to find that the AI paramedics who remained on the scene outside have already taken care of everything, and they report to the Overseer Paramedic that there are no survivors.

"Well," the Overseer Paramedic says to the group of people gathered, "I guess that about takes care of it for tonight. I'll call for a unit of commandos to come in, as I'm sure there will be an investigation."

The people are all shaken and some are crying. The Overseer Paramedic says in nearly a whisper, "It's alright everyone, you can go home now."

The Cloudambulances leave and the remaining folks who linger a little while longer notice something in the distance.

"Look! The Holy Ones!" one of the people exclaims.

Tafari looks up and sees Eve Zula and Adam Makena walking with 10 other Chrysalenes, and Tafari's heart is greatly uplifted. As they approach, everyone can hear them gently singing soft tones from heaven. No one has noticed that another pair of eyes has been watching from the Big House. When the Chrysalenes arrive, the little boy whose eyes witnessed the night's tragic event, comes out of the shadows and out of the house to fly from the horror that just surrounded him.

Eve Zula sees the terrified eyes of Emeka as he runs toward her. When he reaches her, the little 5-year-old boy who just lost what was left of his family, throws his arms around her waist, and starts to cry his heart out. Eve Zula lifts him gently and holds him in her arms, as she whispers to little Lord Emeka, "They are all in Heaven now, and with your help we can bring your papa to them, as well."

Emeka stops crying for a moment and says, "How can we do that Mama Eve Zula?"

The 12 Chrysalenes hold Emeka, passing him from one to the other.

Adam Makena says to him, "With love, my child. We will show you how."

The Chrysalenes take turns holding and loving little Lord Emeka as they carry him with them, back to the Village of the Holy Ones.

* * *

The Major was able to use Kookie's code on the boxes of poison, just in the nick of time. Once they were zapped, the neurotoxins in the juice were completely neutralized. While the Major and Vi have gone back to Master Howard's main plant, Mimi and Ryan are still in the shipping department of the Silver Beach plant of Howard Pharmaceuticals. Their mission now is to snoop around and keep the Major informed. It is Ryan's fantasy come true; he is now officially a mole!

"Hey honey," Ryan says to Mimi as soon as they leave their posts at the end of the day and are safely outside. "Did you hear the rumor going around in shipping today?"

"What rumor, sweetie?"

"They think something happened in Johannesburg. It is believed to be another mass suicide."

"Good heavens! Another one?"

"I'm afraid so," he says. They both stop walking for a moment and bow their heads. Then they look into each other's eyes and in a voice barely above a whisper Mimi says, "Ryan, we have got to do something. These deaths cannot continue."

"I know honey, but what else can we do?"

"Something has been speaking to my gut lately," Mimi says, "And I believe that we are going to find out soon. Also, I have been getting a strong feeling that we need to do some snooping around tonight."

"Okay," Ryan asks her, "Where?"

"You know that detention area, the place where they held Eve Elli, Eve Lydia, Adam Sam and all the other Chrysalenes?"

"That's the place, huh?"

"Yes," Mimi says. "So why don't we go to our dwelling, have some food, get ourselves all self-cloaked and then go to the detention area."

"Okay," Ryan says trying not to sound too excited. He really does love being a mole!

* * *

Vi comes running into the Major's office at the main plant, hardly able to hold back her tears. Fortunately, no one is with him. He takes one look at her and says their usual code words for these situations, knowing that they are under constant surveillance.

"Another problem with the autodelivery van then, huh?"

"Uh *huh!*" she says, trying not to sound so upset over a van.

"Oh, alright then," he says with an exaggerated sigh. "Go on out there and I'll be right with you."

A few minutes later, the Major and Vi meet each other at the shipping vans outside. There is a blind spot to the security cameras that the Major is aware of, although they still must keep their voices down.

"Oh John!" Vi cries collapsing into his arms.

She hardly ever calls him John, so he knows this is serious.

"I just heard of another mass suicide," she is sobbing, "a group of 23 people somewhere in Johannesburg."

"Dear God. I guess I didn't get to all the boxes fast enough," he says sadly, burying his face on the top of Vi's head.

The two of them stand there for a minute without words, trying to be a comfort to each other in their grief. Finally, Vi gives the Major the rest of the story as it has come down through their contacts.

"There's more," she whispers to him, ever so gently. "Apparently, there is a child who is unaccounted for. I mean, he seems to have gone missing."

The Major squeezes his eyes shut fighting back tears.

"John, there is also a rumor going around. . . something about *Holy Ones*. I'm wondering if there might be some Chrysalene involvement and that the child may still be alive and safe."

The Major looks at Vi with a bit of hope. "So, you think we should make a trip to Judy's and check in with our friends there?" he asks.

"Sound like a plan to me!" Vi says, with hope returning to her as well.

"If we leave now, we can be there for dinner. Why don't you let her know that we are coming, and I'll get the Autocar."

"Okay, Major," Vi says with a little smile returning.

* * *

Judy is in the garden walking around from one seedling to the other. She is blessing them the way the Chrysalenes have been teaching her to. Although they have told her that it is okay to bless them by sending them loving energy through her hands from a standing position, Judy is determined to do it the Chrysalene way. Despite her achy back and knees, Judy gets down on her hands and knees and kisses the little guys. When she stands back up, she holds onto her back and lets out a long, "*OOYY!*"

She sees a pigeon coming in for a landing and gets excited, helping her forget about her achy back and knees. Judy gets to the coop just as #5 arrives. "Well, hello, hello #5, sweetie! Let's see what you've got for me today!" Judy takes off the note and reads the following message from Vi:

TWO FOR DINNER – BUTTERFLY

"Oh my! They'll be here very soon then!" Judy exclaims and scurries off to the kitchen, taking #5 with her. Judy loves having the birds to talk to, especially the visiting ones. It feels like they are having a conversation with her when they sit on her shoulder and listen to her talk about the events of the day. In fact, Judy is sure that there are times when she is uncertain about something, #9 and #10 will whisper to her heart and give her the answer.

Looking at #5 she laughs, "You know, there are times when I really do think that you guys are smarter than me!" Of course, #5 cocks his head to one side as if he is in full agreement with her.

Judy is pulling out three loaves of bread she baked fresh this morning when there is the familiar sound of the Autocar out front.

"They're here #5! Let's go to greet them at the door, shall we?"

She opens the door and sees the sullen looks on Vi and the Major's faces and knows that this is not going to be a fun social visit.

"Well, hello there," Judy begins on a pleasant note. "It's so nice to have you both stop by."

They give her a barely audible "Hi," with two weak smiles.

"Okay," she says, "So come on in and tell Mama Judy what's going on."

Vi and the Major just look at each other as they walk inside and sit down.

"Oh," says Vi, with a slight grin. "I see #5 has landed on your shoulder."

Judy chuckles, "Oh aren't the pigeons just the sweetest things!" Then she adds, "Why don't I get some food on the table and we can break bread together."

The Major finally speaks up, "Thank you, Judy, that is most welcome, and um, do you think perhaps a couple of the Chrysalenes could join us?"

"Oh, why yes, of course," Judy says, and heads back out to the garden.

The Major looks at Vi and says in a soft voice, "This is not easy to talk about, is it, Violet." Vi just looks down and nods in agreement.

Judy comes back a few minutes later with Adam Tate. "Adam Tate and I have been enjoying some very interesting conversations lately," says Judy, "So I thought you might like to talk to *him.*"

The Chrysalenes have a heightened sense of intuition, but when something is particularly disturbing, they pick up on everything.

"Good evening to you Major and to you Vi; it is so good to see you both again," Adam Tate says.

"Thank you," they both nod. "You too."

Adam Tate closes his eyes for a moment and listens to their hearts since he can see they are having difficulties speaking with their tongues. When he opens his eyes he says, "I understand you are both wondering what happened in Johannesburg, to those who died from poisoned juice, as well as the whereabouts of the child."

Judy is shocked as she had no idea what was going on. "*What? Who? Poisoned juice in Johannesburg? How did they get poisoned juice in Johannesburg? What child? Who is he?*"

The Major and Vi are waiting to hear the details as they turn to Adam Tate in their grief and bewilderment.

He smiles with compassion at the three of them, knowing how horrible all of this is for them. Adam Tate explains, "The place where this happened was the estate of the late Lord Ekene, who already had the poisoned juice in his possession. It was provided to him by the Council for experimentation purposes, along with the toxic tea cakes. His wife and family did not believe the official story of how he died so they went into his office suite to try to put the pieces together. There they found the juice, tea cakes and the recordings that he was working on. They helped themselves to the snacks and then listened to the recordings, and suddenly had complete emotional breakdowns from the effects of the drugs and subliminal torture. Following the command on one of the recordings, combined with the effects of the mind control drugs in the juice and tea cakes, they left this world through open windows."

"Oh my!" cries Judy. "That is so horribly sad!"

"What about the child?" Vi asks.

"There is a small village near the late Lord Ekene's estate. There are 12 Chrysalenes living there who were summoned to come for the child."

"Who summoned them?" the Major asks, "And how have you come to know all of this, Adam Tate?"

With a look of pure peace on his face, Adam Tate says, "Good Master John, we, the Chrysalenes, are connected to each other all throughout One World. When I closed my eyes just now, I called out to the ones who were there. We speak the language of the heart to each other which travels much quicker than words.

"The child is the late Lord Ekene's son, and his name is Emeka. He is five years old and a true wakanjeja. The Chrysalenes of Johannesburg have been charged to take care of him."

Vi, Judy and the Major are spinning with the sudden onslaught of information. But at the same time, they are also grateful to be hearing all this news, especially the Major who is now beginning to understand things on a much deeper level. He feels more hope now for Operation Monarch and all the people of One World.

Vi is also beginning to understand things more and she asks Adam Tate, "Please sir, won't you tell us more about the child Emeka and why he is so special?"

Adam Tate's smile beams. "He is you, dear lady, and you dear Judy, and he is also you, kind sir."

"I'm not sure I understand you," says the Major.

"Neither does Emeka. But in time, you will learn, all of you, and Emeka will too."

Vi realizes there is one question Adam Tate has not answered yet.

"Oh, by the way," Vi says, "you said that the Chrysalenes were summoned. Um, so who summoned them."

Leaning forward with laughter in his eyes, Adam Tate says, "Why, it was little Eve Elli, ma'am!"

"WHAAAT?!" Vi, Judy and the Major all shriek at the same time.

"And a little child shall lead them!"[10] says Adam Tate.

After a little while, when they have all had a chance to digest things a bit, Judy says, "Are you folks ready for food yet?"

"Does that include your fantastic bread?" asks the Major.

"Actually, it includes one loaf for all of us to share, and one for you all by yourself!" Judy says, remembering how much the Major loves her bread. Then turning to #5 who is still hanging out on her shoulder taking everything in, Judy turns to him and says, "Now isn't that right, #5? That the Major here should get one whole loaf of bread all to himself?"

Number 5 cocks his head to the side letting everyone know that he is in full agreement. Judy goes into the kitchen to get the food while something occurs to the Major.

---

[10] Isaiah 11:6 NKJV

Turning to Adam Tate, the Major asks, "So, you are telling me that all of the Chrysalenes can communicate with each other the way you just described?"

"Yes, sir."

"Hm, I see. So, um, how exactly do you do that then?"

Adam Tate explains, "It's like whispering to someone's heart."

The Major is thoroughly intrigued, although he does not really understand. He looks at Vi, who is nodding at Adam Tate, fully appreciating what the Chrysalene is talking about. When Vi catches the Major's eye he says to her, "I knew that!"

She laughs at him, "Here, you silly, let me show you. Turn your chair around and face me. Get as close as you can but without touching me. Now close your eyes and relax and let your breathing slow down." They are doing this together and after a few moments when they are both relaxed and breathing in sync, Vi says to the Major, "Okay now, keep your eyes closed and just tell me what I am feeling right now. What is going through my heart? Don't think about it, just feel it."

"Okay," he says, and in less than a minute he can feel the warmth and love radiating out of Vi's heart, followed by an image. "I see a little five-year-old child, with eight butterflies fluttering all around him."

"Yes," says Adam Tate. "Vi's heart just whispered to yours that Emeka is being protected by Angel and her friends."

"Wow!" the Major says as he opens his eyes.

"Yes. Isn't that amazing?" Vi says, "And just imagine being able to do that many times greater than we can. THAT, my dear is just a part of the power of the Chrysalenes."

"Wow!"

"I know, *right?*"

"Vi!" exclaims the Major.

"Yes?"

"VI!"

"WHAT?"

"This is it, woman!"

"This is *what, man*?!"

The Major turns excitedly to Adam Tate. "Good sir, would you and the Chrysalenes be willing to help us with, you know, all of those gifts of yours, like communication, and maybe a little healing?"

Thinking of Master Howard, the Major adds, "And maybe even some loving on, you know, difficult people?"

Adam Tate starts beaming and before he can say anything Vi pipes in, "Honey, I think that is exactly what they have been doing!" and she too gives the Major a great big smile.

Judy comes out with the food and senses a different atmosphere around the table. "Well, it looks like we have found our appetites!" Judy says.

"All ready to dig into that loaf of bread, Judy!" the Major says with his eyes glued to it. "Thank you very much, kind lady. Let the feast begin!"

The Major expresses his gratitude to Adam Tate as well and is beginning to see a glimmer of hope for his father. As always, Judy's meal of soup, fruit and pastries is wonderful, and, of course, she packs more bread for him to take with Vi when they leave.

Then, something deep inside the Major hits him. Looking at Vi, he is feeling something for a woman that he has never truly felt before. Suddenly, his heart opens, and he looks at his Violet with great passion.

He sparkles . . .

She twinkles . . .

They both sigh . . .

And they eat homemade pastries together with Judy and Adam Tate.

* * *

Mimi and Ryan slip out of their dwelling unit unseen and make their way to the detention center. The original use for the detention center was for untested chemicals and new drugs that were still in the trial phase. It was necessary to keep them in a separate area from the other pharmaceutical products, so the locked cages were a way of maintaining drug safety. They were never intended to be used as cages for human beings. As Mimi and Ryan enter the detention center memories come flooding back to her of seeing her precious little Elli behind those bars. It is almost more than she can handle, and when Ryan sees Mimi starting to become upset, he puts his arms around her and says, "It's okay, honey, you can do this."

Mimi takes a deep breath and sighs, "Yeah, I guess so," as they press forward.

Just at the end of the hall they see a room with a light inside. It is the Security Overseer's room, and as they approach, they can hear voices coming from within. There are two male voices, and they seem to be arguing about something.

Ryan whispers to Mimi, "Stay well cloaked, honey, and do not make a sound. I want to get close enough to see who they are and hear all of what they are saying."

"Okay," she whispers to him, "And I'll let you know if I see anyone coming down the hall."

Ryan peers into the room and sees two men talking. As Ryan is self-cloaked, the two men do not see him. He hears one man saying to the other:

"What was he doing in here?" the first Security Overseer asks.

"What was *who* doing in here?" the second Security Overseer replies.

"Master John. You know, the *Major!*"

They both laugh, "Aw, who knows, and who cares. It's his factory, isn't it? He can do whatever the **bleep* he wants to!"

"I suppose so. But you know there are rumors of some strange things going on around here."

"Hey! You know the rules about all that. It's the old saying our ancestors used to use: *See no *bleep, hear no *bleep, speak no *bleep.* I mean when have there *not* been strange things going on around this place, anyway?"

"I don't know, man, I just don't know. Well, I suppose you're right."

The two men are going over some clip boards in front of them, checking things off as they inspect the boxes. Then one of them says, "Oh a little while ago there was one more box that came in from the lab. Looks like they were in a hurry or something. Didn't even bother to seal it shut."

"Well, I guess that explains the missing box on our inventory checklist, and why they must have forgotten to seal it. Hm." They both look at each other and then take a peek inside the box.

"This is for the Coffeehouses. Heard something about it on My Buddy."

"Yeah, I remember hearing about that, too. Said it was supposed to be a kind of healthy additive or something."

They look at each other with curiosity and then at the little bottles in the box. Each one takes out a bottle and sniffs.

"Hmm, smells good! Like cherry pie!"

"Mine smells like grape juice."

Glancing around, making sure that no one is watching, they look at each other and take a swig.

"Wow! That sure is scrumptious! I'm sure the kids are gonna LOVE—" But he doesn't get a chance to finish his sentence because both men go into violent convulsions.

Suddenly Ryan wails, *"MIMI! WE CAN'T GET CAUGHT HERE! RUN!!"*

They only get halfway down the hall when the men's violent shrieking brings security overseers running towards them from every direction.

* * *

The Major and Vi are just finishing up their meal, and afterwards Adam Tate takes them out to the gardens. There they find the other Chrysalenes communing with nature, singing to all of creation around them in beautiful angelic tones, and winding down their day.

Vi says to the Major, "Can you imagine a world that is all *their* world?" she says while holding her hands out to the Chrysalenes. As Vi and the Major are walking through the Chrysalene's gardens, they both feel what it must be like to live in such a beautiful place, close to the Creator and filled with love for all of creation.

"There was a book once," the Major says, "during the days of our ancestors. And it talked about such things."

"You mean about living in a beautiful garden and being at one with all of nature?"

"I think so," the Major says as he tries to remember what he once heard about it. "It talked about love too, I think."

"Hm, sounds like a good book," says Vi.

"Well, I guess it's time for us to get back to reality, I mean to the factory. . . um. . . *honey!*"

The Major likes the sound of that word. Then he pauses and gazes deeply into her eyes . . . "Violet."

Looking deeply into his eyes, Violet whispers softly to him, "Yes John, back to reality."

They both smile at each other, and he kisses her gently on the lips.

Saying good-bye to everyone they pack up #5 to treat him to a luxurious ride in the Autocar. The Major is just getting ready to tell his

AI Autodriver to head back to the main plant when his Master's Communication Device goes off. Taking it out of his pouch he sees it flashing red and the incoming message is from his father.

"Father?"

"*SON! WHERE ARE YOU!!*"

"I, uh, I just took a little time off, Father, just a little relaxation, cruising around and—"

"Never mind that! There has been a terrible accident at Silver Beach! Get up there! IMMEDIATELY!!" Master Howard is in a near panic.

"WHAT?" The Major is suddenly terrified for Mimi and Ryan.

"Give me the coordinates for your present location, son, and I will send a Cloudtransporter to pick you up! You must get there as fast as you can!"

"BUT WHAT HAPPENED?" The Major is fearing the worst for his two friends.

"I don't know! I don't know! It's the neurotoxins! Two people are dead and two more are being held in custody! JUST GET ON UP THERE!"

Chapter 10 – Dreams

ANGEL AND THE MONARCHS look down upon the carnage below. It pains them to see the suffering of the human creatures whom they love so much. They will do anything they can to help their cherished friends survive the nightmare. The Monarchs find that human creatures do not seem able to truly transcending their own misery, but they do see an enormous strength in them. It is this strength which makes humans so lovable and rise above all other creatures of the world. It is a unique gift that only human creatures seem to possess; the way they find hope in moments of despair, cling to life when death beckons, and reach up to heaven when drowning in hell. The Monarchs are especially moved at how the human creatures can feel sympathy when betrayed, forgiveness when harmed, and unshakable love, even in the face of deceit.

But most of all the Monarchs Butterflies know that no matter how far down the path of darkness a human creature has gone, there is always a chance that he or she will come back to the Light. And that is why Angel is now calling upon her swarm; and thousands arrive.

Hear me Monarchs, the time of transformation for the human creatures is approaching. Many are frightened and have lost their way. We must guide them, help them, and give them all the love we can. But most of all we must protect the chosen ones: the 39, the 3 little ones, and the one who will be taken. Go to them, go to them all!

With that the Monarchs fly off to all three Continental Territories, listening for the desperate cries of human creatures calling to the heavens above.

* * *

Kookie and Angie are pleased with the way the Pigeon Boot Camp turned out. Kookie and his tech team also managed to restructure 36 Lord's Communication Devices into 36 Metatron Devices and program all 36 of them with the 369-Program. All the training and instructions for Metatron and the pigeons were accomplished out at Kookie's Kabin, so they were not tracked by the UC. The Lords and Ladies all received training for neutralizing the neurotoxins with Metatron should there still be any remaining that have not already been neutralized. They are also now able to deprogram any subliminal messages on My Buddy. Kookie also knows that he must meet with the Major soon and get caught up with everything. With that positive feeling of hope, Kookie and Angie fall asleep peacefully in each other's arms. Then their nightmare begins:

It is a beautiful day out in the garden. The sun is shining and all of nature is singing to them. There are Chrysalenes planting seedlings nearby and little ones running around playing with the butterflies. Angie is tending to a cactus flower garden while Kookie is entertaining a flock of pigeons with his tuba. Number 3 and #4 are bobbing their heads up and down to the rhythm of the tuba's deep tones and everyone is having a good time.

Kookie stops playing his tuba for a moment and Angie also looks up as they both hear something off in the distance. It is a faint, deep, rhythmic pulsating sound of a djembe drum which seems to be coming from the other end of the garden. Kookie and Angie both stop what they are doing and follow the sound of the drum beat. They approach slowly and with caution as a feeling of apprehension is gradually creeping up on them. As they get closer, the sky begins to darken and the Chrysalenes gradually disappear. The drumbeat is getting louder and a little bit faster as the sky grows darker.

They come to the edge of the garden and suddenly, before them, the ground opens. Kookie and Angie stop short to keep from falling into a black, gaping fissure. The deep booming, pulsating sound is now upon them and seems to be pulling Angie into the fissure. It is almost intoxicating as it seems to have her eerily spellbound. She is moving her body to the rhythm of the beat and leaning forward over the edge of the black hole.

A voice begins to materialize, forming words out of the pulsating tone, and the words say, "Do it! Do it! Do it! Do it!" to the steady beat of the drum. And finally, a pair of red eyes appears from below and a high-pitched voice hisses out, "AAANNGIEEE! DOOO IIIT!"

Just as Angie is about to fall into the abyss, Kookie jumps in front of her shouting, "NOOOO!" pushing Angie back to the ground behind her, as he himself falls in.

A multitude of demonic voices screech below, "WE GOT HIM!! WE GOT HIM!! HA, HA, HA!!"

"*AAAAAA*aaaggghhh!" Kookie and Angie both shriek as they bolt back to consciousness, howling and flailing in their bed.

"Oh, honey, honey, are you okay?" Angie cries out to Kookie, panting and trying to catch her breath.

"I'm okay. I'm okay. I'm okay," he is panting, barely able to breathe.

As the two of them calm down and their breathing returns to normal, they begin to realize that they just came flying out of the same nightmare. For a long time, they do not speak and just hold each other close.

* * *

The Major and Vi have arrived at the Silver Beach plant of Howard Pharmaceuticals and are moving quickly to the detention center. They have had no word as to who died and who are being held in custody; they can only imagine the worst. When they get there, the building is filled with Security Overseers, scratching around for clues as to what happened. But when the Major and Vi walk into the room where the two men came to a violent end, filled with a tornado of shattered glass, blood, and human wreckage, they are horrified. The Major can barely manage to speak to the Security Overseer in charge of the investigation as he asks him, "Excuse me, good man. Kindly tell me what happened here."

"Well," he says, rubbing his face, "for the life of me, Master John, I don't rightly know. I mean none of this makes any sense. We found two servants loitering in the hallway though and figured that they must have seen something. But since they haven't said a word, we've had no choice but to detain them. Got 'em locked up over yonder," he says pointing to the cage area.

"Thank you, my man. Thank you. You have been very helpful," the Major says with tremendous relief, as he is finally able to breath knowing that his friends are alive.

Mimi and Ryan are listening to the commotion going on outside of the detention room when the door opens and in steps the Major and Vi. They are all aware of the security cameras, so it takes every ounce of self-control for all of them *not* to jump up and down and start yowling when they see each other.

"Hi!" says Mimi.

"*Hi!*" says Vi.

"Uh . . ." stammers Ryan.

"*HEY!*" says the Major. "So, I understand that you guys have seen a bit of action here this evening, *eh*?" the Major inquires casually with a self-control he never knew he had in him. Mimi and Ryan nod vigorously.

"Well," the Major continues, and for the benefit of the cameras pointing at them he says, "If I take you both out of here, do you think you will feel more like talking?"

Mimi and Ryan nod *more* vigorously.

"Okay," he says, releasing them. "Let's go talk someplace else then."

"Thank you, Master," Ryan says as he puts his hand out to shake the Major's hand. When the Major takes his hand, Ryan slips something into it.

"I'm going to take these two for a little walk," the Major says to the Security Overseer in the hallway. "I'm sure we can talk things over better in the cool night air."

"You betcha, sir. Just let me know if they tell you anything."

"I sure will, my good man. I sure will."

The four of them head for a nearby outdoor area that has a blind spot from the surveillance system. Then the Major turns serious as he looks at Mimi and Ryan and asks them what happened. Ryan tells him about the box that arrived last minute and was not sealed, and how the two decided to indulge since they saw it was the flavor enhancing, healthy stuff being sent to the Coffeehouses. Then Ryan tells him about the folded-up piece of paper that he placed in the Major's hand, which has a scrawl of numbers on it that he cannot make out.

"What is this?" the Major asks Ryan as he unfolds the paper.

"There were actually two such boxes," Ryan says, "But one of them was still in the hallway, right outside of their room. And as Mimi and I started to run I knew that it might be important, so I ripped off a piece of the labeling from it. And it was that momentary delay that got us caught when the Security Overseers came rushing in."

The Major sighs with a heavy heart as he looks at the piece of paper. He still can't make out too much, but it clearly is a piece of an inventory label.

"And here's the really creepy part, Major," Ryan says. "As the Security Overseers took us to the detention area, I looked back thinking about what might happen to that box. And, well, it was gone!"

"WHAT?!" says the Major shaking his head.

"Were you two aware of anyone going into that end of the hallway?" Vi asks, steeped in heavy thought.

"No!" says Mimi. "That's what is so terribly strange about it. I mean there wasn't any way that anyone could have gotten in and out of there so quickly; especially carrying a box."

Vi asks the Major if she can have the piece of paper for a moment and says, "There are other ways this paper can speak to us. May I give it a try?"

"Sure! Be my guest. I mean, whatever helps!" says the Major and hands Vi the scrap of torn inventory labeling.

She takes the piece of paper, closes her eyes, and holds it against her chest. Images and feelings come flooding to her that are all too familiar. She announces to the other three, "You two were being watched."

"What?!" Mimi and Ryan both yelp together.

"I *mean*," says Vi, "that we have another mole here. And one who also knows about self-cloaking."

"Wait, *what?*" the three of them are all scratching their heads, while a smile creeps over Vi's face.

"Okay Doc! Come out, come out wherever you are!" Vi calls out. And from out of the shadows Doc appears, holding back a laugh and holding out the box that belongs to the torn piece of paper. Mimi, Ryan and the Major just about pass out when they see her.

Turning to Doc, Vi asks, "So what brought you up here then and why the self-cloaking from *us?*"

"It was a dream I had the other night. I know it sounds strange, but Angel came to me. She said that I must leave for Silver Beach immediately and not tell anyone where I was going, except that I just felt the need to spend a little time by myself with the flowers and trees. Then she showed me this box and said that it had to be taken and hidden away, for the time being. She would not tell me why but said that one day I would understand.

"Well," Doc sighs and smiles at her friends, "if there is one thing I have learned, it's to listen to dreams and visions, especially when coming from a Monarch Butterfly."

"And especially when that Monarch is Angel," Vi says in full agreement.

"Okay," says the Major. "So, let's get this box of neurotoxins and ourselves out of here. I am bringing you all back to Bear River Farm, and I will neutralize these neurotoxins here with Metatron once we get there. Of course, I will give the security person here as well as my father the usual story, *no one seems to know anything, blah, blah, blah, etc.*"

Ryan looks at him rather amazed and says, "How is it that everyone always believes your little, um, *stories* so easily, Major?"

The Major rolls his eyes and grins as he says, "It's a secret my man, and maybe one day I'll let you in on it!"

The women all smile at him and shake their heads, and Vi includes an eye roll, but Ryan remains impressed.

The Major thinks to himself, *Actually, I'm just a really good liar.* He goes to have a final word with the Security Overseer as the others all pile into the Cloudtransporter heading back to Bear River Farm.

* * *

Lady Liling is in her garden tending to her White Jasmines. "How do you like your new little companions?" she says to the flowers while holding her hands out to #21 and #22.

The pigeons bob their heads up and down, and the flowers speak to Liling's heart. *Well, it sure does seem as if they like your company!*

Giggling at the cute antics of #21 and #22 Liling takes a handful of their food into the palm of her hand and holds it out in front of them. She was told at Kookie's Birdie Boot Camp that this would help them bond faster to her. Number 21 sticks out his foot and steps onto Liling's hand, followed by #22 who does the same thing in a dainty, lady-like fashion.

Liling laughs and says to the pigeon, "Yes, #22, I am a Lady, too! Anyway, the three of us seem to be well bonded already, don't you think?"

At Boot Camp when the birds first arrived, the 36 Lords and Ladies were told to see which pair they felt most connected to before making their selection. When Liling held #21 and #22 it was love at first sight for all of them.

As she is chatting away, feeding and petting her new little friends, Liling's Lord's Communication Device goes off in her pouch. Accepting the message, her HOC speaks to her:

"My Lady, as you have probably heard by now, there has been a most dreadful accident at the estate of the late Lord Ekene involving his staff and entire family."

"Yes," Liling says, bowing her head with great sadness.

"Are you also aware that the child, Ekene's son Lord Emeka, has been missing since that horrible night?"

"Yes sir, I am aware of that, too. As you know we do keep track of all such things," Liling says.

"Yes, well, I have been contacted by SPA and while they are figuring out what to do with Ekene's estate, they would like you to move in there; you know, sort of keep an eye on everything and everyone in the area. Perhaps if you go through his office files you might come up with something."

"I see," says Liling, suspicious, and rather surprised. A myriad of questions pop into her head, but she knows much better than to ask anything, so she keeps her mouth shut.

"SPA has requested that you leave on this very day. Pack whatever personal things you need quickly, My Lady. You can have the rest sent for later."

"Very well," she says, although it is most definitely *not* very well with her.

"Your Cloudtransporter has been programmed to take you there. You are to leave in an hour."

And he disconnects.

While they were at the Kabin, all 39 of the Lords and Ladies had decided to use a special code amongst themselves if they ever needed each other in an emergency. Kookie tested out the code the morning of their Pigeon Training. He sent everyone to the Kabin for their clandestine work by saying that they would take a fun walk together around his garden. It apparently worked out just fine. Their code is always to say they are going to do something fun in a ridiculous tone of voice, sounding like an Overseer on My Buddy.

They all agreed that using their Lord's Communications Devices as usual would also be a good way to throw the Council off their guard, especially when it is most necessary to do so. And Liling now knows that she must bring Kookie and Yakov to Johannesburg immediately. There is a terrible foreboding in her heart that the Council is up to something nefarious, and she knows that they must all be together right now. She sends out a quick message on her Lord's Communication Device to Kookie:

"Hello brother, no time to talk. Making a quick dash to my new special assignment. Sounds like an easy and relaxing one, Woo Hoo! Yes indeed! Lord Ekene's beautiful, luxurious estate in Johannesburg. Thought you and Yakov both might like to join me for a bit. We can take lovely walks together in the beautiful gardens there."

Kookie receives the message and shares it immediately with Angie.

She takes one look at it as Kookie says to her, "I'll get the Cloudtransporter!"

"I'll get the birds!"

"I'll get Yakov!"

"I'll get your tuba!"

The two of them are all packed up in the Cloudtranporter, on their way to Johannesburg.

* * *

A terminal activates in a secured location, somewhere in Sinopacifica. The incoming message is received:

HOC: Greetings to SPA, the Highest of the Council.

SPA: Greetings, High Overlord Contact of Lady Liling. What news have you for me?

HOC: The three are on their way to Johannesburg. Our plans are all in order, running right on schedule.

SPA: *EXCELLENT, most loyal HOC! TRULY EXCELLENT!* I shall send word to my Brethren PA and ES immediately! MOST EXCELLENT WORK!

HOC: Thank you very much, Highest One. What would your Highest have me do next?

SPA: (grunts and snorts) Wait . . .

* * *

Lady Liling is sitting comfortably in her plush, Cloudtransporter recliner. Number 21 and #22 are in their little coop snoozing, nearby. Traveling in a southwesterly direction, the sun will begin to go down soon, making it a shorter, not to mention more tiresome day. Liling looks out the window at the majestic orange and golden colors of the sky, as she glides swiftly and silently above the clouds. Her mind is wandering, and wondering what lies ahead for *all* of them, the UC, and people all over One World. Sleep comes gently upon her.

Looking down below, Liling sees the ocean, shining and sparkling with the red, orange, gold, and violet of the setting sun. High up above, she can make out the silhouettes of celestial beings soaring through the heavens as the sky gradually darkens and the stars come out. When Liling looks down again, the ocean is all dark, except for a few stars that are twinkling down upon it. Liling then finds herself outside of the transporter, floating through the night air with the starlight guiding her way, until one by one the stars go out, and she is left drifting in a dark space of nothingness.

Fearful now, Liling tries to cry out for help, but discovers that her voice is gone and all sounds around her have gone silent. A deep, distant boom comes from below as she looks down into the black, bottomless ocean. The deep boom gets a little bit stronger when a small, dark red glow appears. It seems that the red glow and the heavy boom are both coming from the endless depths of the ocean below. Liling sees the glow and hears the boom growing stronger and louder. Suddenly she realizes that she is going down, down, into the ocean, into the red, into the increasingly heavy, dark, booming, below.

Fear is overtaking her as she becomes aware of a growling voice coming from deep within the ocean, saying DO IT! DO IT! DO IT! DO IT!

And with one last cry of freewill, Liling finds her voice, and bellows down into the darkness below, NO! NO! NO! I WILL **NOT** *BE TAKEN!*

In the darkness Liling hears another voice as she slowly emerges from her sleep.

It is the AI on the speaker of the Cloudtransorter announcing, "Destination Johannesburg, almost completed. Arriving in 10 minutes."

* * *

Later that evening the Major, Vi, Mimi, Ryan and Doc go to Bear River. Taking the Cloudtransporter from Silver Beach to Bear River is a fast trip, but the group is wiped out nonetheless from the exhausting day, and they are glad to be able to relax for the rest of the evening, if only for a little while. They all know what lies ahead and that there will not be much time to relax in the days to come.

At the farm, everyone has pretty much settled in for the evening. Lisa is finishing up in the kitchen, Kenny is getting the pigeons nestled in their coups, the Chrysalenes and other farm helpers are finishing their day's work out in the fields, and the little ones are all tucked in and fast asleep. The Major and company have had an exhausting day, but they all feel too unsettled to turn in just yet. Lisa is a welcoming sight when they arrive at her cottage, and she opens the door to greet them.

"Well, hello!" she says to the Major and Vi, "It's so good to have you all back!

"Thank you, Lisa," says Mimi, "It most certainly is good to be back."

"How did everything go over there at the Silver Beach plant?" Lisa inquires.

They all just look at her with a worn-out expression. "I will fill you in on everything Lisa and would seriously appreciate a flask of coffee if it's not too much trouble," says the Major.

"Oh, not at all," Lisa says as she goes to prepare enough coffee for everyone, with a plate full of cookies.

"If you would all pardon me," says Mimi, "I am rather exhausted. I would just like to see Eve Elli and then turn in for the night."

"Sounds like an excellent idea," says the Major. "I will fill you in briefly Lisa and then if it's alright with you, Vi and I would seriously appreciate turning in and continuing in the morning."

"Oh absolutely," says Lisa most graciously.

"As you will discover, much has happened and there are some decisions that will have to be made. But I sure wouldn't turn down some cookies and coffee first!"

He chuckles and proceeds to fill Lisa in on everything that they experienced that evening.

Mimi and Ryan excuse themselves and say good night to everyone, while Doc hangs out with the rest of them for a little while. She too is very anxious to be updated on all the goings on, especially since Doc was also witness to the grisly deaths of the two men at the plant earlier that evening.

"Honey, let's go and check on Eve Elli before we turn in, okay?" Mimi says to Ryan.

"Okay," Ryan says affectionately to his Woman. The experience of being a mole for a little while was an exciting adventure for him. And although he is exhausted like everyone else, Ryan is also feeling particularly amorous.

Knocking gently on the door of Adam Sam, Eve Lydia and Eve Elli's little hut, Mimi and Ryan are greeted by Eve Lydia. In a hushed voice she says, "Hey mom, when did you guys get back? Oh, Eve Elli is sound asleep."

"We only just got back," Gramma Mimi says, as she peers in and sees her little sweetheart sleeping peacefully on her soft floor mat. "Just wanted to have a quick look at our little girl, then I expect to be out like a light myself," Mimi says.

"Sure, thing mom," Eve Lydia smiles.

Gramma Mimi goes over to her little snoozing bundle and sits down for a moment beside her. Ryan sits down beside Mimi and puts his arm around her shoulders, loving the love he sees in a grandmother's eyes. In that moment, they both know there is nothing in the world they would not do for this dear little angel, as they sit there together gazing upon her in the peaceful stillness of the evening.

* * *

Mimi and Ryan turn in for the night and as Mimi falls asleep, she begins to dream:

She is in a large mansion with lots of other people. Eve Elli is there, and she is playing happily with some new friends. They are running from one room to another exploring all the wondrous things they come across. The kitchen is full of cakes and cookies and candy. Mimi is enchanted as she watches Eve Elli and her little friends eat all the goodies, laughing themselves silly. The adults in the large mansion seem relaxed, enjoying each other's fellowship of good conversation, excellent cuisine, and merriment. In one room there is a small pool that is very hot, but soothing. Mimi goes into the hot tub, sits down, turns on the jets and feels the soothing waters massage her as the hot jet streams hit her body.

Mimi smiles and feels at peace within herself while her body relaxes more and more, deeper and deeper. And as she goes deeper, the room begins to get darker, deeper and deeper, darker and darker . . . deeper and deeper and darker and darker, until the room is pitch black and Mimi cannot see anything. She begins to panic in the pitch-black that is enveloping her. Then she looks down and sees a faint red glow. At the same time, she begins to hear a deep booming sound coming from the depths of the darkness below.

Gradually the red light grows brighter, and the booming sound becomes louder and faster. Mimi's heart beats hard and fast as she is now filled with terror. The red light takes on a shape, and the form is moving towards Mimi. Boom . . . Boom . . . Boom . . . the form becomes a large face with an evil grin and demonic eyes staring right into hers. Boom . . . Boom . . . Boom . . .

Suddenly the demon opens its mouth wide and starts screaming in Mimi's face while the booming becomes deafening BOOM! . . . BOOM! . . . BOOM! . . . DO IT! DO IT! DO IT! BOOM! . . . BOOM! . . . BOOM! . . . DO IT, MIMI! DO IT, MIMI! WE ARE WAITING FOR YOU! BOOM! . . . BOOM! . . . BOOM! . . . WAITING FOR YOU! BOOM! . . . BOOM! . . . BOOM! . . . HERE! — IN! — HELL! HAHAHAHAHAHAHA!

"WHOA!" Mimi jolts out of her dream, jolting Ryan at the same time.

"Honey! Are you okay?" he asks her.

"Not yet," Mimi whimpers. "Just a sec. Gimme a sec."

"Shhh, it's okay, honey. I'm here." Ryan says to his Woman, holding her and kissing her hair softly as she begins to calm down.

The nightmares are coming more and more frequently to Mimi, and Ryan already knows the drill. They lie there for a while until she is calm again and they gradually both drift off back to sleep.

* * *

The Major wakes up early the next morning with the birds singing and the warm fragrances of the sweet earth beckoning him to the fields. The Chrysalenes are already among the crops giving the growing plants their own sacred nectar in the misty, magical dawn.

The Major tossed and turned most of the night with the turmoil of the choices that lie before him this morning. He seeks council when he comes across his friend Adam Mark who is loving on the tomato plants.

"Good morning, Brother" Adam Mark calls to the Major. "So nice to see you bright and early this morning."

"Thank you, my good man. It is nice to see you too. Mind if I have a word with you for a moment?"

"Why, not at all Major," Adam Mark says, while patting the sweet earth that he is sitting on, inviting the Major to join him. "What can I do for you, sir?"

Sitting down on the soft plant bed next to Adam Mark and the growing tomatoes, the Major is already beginning to feel the answers to his questions being spoken to his heart. Looking into the eyes of the Chrysalene, he can see that Adam Mark already knows what is troubling him, and the Major speaks the words that have kept him awake most of the night:

"As I watch people die from every stratum of society, completely unaware of what is happening to them, or why, I want to yell out to our Heavenly Father and say *WHY! WHY! WHY, Dear Lord! WHY are You letting this happen?! WHY are you allowing all the pain, suffering and murder to continue?! WHY have you allowed us to become so badly divided that we are unable to even communicate with each other, let alone help each other? Are you unable to hear the agonizing terrified cries of your people, Lord? Do you not love us? Why must you allow all this to continue? Why have you not helped me so I can better help your people? Father in Heaven, I feel so helpless! What can I do? What can I do?'"*

Adam Mark is filled with much compassion for the Major. He reaches out with his hands and the Major takes them immediately.

Adam Mark closes his eyes and speaks not a word. Suddenly he begins to glow and becomes transparent; with a soft light emanating from his very being. While the Chrysalene is transforming right in front of him, the Major feels an inexplicable peace and ecstasy filling his body. The peace is moving from Adam Mark's hands into the Major's, traveling up his arms and into his body until it reaches the very deepest part of his soul. When he looks at his hands still holding Adam Mark, he notices that he too is becoming transparent and glowing. The feeling of ecstasy is indescribable, bringing tears to the Major as he knows and understands the answers to all his questions.

Adam Mark gradually releases the Major's hands and opens his eyes. Smiling at him he bows his head and says, "He truly does love us, my friend, as you have just felt that love flowing through your own spirit."

"Yes," the Major says, barely able to speak. "And I also know that he has given us all the ability to make things better, to change the things that need changing in this world and to help and care for each other. I now understand what is stopping us from doing that, Adam Mark," the Major continues.

Looking at the Chrysalene he says one word: "Fear."

Adam Mark responds, "When we replace fear with love, then my friend, all things are possible."

The Major continues, "It is *I* who has not heard the voice of my people as I have been wrapped up in my own self-doubts of not being good enough . . . not ever being good enough for my father. I have allowed my own shame to stop me from jumping in and giving it my all."

Hanging his head low the Major says, "I have especially allowed the fear of my father to get in the way." Then, with a warm and loving smile, looking directly into the eyes of Adam Mark, the Major finally says, "But not anymore. My prayer has just been answered as the Lord has taken my fear away through *you* my amazing friend. Thank you, thank you! I will fear no evil."

* * *

"Vi! It's time for us to get going. We've got a few errands to run, honey!" He calls out to her as he walks into Lisa's kitchen where Vi, Mimi, Ryan and several of the others are all breaking bread together.

"Oh, Major!" Vi sighs, "I had the most incredible dream last night! The Monarch Butterfly, Angel, came to me with a message. Only she was not a Monarch at all; she appeared to me as a real angel!"

"No kidding," says the Major, with an affectionate grin plastered on his face at Violet.

"Yes!" Vi continues, "And do you know what Angel told me? She said that we are to go to Johannesburg at once and take Eve Elli with us! So, I went into their hut to tell Adam Sam, Eve Lydia and Eve Elli about my dream not knowing how they would react to it, and would you believe, they had Eve Elli all dressed and ready to go! Oh honey! They all had the same dream!"

"Me too," the Major confesses, his smile broadening at her. "It is one of the reasons why I didn't get much sleep last night."

"WHOA!" The group seated around the table laughs.

"Yes, whoa. And I didn't know what kind of yarn to spin with my father. But now I *do* know what to say and I am not afraid to say it anymore."

"Oh Major!" Vi says with all the love in her heart as she wraps her arms around her sweetie.

After embracing each other, the Major looks at Vi and says, "Well, honey, you go get the kid and I'll go get the Cloudtransporter. While we are enroute, I will give the old man a call."

Mimi and Ryan cannot bear to be left out. Mimi jumps in and says, "Major, Ryan and I have talked it over and we both feel like we just *have* to go with you. We know that we will do whatever we can to be of help but most of all, I want *so much* to be there for my Eve Elli!"

"So," the Major says with a wink and a smile at both of them, "Let's get going then! Our next stop is Johannesburg!"

Chapter 11 – Fathers

LITTLE LORD EMEKA IS JUST WAKING UP in his small grass hut. The sun is shining, and so is Emeka. He has been in the constant care of the Chrysalenes from the Village of the Holy Ones, near his late family's estate, and they have been loving on him non-stop. Last night was the first time since the death of his family that Emeka was able to sleep peacefully through the night without nightmares; and for this he is truly shining brightly with the morning sun.

With the Divine energy of the Chrysalenes pouring into Emeka every day, his soul is healing rapidly. The people in the village notice the little Lord has grown in wisdom beyond his years which defies all logic, and it is magical to behold in the five-year-old Lord.

"Emeka? Emeka?" Mama Eve Zula calls out to him, "Why, there you are, my precious child! My goodness, you do look radiant this morning."

Emeka runs to her arms, and she bends down to give him a big hug. As she does so, Mama Eve Zula becomes transparent and starts glowing, sending the loving Light of the Divine into Emeka's soul. The little Lord's face begins to glow as he receives the healing energy of his Heavenly Father.

"Come now, child," Mama Eve Zula says to him. "There is much for you to do today."

"Yes, Mama," Emeka says to her. "Angel came to visit me again last night, and she told me that I must prepare myself for them today. But I do not know who *they* are, Mama. Angel did not tell me any more than that. She just said, *you will see, young human creature,* and then she flew away. Who are they Mama? And when will I meet them?"

With a gentle voice, Mama Eve Zula says to little Lord Emeka, "They are your destiny, my child. They are on their way here now and you *are* going to meet them today."

* * *

Lady Liling is the first to arrive at the late Lord Ekene's estate. She knows Kookie and Yakov will be arriving shortly, as well as the others who have been called. Her Lord's Communication Device is pulsating with an incoming message. She accepts the message and Yakov appears on the screen.

"Well, my Sister, we are here! And I do believe that Kookie and Angie are right behind us."

"We?" says Liling, looking out of the window facing the back field of the Big House. There she sees a newly arrived Cloudtransporter parked right next to her own.

"Well, we *do* need all the help we can get in our efforts to help the Council, do we not, dear Sister?"

"Oh yes, Brother! Yes, indeed we do!" Liling says as she notices two people emerging from the Cloudtransporter. "I will come down and meet you both," she says to Yakov on her device.

* * *

"There they are!" Angie says to Kookie. On their descent, they look down from the window of their Cloudtransporter and see a group of people on the ground below waving up at them. Angie gets #3 and #4 out of their coop and puts one on each of her shoulders. "We're here, my little darlings!" she says to the birds.

The Cloudtransporter settles gently to the ground, and Kookie, Angie and the two pigeons go out to greet everyone. Kookie goes over to Yakov and Liling to give them each a hug and do their ritual greeting. With hands joined, they hold them up in the air and say, "Ni Hao, Privyet, Hey!" and drop their hands down at their sides.

Smiling at each other, Kookie notices a familiar face with Yakov.

"Well, my goodness, if it isn't Lady Neely! So glad you could join us!" Kookie says, with a sideways glance, raised eyebrow and a smirk at Yakov.

"Thank you kindly, Lord Kookie," says Lady Neely most graciously. And then she adds, "I don't suppose you remember me, sir, from our youth, that is?"

"Actually," says Kookie, "The answer to your question is, *yes*. And the answer to your question on *that day* is, *no.*"

Lady Neely laughs out loud and is taken by surprise.

Yakov is just standing there scratching his head. "Mind letting *me* in?" he asks.

"When we were young folks at summer camp, I took off one day with my tuba and headed for the lake. A group of other kids came looking for me out of concern and when they found me, one of them asked if I was okay. Well, I never did answer her, until now."

Smiling at Lady Neely, he adds, "And I never did thank you for caring about how I felt."

"I remembered that incident too," says Lady Liling, "when I saw you at the Gathering at the polar location. I remembered the kindness you showed to Kookie on that day, and the concern you showed in the Great Dining Hall at Lady Bella and Lord Ekene's *suggestions* for genocide. That is why I contacted you to be a part of our Alliance."

Bowing her head to Lady Liling, Lady Neely says, "Thank you, Lady Liling. It is an honor to serve in this Alliance."

Yakov looks at his lovely Lady, takes her by the hand and says, "My dear, sweet Lady, the honor and pleasure are all mine."

He kisses her hand, she smiles at him, and everyone sighs, including #3 and #4 sitting on Angie's shoulders.

Lady Liling beckons to the group with her hands saying, "Well, my Brothers and Sisters, let us go inside and break bread together while we are waiting for the last party to arrive, shall we? Then we can discuss the reason for my calling you all together."

"Ooo! Another party!" Angie exclaims. "Who else is coming?"

"The Major and his entourage, along with a very special little girl," Liling announces proudly.

"Woo hoo!" everyone cheers.

Kookie smiles at Liling and Yakov. "Yes, the time we have been anticipating, the time of the sacred children, has come."

* * *

Master Howard is receiving an incoming message on his Master's Communication Device. He has been anxiously awaiting some communication from his son regarding the deaths at Silver Beach.

"Hello, John!" Master Howard says to the Major. "What were you able to find out at Silver Beach?"

"Hello father," says the Major. "Apparently there was an open box of neurotoxins, and two of the Security Overseers who found it saw that it was the added flavoring for the Coffeehouses—"

Master Howard cuts him off, "And they suddenly got thirsty, *eh?*" he laughs. "Well, I'm sure they can be easily replaced. Have you taken care of everything?"

"Yes father, I have taken care of everything."

"Good, son, good."

"There still is one thing, though," the Major adds, "that has to be dealt with in this matter. I am on my way now to finish up my investigation and *cleanup* of the matter."

"Fine son, fine. You do that. Will your mother and I be seeing you for dinner then?"

"Not this evening, father. I will let you know when I get back. Right now, I am on my way to see my Overlord."

"Ah yes!" says Master Howard. "The Lord Kenneth is a good man, a very good man. Then I shall have to share my news with you right now."

"What news is that father?" the Major asks, feeling a bit leery.

"Word came down today from the Council. We are to roll out the final phase of Operation Pied Piper.

"It is quite the finishing touch, *eh?*"

"Yes father, it is *quite* the finishing touch."

"Let's be absolutely certain that all the water purifier tablets are fully in place for the UC reservoirs, along with our secret pipelines, first. Then we will be all ready to roll out our *little surprise!*"

"Absolutely," says the Major. "In fact, I will be sure to discuss all of that with Lord Kenneth when I see him, so thank you for letting me know about it, father."

"Indeed, son, indeed."

The Major and Master Howard disconnect. Vi, Mimi and Ryan, who have been staring at him during that whole conversation, are absolutely flabbergasted at what they have just heard.

"Water *what?*" Vi asks incredulously

"Good Lord! Now what?" exclaims Mimi.

Looking out the window of the Cloudtransporter, the Major is grateful for one thing: that they will all be arriving in Johannesburg soon and he can share everything with Kookie, Liling and Yakov.

"Don't worry Gramma, it's gonna be okay," Eve Elli pipes in.

The others almost seem to have forgotten the little angel sitting there amongst them until they hear her reassuring voice of calm and compassion. They all look at her and smile.

"Yes, like Eve Elli says, it's gonna be okay," reassures the Major.

* * *

Bem, Tafari, Dumaka and Nassor are tending to their blossoming fruit and vegetable garden when a servant from the Big House comes rushing out to see them.

"Overseer Groundskeeper, sir! Overseer Groundskeeper!"

"Yes?" says Bem, as all four of the men look up.

"Our Lady Liling of the Big House would like all of the servants to come to a gathering at the back field this afternoon. There will be tents set up and food will be served. Please let everyone know that they are all invited."

"I sure will," says Bem and the servant scurries off back to the Big House.

"I wonder what that is all about?" asks Tafari.

"I guess we will have to wait until this afternoon to find out!" chuckles Dumaka.

They all get back to work, looking forward to whatever it is their new Lady has in store for them.

The servant rushes back to the Big House and is put to work right away with the others, that is, with Kookie, Angie, Yakov and Lady Neely, all of whom are setting up tents and tables. Lady Liling is busy with her crew in the kitchen, cooking up a wonderful meal for the entire staff of the estate. Kookie and Yakov have both moved their Cloudtransporters to another part of the grounds, and not a moment too soon either, because their next guests are coming in for a landing. Everyone stops what they are doing to greet the Major and his companions, which includes one very excited little girl.

Eve Elli's love and happiness radiate to all around her, and everyone simply must have a turn at raising the little angel into the air, hugging and twirling her around. When it comes Angie's turn, #3 and #4 fly off Angie's shoulders as she tosses Eve Elli in the air. They circle around their little angel as if they are all playing together in an earthly paradise, totally enchanting all who are present.

Liling comes out just in time to share the magical moment of *Angie, the Cherub, and the Doves*. She suddenly becomes aware of a heavenly glow radiating all around the four of them as if they truly are in Paradise.

"Okay folks, now that we are all here, let's go inside for a little while, shall we?" Liling announces. She leads the group inside and into a large living room, comfortably furnished with several overstuffed chairs and sofas, as well as various plush floor cushions. Eve Elli dives into one of the floor cushions, but then notices the trays filled with sandwiches, pastries, and confections of every description.

Mimi is reminded of another dream she had of Eve Elli when she hears her little baby saying, "Ooo Gramma, I want this! Ooo Gramma, I want that!" She is, of course, pointing to everything on every tray around the living room, skipping from one to the other.

Almost in tears, as Mimi remembers the rest of the dream, she repeats what she said to Eve Elli in the dream, "Well then my little angel must *have* everything!" Finishing off that particular dream sequence, Eve Elli giggles, "Hee, hee, hee!" and proceeds to grab a scrumptious chocolate chip cookie, beating Kookie to it within a matter of seconds.

The High Lady Liling knows it is time for her to reveal why they have all been summoned so suddenly to Johannesburg. Donning her Universal Translator pendant necklace for the benefit of the Major and company, she stands up and addresses the group.

"Isn't it just lovely here!" Liling begins with their coded message, knowing that she must get Kookie's Holographic Imager going immediately. She looks at him and says, "My High Lord and Brother Kenneth!"

He is now on code alert as Lady Liling continues. "Thank you so much for taking the time to come here today. *Indeed*, it is quite the trip for you to come all that distance, yes, *INDEED! Brother!*"

Kookie has just turned on the Holographic Imager to project in seamless fashion, the image of a pastry party among friends.

"Okay," Kookie says with a wink and a nod at Liling. "You may proceed now, Sister."

* * *

Somewhere in a secret location in Sinopacifica an incoming signal is activated on a security alert system. A Security Overseer is messaging SPA who accepts the communication.

SPA: Yes, my Security Overseer. What seems to be the problem?

SO: Thank you, Oh Highest SPA, for receiving my transmission in this unexpected and sudden manner.

SPA: Yes, well, what is it then, Security Overseer?

SO: I'm not exactly sure sir, it's hard to say. There was just a sudden blip of some kind in the system.

SPA: I am assuming that you are referring to the Gathering in Johannesburg of the treacherous nine and their unholy child?

SO: Yes, indeed sir, that is correct. I do believe that there might be something going on with their technology which is sliding just under our radar, sir.

SPA: Hmm, very well then Security Overseer. It seems we will have to send in our very best mole to. . . how shall I say, join their party.

SO: Yes sir, I do believe that would be best at this point. And perhaps we can get an insight into exactly what the technology is that Lord Kenneth has which keeps alluding us.

SPA: Yes, Overseer, that is an excellent idea.

SPA abruptly ends the transmission. He then sends out a message to PA and ES who accept the communication.

SPA: Hello, Brethren, there is something urgent we need to talk about.

PA: Yes, my Brother, what is it?

ES: Indeed, SPA. What is happening?

SPA: I have just spoken to a Security Overseer regarding the need for a mole at the Johannesburg Gathering.

PA: Yes Brother. Surely that can be arranged.

ES: Without a doubt, Brethren.

SPA: You do understand however, the nature of this group, and who they are.

PA: Yes indeed.

ES: Indeed, we do.

SPA: Then I think you can agree that this must be a truly special mole, suited to the situation.

PA: Yes, that is quite understandable.

ES: Absolutely, Brother SPA.

SPA: Then I choose Master Howard as our mole.

PA & ES: OH, MOST EXCELLENT!!

SPA: We let him in on all that is going on with his son and tell him that the only way to save his miserable son is to cooperate with us. Master Howard will then go to Johannesburg and present himself to his son Master John as one who wishes to *repent*, as the treacherous ones are so fond of saying.

PA & ES: OH YES! YES! THIS IS DELICIOUS BROTHER SPA!!

SPA: Once Master Howard has their trust, it will be all over for their treacherous Alliance!

PA: And of course, do not forget the one in their group who must be *TAKEN*!

PA, ES, and SPA all erupt into sinister laughter. Then they disconnect.

* * *

Lady Liling begins, "First, I would like to offer each of our friends from Panamerica a Universal Translator pendant necklace. It will be very helpful to you all as you get to know the people here."

She passes around a box to the Major and his companions as each one of them excitedly picks out a UT necklace and puts it on. Liling then continues; "I have brought you all here to share with you what has happened in this house and what I believe is going to happen here. I understand that you have already heard of the recent and tragic mass suicide of Lord Ekene's family. And I believe you are also aware of the fact that Little Lord Emeka has been reported as missing since that night." They all nod, sadly.

"What you probably do not know is that following the tragedy I was told by the Council to come down here and manage things until further notice. Although they gave me no specific instructions, I am sure that they would be happier if Emeka was located and brought back here. However, I am not so sure that is a wise thing to do right now. Whatever the Council has in mind, I feel that this place is central to their plans and that we are being called upon to protect this child."

"Eve Elli and I are having all sorts of dreams regarding the Little Lord Emeka and this place," says Mimi.

"The Chrysalenes and my dreams have also led me to this place, and the importance of bringing Eve Elli here," says the Major.

Everyone else has their own story to share about similar dreams, visions, and nightmares. They are astounded by the similarities of their dreams.

"Yes," Liling says, "That is why I felt that we all needed to be here. I believe it is crucial that we find Little Lord Emeka. My heart tells me that he is not in any danger at the moment and that he is in fact, someplace nearby. But I also feel that he needs us, and that we all need him, too."

"So how do you propose we go about finding him, Sister?" asks Yakov.

"Well," Liling says, "I am quite certain that the people of this estate know what is going on and probably where Emeka is. I have invited them all over for a gathering this afternoon where we can all get to know each other, and hopefully where they will trust us enough to tell us some of what they know."

"That sounds like a good place to begin," says Kookie, "And I would like to run an article of Emeka's clothing through my surveillance system. We'll see what that turns up."

"Sure thing," says Liling. She goes to Little Lord Emeka's suite to fetch something appropriate and returns with a pair of slippers from underneath his bed.

Kookie turns on the tracking system on his Lord's Communication Device, and he passes the security scanner over Emeka's slippers.

"We have a green pulse right around this area." Kookie says as he shows everyone the map. "Little Lord Emeka is alive and well, and very close by!"

"That's perfect!" says Liling.

Everyone agrees that it will be best to proceed with caution, as they do not want the Council to know of Emeka's whereabouts.

"We must find someone from among the people here who we can trust to help us find him," Liling adds, and everyone nods in agreement.

* * *

Bem, Tafari, Dumaka and Nassor are just finishing up with their work for the afternoon. They are very much looking forward to meeting their new Lady of the house and enjoying some time gathering with their fellow servants of the estate. Some folks have already begun to drift over to the tents, and the four gardener friends are now ready to join them.

"I am hearing some very nice things about our new Lady," says Bem. "People who have met her say she is a very kind woman."

"And I am feeling good things about her in my heart," says Dumaka.

"And I am smelling good things coming from the tents over there," says Nassor."

The men all laugh. Tafari says, "Well, then let's get on over there!" and the four of them head over to the gathering at the tents on the back field.

They arrive to an informal gathering where everyone is eating and relaxing and enjoying each other's company. While they are doing so, Liling's companions begin to mill about among the people, introducing themselves, telling everyone who they are and where they are all from. They set the tone for warmth and trust, and a new way of relating to the five members of the UC: Kookie, Yakov, Liling, Neely, and the Major, who are reaching out to the people in genuine friendship.

It is something that the people have never experienced before, and while some of them are skeptical and cautious, others, such as Bem and his companions, are truly touched. Even #3 and #4 are getting friendly with the people as Angie introduces them from her shoulders. Going through the pigeons' "handshake" routine, #3 and #4 each put a foot out, thoroughly delighting the servants of the estate.

As the afternoon progresses, a bond is forming between Bem, his gardeners, Lady Liling, and her companions. Liling feels in her heart that she can trust these men and ask them to take her to Little Lord Emeka. Taking the four of them aside, Liling says, "I know that you have all been through a terrible nightmare here, and I am so very sorry for your suffering."

They lower their eyes and nod. Bem says to her, "Speaking for all of us, My Lady, I would like to say thank you for that, and especially, thank you all for the kindness which you and your people have shown us here today."

"You are quite welcome," says Lady Liling. "And we wish to do much more, if you would be willing to help us."

"What is it we can do for *you,* My Lady?" Tafari asks a bit surprised.

At this point, Kookie and Yakov have gathered around Liling and the four men. Hearing Tafari's question, Kookie takes out Metatron and turns on a special Universal Translator program designed for a group of people to all be able to speak together in their own languages.

Kookie then speaks up. "We have been brought here to find a very special child, and to help and protect him."

Pointing out Eve Elli who is with Mimi and Ryan nearby, Kookie continues, "The little girl who you see over there, Eve Elli, has been brought here for the sake of this child as well. The child we are speaking of is Emeka, the new Lord of this house."

Bem and the others suddenly look at each other and realize what is being asked of them. They instinctively turn to Dumaka, who looks into the eyes of the High Lords and High Lady.

Dumaka says, "I see a goodness in the three of you which I have heard of but have never seen. My grandmother used to do this thing which she called *praying.* She said that someone or something very kind was always listening and that someday the Kind One would answer. I believe that day has now come. I believe that the Kind One has sent you to us."

Mimi and the rest of the group have joined in listening to Dumaka. With much compassion Mimi says to him, "Thank you kind sir. Thank you from all of us."

Eve Elli is smiling and beaming forth her loving light.

Dumaka finally says, "Well, then, let us take you to our Lord Emeka."

* * *

Little Lord Emeka is tending to the crops out in the field of the Village of the Holy Ones. Papa Adam Makena is walking around with Emeka going from one fruit and vegetable plant to another, gently guiding the little boy in his lessons of loving on the growing food. Emeka comes to a tomato plant and gets down on his knees.

Touching the newly sprouted tomatoes Emeka says, "Thank you, my Brother and Sister tomatoes, for giving us your life, your love and your nutrition," although somewhere in his heart he is hearing the word *nutritious*. He leans over and kisses the plant, trying to kiss each and every little sprout.

"Papa," he says gazing up at Papa Adam Makena. "Is it important for me to kiss each and every little sprout, or can I simply kiss the whole plant with one great big kiss?"

Papa Adam Makena laughs heartily. He says, "Well my child, consider that one day you will be the grown man Lord Emeka of your estate. You will have many people to take care of on your estate. Imagine that these little tomatoes are like those people. They need sunlight, nourishment, and lots of love, just as you are giving to these tomatoes. How do you think you will do that with many people to take care of?"

Little Lord Emeka's eyes grow very wide, and he says, 'Gosh! I don't know, Papa! I just don't know!"

"Ha, ha!" laughs Papa Adam Makena. "Well then, do you think that the people will know what they need from *you?*"

"Oh, I'm *sure* of that!" says the Little Lord. "They are much smarter than me!"

"Ha, ha, ha! Well, perhaps the tomatoes also know what they need from you, too."

"So, you think I should ask them?" inquires Emeka, as everything suddenly seems to make sense.

"That sounds like a very good idea, child. You are indeed most wise!" Papa Adam Makena says, beaming down upon Little Lord Emeka with all the love of a father.

"Thank you, Papa! I will do just that!" Emeka says very happy to please his Papa and the tomatoes.

At that moment, little Lord Emeka and Papa Adam Makena are aware of something going on behind them. They turn around and see a group of people coming toward them led by four men whom Emeka recognizes from the estate. And then he sees her. Coming up from behind, he sees the little angel who has been comforting him in his nightmares.

Suddenly Emeka cries out, "Angel! It is my angel!" and he starts running towards her.

And as she sees him, she cries out, "Emeka! Emeka!" Eve Elli starts running toward him, and everyone else stands still for a moment as they feel themselves witnessing a sacred moment.

The others in the village approach the scene slowly with a deep awe and reverence. Every heart present, every human creature, from the Lords, Master, people, Chrysalenes, and even #3 and #4, circle around the children and bear witness to the purest and highest form of love they have ever seen.

Emeka and Eve Elli lock arms around each other, jumping up and down, laughing and squealing with delight. All are moved to dance and sing, clapping their hands and laughing, while the two young ones are spreading their love and happiness all around.

High up above, a flutter of Monarchs smile down upon the human creatures below. Angel says, *Thy will be done, Kind One, Thy will be done.*

* * *

An AI voice comes over the intercom of the Cloudtransporter.

"Arriving in Johannesburg; 5 minutes."

However, Master Howard has been listening to another voice in his head for the last several hours.

Your son, Master John, has deceived us, and in so doing he has also deceived you. Your son, Master John, is working to take us all down. Your son, Master John, is working to take YOU, his own father, down. Your orders from the Council are very clear now, Master Howard.

"Yes. Very clear, indeed," Master Howard says, and looks out the window to see a mansion, tents and three other Cloudtransporters below, as he makes his final descent.

Chapter 12 – Forgiven

"WELCOME TO OUR VILLAGE," Papa Adam Makena says to Bem, Kookie and all their companions. "I am Adam Makena, and the child here is little Lord Emeka. It seems that the children already know each other!"

Everyone laughs and nods in agreement.

"We have all been called to this child, little Lord Emeka," Lady Liling says. "Each in our own way. I am Lady Liling who is now the caretaker of his Lord's estate." Turning to Emeka she says, "We are all glad to see you here Emeka, safe and protected."

"Thank you, Lady Liling!" Emeka says.

"My name is Kookie," he says, bending down to shake Emeka's hand. He is using his multi-person Universal Translator for everyone's benefit. "It is very nice to meet you, Lord Emeka."

"Thank you, Kookie!" Emeka says with a grin on his face. "It is very nice to meet you, too!"

The others make their introductions to the little Lord as well as to the people of the Village of the Holy Ones. Mama Eve Zula is touched by the love and kindness that she sees in all these people who have brought a little angel to Emeka.

"Won't you come into our hut and break bread with us," Mama Eve Zula says. Everyone bows humbly before her, graciously accepting her invitation.

Once inside the hut, with everyone seated around the two children, Mama Eve Zula says to Emeka, "These people have come here to help you, my child."

Emeka lowers his eyes with sadness.

"What is it?" asks Vi.

"What can we do for you, Emeka?" says Neely.

"I am so sorry to see that you are sad," says Angie.

"Is this about the dreams, Emeka?" asks Dumaka.

At the mention of dreams little Lord Emeka looks up.

"Yes, Dumaka. It is about the dreams about my father."

"Can you tell us about your dreams?" asks Mimi, feeling much compassion for the little Lord.

Emeka begins to give everyone an accounting of his nightmares, and his tears come quickly. "It is always the same," he says. "I am very scared, being chased by something very bad with red eyes. It is laughing at me. I hear screaming and the bad thing says the screaming is my father. That he is in a very bad place where he is being hurt."

Emeka is sobbing heavily now and pauses.

"It's alright," says the Major, putting his arm around Emeka's shoulders. "Take your time. We are here."

"The bad thing with the red eyes says that my father is in a place called hell." Emeka breaks down completely and cries, "Oh please, please help! I do not want my father to be in that bad place."

The little Lord is inconsolable while the Major holds him close. Tafari, Kookie, Angie, Yakov, Neely and Liling are all remembering how Emeka's father, Lord Ekene, almost murdered them, and their hearts are filled with nothing but compassion for Ekene's son.

Mama Eve Zula feels their love and is very moved by it. She says to them, "There is a way that you all can help Emeka, my good people."

"How is that?" asks Kookie.

"It begins with forgiveness," she continues. "As six of you here were almost murdered by the late Lord Ekene, you all have the power to forgive him."

"Actually, make that seven," Angie says taking #4 off her shoulder and holding her up for all to see.

"Yes," Mama Eve Zula smiles at #4 *and* #3, "that definitely includes the pigeons. And especially #4."

She takes the pigeons from Angie and holds them against her chest. With her eyes closed, Mama Eve Zula is listening to the pigeons speaking to her heart. When she opens her eyes, she says, "It is okay. The pigeons say they will help. They too have forgiveness in their hearts and know that they have also been called here to help Emeka, just like the rest of you"

"But how can we help?" asks the Major. Is it enough just to forgive Lord Ekene to rescue him from hell?"

"Almost," says Mama Eve Zula. "Having your forgiveness is enough to light Ekene's way. But the *rescue,* as you put it, especially for one who has done so much evil to so many, is another matter."

"What does that mean?" asks Tafari, the one in the group who undoubtedly suffered the most at the hands of Lord Ekene.

"It means that it is going to take a village of loving people, Chrysalenes, and one pure son who loves the condemned one very much, to go down into hell and get his father out. The son can guide the redeemed one back up the dark tunnel and into the light, releasing him to the Heavenly Father."

The group lets out a collective gasp. "I think the pigeons just fainted!" Angie blurts out.

Mama Eve Zula continues, "Oh yes, #3 and #4 can help too!"

"Good grief!" Ryan pipes up. "How's that?"

"Pigeons are also doves and doves are very special birds to the Lord."

"Yes, they sure are very special to me," quips Kookie.

Kookie's friends groan and roll their eyes.

"You just couldn't resist that one, could you, bro'!" says the Major.

Kookie smiles, looks up, and taps the tips of his fingers together. "Sorry," he says.

Meanwhile, little Lord Emeka is feeling heartened by what he is hearing. Seeing Emeka smile and laugh a little at the antics of his new friends, they all gather around him forming a circle, seated on the floor. The little Lord stands in the center of the circle and puts his hands out to invite Eve Elli to join him.

Papa Adam Makena steps forward and asks everyone to close their eyes and just listen to their hearts for a moment as he prays.

"Oh Lord, hear our prayer. That there are those here who may be moved to forgive your son Ekene and help him and his son Emeka to find peace, through your love and your mercy. May they step forward and proclaim themselves in your service. Thank you, thank you, Heavenly Father. Amen."

The first one to speak is Dumaka. Opening his eyes and looking around the circle he is moved to tears and says, "Thank you for bringing me here today, that I have now learned how to address the Kind One as the Lord and the Heavenly Father. Thank you!"

Putting his hands out to Little Lord Emeka, Dumaka says, "I offer my services to you, My Lord, in whatever way I can be of help."

The next to speak is Lady Neely, "In your soul Ekene I can see the Light of who you might have been in life, and how you must be suffering now to have left the world behind having never truly known what love is."

Lifting her hands to Heaven and bowing her head, Lady Neely says, "I am truly sorry for your loss and for this I forgive you, Lord Ekene."

Yakov listens to Lady Neely and sees a beauty deeper in her than the superficial one which he has already fallen in love with. And for this, he also expresses deep gratitude and pledges himself to help Little Lord Emeka.

One by one, the others do the same; each one expressing gratitude for what they are experiencing, sadness for Ekene's loss, forgiveness for what he has done in life, and a pledge to help his son. And in so doing, to help Ekene. Last but not least, it is Tafari's turn. All eyes are upon him unable to imagine what he could possibly say after the cold-blooded brutality that Ekene perpetrated upon him.

Tafari says, "Before I came to be in your service, Lord Ekene, I was but an arrogant, mindless, irritating voice on My Buddy. And although you knew not what you were doing when you drove me out of your window that day, my life of being truly human, decent, and kind *began* on that day. I can only thank you for that, feel sad for the suffering that you now endure, and for the sadness that your son holds in his sweet and gentle little soul. For that, I completely forgive you. If I can be of help, I am willing to go down into hell with your son to go and get you out of there. Together may we all bring you to Heaven's door."

In the depths of the underworld, a pair of angry red eyes are snarling and growling, as Lord Ekene has just received a gift from above. He has been allowed to hear every single word that was just spoken on his behalf.

In the depths of hell, Ekene's soul is filled with shame. . . and he weeps.

* * *

Stepping out of the Cloudtransporter, Master Howard notices the tents straight ahead and walks over to see what he can find out.

One of the people milling around the tents approaches Master Howard, "Is there anything I can do for you, sir?"

Master Howard looks around at all the food still left over on the tables and people still lingering about, eating and socializing.

"Are you with the others, sir?" asks the man.

"What?" Master Howard asks, as he turns on the Universal Translator pendant necklace that was given to him by the Council.

"The others who came in the Cloudtransporters over there, sir," he says, pointing to all four of the vehicles.

"Oh, uh, yes, yes," the Master stammers. "Yes, I am with the others. Do you happen to know where the others are, my good man?"

"They were here earlier, having a wonderful meal with all of us. But then a group of them left and said they would be back a little later. That we should all continue with our gathering and fellowship with each other and just leave whenever we feel like it. They are very nice people, sir, very kind. I say, if you know them, then you must be very kind too."

Don't bet on it. Master Howard thinks to himself.

The servant smiles warmly and says, "Well, why don't you just grab some food and make yourself at home until the others get back."

"Thank you," Master Howard says, "I shall do just that."

He really doesn't have much to say to anyone and would rather just sit quietly and wait for the Major's return. *Useless eaters.* He looks around at the people eating, talking with one another, and laughing together, seeming to have a good time.

Useless eaters are the words that keep going through his head as he sits there surrounded by gaiety and the simple pleasures of people who are enjoying each other's company.

A little girl walks by with her mother. She is eating a large cookie and Master Howard realizes that he has not eaten for a while. He eyeballs the little girl's cookie and thinks about what food might be left on the tables. But before he can make a move, the little girl stops and smiles at him. She offers her cookie to Master Howard.

The girl's mother says, "My child seems to think that you are very hungry, kind sir." The mother's smile is just as sweet as the daughter's. "Won't you come over to the food and help yourself? Yes?"

For a moment, Master Howard feels a lump in his throat. He bites down hard on his lip and furrows his brow, hoping the lump will go away. But it doesn't. He lowers his head and stares at the ground, fighting with all his might against a single tear drop that is trying to fall from his eye.

When he manages to regain his composure, Master Howard looks up and sees that the mother and child have gone over to the nearest table. They are filling a plate with food and within moments return to Master Howard with a plate full of exquisite pastries and fruit. The mother puts the plate down on the empty chair next to Master Howard. They both nod, smile at him again, and walk away. As hungry as he is, it takes the Master a few more minutes before he is able to eat.

* * *

Liling's group of 14 people and two pigeons are on their way back to the Lord's Estate. They all glow with the light of love and a flame of hope that is growing inside each of them, including the pigeons. As they are walking along the dirt road, lost in thought about all that now lies ahead of them, it occurs to Kookie that in all the excitement since their arrival at Johannesburg, he has not shared his good news with the Major and several others present.

He stops walking for a moment and asks everyone else to do the same so he can make his announcement, "My dearest Brothers and Sisters, and pigeons, in all the hustle and bustle since our arrival I have not shared some very important and wonderful news with you all."

Everyone looks at each other curious at what Kookie is about to tell them. Of course, four of them already know. Putting his arm around Angie and smiling tenderly at her, he announces to the group, "My beloved Angie and I have recently taken our vows with each other."

A collective gasp rises up and joyous shouts of, "Woo hoo! Yay! Way to go, Bro!" with handshakes, back-slapping and hugs all around.

Ryan puts his hand up in the air to get everyone's attention. Putting his arm around Mimi in like fashion to Kookie and Angie, Ryan announces to everyone, "My darling Mimi and I have also taken our vows with each other. And one day, when we are all free to do so, I hope to make her my wife."

"Aww!" the group exclaims, followed by more hugs, congratulations and big smiles all around.

Kookie says, "Well, I guess we had better head on back now and celebrate all the good news tonight, shall we?"

"Amen to that, Brother!" says the Major; everyone nodding in consent.

With one more hand in the air and an "Echem!" all eyes are now turned to Yakov.

"Just one more thing," Yakov begins. "Before coming here, I asked my lovely Lady Neely to marry me, as Lords are permitted to do such things. And she told me that until *all* men and women are free to marry each other, she would be happier taking her vows with me, as one of the people."

Putting his arms around Lady Neely, looking deeply into her eyes he says, "And I fell even more deeply in love with her, as we took our vows."

The little group is teary and speechless as they gather around Yakov and Neely giving them both warm hugs.

Mimi hugs the two of them and wiping away her tears says, in English and in Russian, "Thank you. Spasiba."

The Major looks at Vi and smiles. Taking her by the hand he says to everyone, "Well, I guess we had better get back to the house. It does seem as though we have much to celebrate this evening!"

Everyone nods and chuckles.

Liling turns to Bem, Tafari, Dumaka and Nassor and says, "I do hope you will join us all this evening. In addition to our celebration for these most blessed events, we also have much to talk about regarding Emeka."

"Thank you, dear Lady," says Dumaka. The four of them graciously accept Lady Liling's invitation.

As the estate comes into view, the group is in high spirits. Everyone is thinking about the most precious gifts that they have all been given, including the gift of forgiveness. They think about how they will be helping Emeka, and the Alliance will move forward with renewed strength for all the people of One World. All of this and so much gratitude is on their hearts and minds as they come to the big field behind the estate.

And then the Major sees him. Sitting under a tent, nibbling on a plate of food, Master Howard looks up and locks eyes with his son.

* * *

The screens of ES and SPA are activated and an incoming message is accepted from PA.

> PA: Greetings, my Brethren, and a most auspicious hello!
> ES: Greetings, PA! What is the auspicious occasion?
> SPA: Yes, Brethren, Greetings! And do tell us of this news, PA!
> PA: It is beyond mere words, my Brethren. Therefore, I simply invite you to tune in your surveillance system to the implant in our prize mole, Master Howard. And in real time, do as the slaves are so fond of saying, *ENJOY THE SHOW!*

* * *

The Major stops dead in his tracks and so does Kookie, who catches a split-second glimpse of a tiny, pin-spot flash of red at the base of Master Howard's throat.

"*FATHER!*" the Major cries out.

Everyone stops moving.

A calculated, well-rehearsed response comes from Master Howard as he holds out both arms and says, *"My Son!"*

The Major is moved beyond comprehension, and with every fiber of his being he wants so much to believe what he is seeing.

Master Howard walks over to his son with open arms. "Please John, forgive me," Master Howard says softly.

The little boy John breaks down completely in his daddy's arms, receiving that which he has wanted and hoped for his whole life: his father's love.

"I am so sorry for being selfish and greedy all of these years. I have always seen how you care about people, and I have never appreciated you for that. Instead, I have given you horrible tasks to perform, for me and for Howard Pharmaceuticals. I have made you do all those things knowing that it was against your nature and knowing that you were just trying to please me. And now I have seen some of the terrible effects of our greed and learned the error of my ways."

Master Howard looks straight into the Majors eyes and finishes the monologue that was written for him by PA. The words which he just memorized on the Cloudtransporter, enroute to Johannesburg. "Son, with all of my heart I am sorry, and I wish to help with the work you are now doing. Can you forgive me, John? Will you let me in?"

The Major is speechless and beside himself with emotion.

The others just don't know what to say. Lady Liling interjects with, "Master Howard, won't you come in and join us for dinner? There is much we have to share with each other, and you are most welcome."

"Why, thank you, Lady Liling. You truly are a very kind woman," Master Howard responds.

The Major looks at his father and finally says, "Bless you father, bless you. Please come in and join us."

The group lets out a collective sigh and each welcomes Master Howard. Everyone seems to be quite touched and happy. Everyone that is, except Kookie.

Later that evening, the companions are sitting around after dinner, getting ready to discuss the business at hand. Eve Elli has fallen asleep, curled up into a little ball on one of the plush, overstuffed cushions. The others are all hunkered down in their favorite cozy spaces in the living room.

The only one not present for the moment is Master Howard, who excused himself saying that he had some things to attend to in his Cloudtransporter, but would return just as soon as he could.

Kookie jumps on the opportunity. He gets the Holographic Imager going again and calls everyone to his attention. The Major is still in a state of shock over his father's sudden and most complete turnaround that he is still not 100 percent sure that he believes what he is seeing. But he wants to so desperately that he ignores any gut-feelings to the contrary.

"I would like for all of us to discuss how we are going to proceed with all that we have learned this afternoon, and the needs of Little Lord Emeka. I have been thinking about his desperate need to rescue his father from hell and help bring him to the Light. In consideration of how this is affecting Emeka, that is, the way the beast seems to be baiting him in some way, I do believe that we should get moving on this right away."

"What do you mean by *the beast seems to be baiting him?*" asks the Major, as a cold feeling settles into the pit of his stomach.

Kookie answers him gently, fully aware of that which the Major is not yet able to see. "Little Lord Emeka must be important to us, or we would not have all been called here on his behalf and the beast would not be coming to him in his dreams and frightening him. He is very likely being set up by the beast to become like his father rather than like the Chrysalenes.

"I see," says the Major, but the cold feeling in his stomach has not faded.

"So, what do you propose, my Brother?" asks Liling.

I propose that a few of us go back to the Village of the Holy Ones this very night and follow through on our promise to Emeka. For those of us who stay behind, we maintain a prayer vigil for him and for Ekene, that all goes according to plan." Kookie says.

"I totally agree with that," says Angie. "And I for one would like to go and bring #3 and #4 with me."

Tafari speaks up and says, "And I would like to fulfill my promise to be with Emeka on his journey."

"I would like to bring my precious little granddaughter." Mimi says smiling at the sleeping bundle on the cushion.

"And I would like to be at your side, for whatever support you need from me," says Ryan to Mimi.

There is a pause and Kookie says, "I guess the rest of us can stay here and do a whole lot of praying."

"That sounds very good to me," says Lady Liling, and the others all nod in agreement.

Kookie sees Master Howard returning to the house at which point he quickly turns off the Holographic Imager. He goes over to Angie and kisses her ear, while whispering to her softly, "Get everyone out of here quickly and quietly. Go *now*. I love you."

"Ah! There you are Master Howard!" says Kookie, all surprised and *happy* to see him. "You know, we always like to have an after-dinner relaxation time together. I have just the thing that I always like to do."

Behind Master Howard's back, Kookie holds up his hand waving at Angie. He looks at her one more time and blows her a kiss.

Turning to Master Howard he says, "Why don't you come with me to my room and I'll share a little secret with you."

Hearing the words "little secret," Master Howard perks up and is all ready to go. Holding his tuba mouthpiece up for Angie to see, Kookie turns around and winks at her. Then he disappears with Master Howard to go fetch his tuba.

* * *

It is dark outside with a few stars shining as the little group reaches the Village of the Holy Ones. Mimi is holding a sleeping Eve Elli while Ryan has his protective arm around them both. Angie is walking proudly carrying #3 and #4 on her shoulders. And Tafari has the light of the Lord in his eyes as he is remembering his pledge and the forgiveness he gave to his former Lord and task master, Ekene. They reach the hut of little Lord Emeka and the twelve Chrysalenes are all inside waiting for them.

"We are all ready for you, and here to serve," says Mama Eve Zula.

The rest of them smile and begin to glow, becoming slightly transparent. Looking down at her sleeping little angel, Mimi sees Eve Elli glowing too, just like the time she first saw her glowing behind bars in the cage at the Howard Pharmaceuticals Silver Beach Plant.

The glow from the 12 Chrysalenes and Eve Elli brightens like a morning star. Suddenly, the little sleeping bundle wakes up. She is wide awake and ready to go. Looking at Mimi who is now crying with a mixture of joy and awe at what her little granddaughter is about to do, Eve Elli says to her, "Don't cry Gramma, everything is gonna be okay. Eve Elli loves you. Eve Elli will be just fine! Don't cry Gramma."

Eve Elli goes over to Little Lord Emeka who is sound asleep. She kisses him gently on the forehead and beckons Tafari to come over. She then looks at #3 and #4, smiling and nodding at them. Eve Elli puts out her hand to receive the Monarch Angel who just joined them. As she does so, everyone notices that there are seven other Monarchs who have just landed on the shoulders of other Chrysalenes. They all form a circle around the sleeping Emeka, and Eve Elli says to the sleeping child, "Okay Emeka, it's time to go get your daddy."

Eve Elli and Tafari raise their hands up to the heavens as the two of them bring forth words in their own languages, which neither one has ever heard before, but are imprinted in their souls . . .

"Yeah, though I walk through the valley of the shadow of death, I will fear no evil."

The birds and the Monarch Angel fly up into the air over their heads, and all lights go out.

Little Lord Emeka wakes up to a deep booming sound.

Tafari moves behind him, holding him around the waist as he and Eve Elli continue,

"I will fear no evil, for thou art with me."

Deep in the depths of hell, a red glowing light appears.

Comforted by the presence of Eve Elli and Tafari, Emeka leans forward over the chasm of doom.

The sound of rumbling thunder below turns into angry red eyes, glaring and snarling at Emeka.

Eve Elli raises her hand against the fiery eyes of hells creature and says, "Thy rod and thy staff they comfort me, in the presence of mine enemies."

Eve Elli holds Tafari, who holds Emeka as Angel and the two doves are circling overhead. Love and courage guiding their way.

Emeka, Eve Elli, Tafari, Angel and the doves plunge down into the snarling, evil eyes of the darkness below.

The thunderous boom is pierced by the screams of Ekene, as Emeka calls out in the cold void of fear; "Father! Father! I am here!

Come to me, my father!"

Eve Elli proclaims, "I will fear no evil, for thou art with me."

Emeka cries, "I have come for you, my father!"

Tafari calls out, "We have come for you, My Lord Ekene, to bring you to the Father in Heaven."

Ekene's cries resound as Emeka thrusts his arms straight into the demonic, fiery red fear.

Suddenly, a pair of arms reach up from hells darkness crying, "My son, my son! Please, help me, my son!"

Emeka answers, "We are here for you, my father"

As his loving little hands reach out to Ekene, father and son clasp hands.

Eve Elli looks up to Angel and the doves and she says, "We will now go to the House of the Lord."

The winged messengers of the Light begin to spiral upwards raising Eve Elli, Tafari, Emeka and Ekene out of the cold darkness of hell.

Slowly they rise from the eyes of the demon into a long dark tunnel.

As Ekene looks up he sees two white doves, a sparkling golden angel, and the Light of his journey's end.

"Do not be afraid human creature," the golden angel says, "We have come to take you home."

Ekene is crying tears of joy as the Light of Heaven is getting near, and he speaks with tenderness to his son:

"Thank you, my son, I love you, I am so sorry. Please forgive me," Ekene pleads.

"I love you my father, and I forgive you," Emeka declares from his heart.

Looking at Tafari with tears overflowing, Ekene implores:

"Thank you, my faithful friend. I love you. I am so sorry. Please forgive me."

"From the depths of my soul I forgive you, my Brother." Tafari avows with compassion.

The Light of Heaven streams down upon them,

And Eve Elli says to Ekene, "You are now at the House of the Lord. Until we meet again my friend."

They all smile at Ekene as he rises above them and enters the House of the Lord forever.

PART 3
RAGING BEAST

Chapter 13 – Water

WHILE EVE ELLI, TAFARI, AND EMEKA are descending into hell, the others in the hut are left watching and waiting.

Mimi, Ryan, Angie and the 12 Chrysalenes listen to Eve Elli speak the words, "Yea though I walk through the valley of the shadow of death, I will fear no evil."

Eve Elli, Tafari, Emeka, the Monarch Angel, #3 and #4 all become transparent and then they disappear. Mimi is frightened having just seen her granddaughter vanish, but the Chrysalenes reassure her that Eve Elli is in the hands of the Lord, and that she is quite safe.

As the Chrysalenes sit in a circle, glowing with the Light of Heaven, they begin to sing a song of the angels. There are no words, simply tones of beauty and purity. Mimi, Ryan, and Angie lie down on the soft earth in the hut and let the angelic song of the Chrysalenes fill and comfort their hearts. They feel themselves being transported to majestic mountains, crystal clear rivers and sparkling lakes. They feel the warmth of morning meadows and inhale the fragrances of a garden in the springtime. They experience a peacefulness as if they are lying beside still waters. They can each feel their souls rising to a loving, bright White Light above, experiencing the bliss of being in the House of the Lord forever.

The singing gently ceases, and Mimi, Ryan and Angie are opening their eyes. Standing before them are Eve Elli, Tafari and Little Lord Emeka beaming with joy as if they themselves have just been to Heaven's door. The Monarch Angel is nestled in Eve Elli's hair, #3 and #4 are snuggly perched on Tafari's shoulders, and Little Lord Emeka has a great big smile on his face.

"My father is in Heaven now!"

He rubs his eyes, yawns, and says to everyone, "Can I go back to sleep now?"

* * *

Back at the Big House, after Kookie dismissed Angie and the others to go to the Village of the Holy Ones, and he escorted Master Howard out of the room, the others are left in a state of uncertainty.

The Major is overwhelmed by all that has just happened with his father. He looks to Vi for a sense of stability amidst the turmoil he is experiencing in his guts.

Is this really happening? he questions. Could his father truly have changed so dramatically, so suddenly? Is this really the manifestation of everything he has ever wanted with him? And if not, then what else *could* it be?

Vi can see the internal struggle going on in her man, and she is at a loss for words. She simply sits down in silence next to the Major, offering him her calming, loving presence. Kookie and Master Howard eventually walk back into the living room. He is carrying his tuba and is all smiles.

"Well!" Kookie announces with delight. "I just shared my huge secret with Master Howard here!"

"Really?" says the Major, "And what secret might that be, bro'?"

With a sly expression and a wink, Kookie replies, "I showed him how to get a mellow, rich sound out of a tuba." Kookie says, smiling and tapping the tips of his fingers together with great delight over his "accomplishment" with Master Howard.

The Major sadly understands what Kookie is hinting at. He does not quite trust his father yet either, and appreciates the fact that Kookie is exercising caution with the man.

As Kookie nods at Yakov and Liling, the two of them get up and go into the study, with Lady Neely following behind. Those now left with Kookie in the living room are Master Howard, the Major, Vi, Bem, Dumaka and Nassor. Kookie says to them, "Well while the others are off for the moment doing their thing, why don't we have some fun with a little favorite concerto of mine."

From the study, Yakov, Liling and Neely can hear Kookie playing his beloved Concerto in F minor. Without saying another word, Yakov takes out his Lord's Communication Device and activates the Holographic Imager, making it appear as if they are going through some of the late Lord Ekene's files.

"What was that all about, honey?" asks Neely.

"Well, my dear, when our brother gives us the old Kookie Eyeball, we know enough to just shut up and do what he says!"

"I see," Neely says. "And what exactly does *that* mean in this situation?"

Lady Liling says, "It means that we should proceed without him and pray for what is happening at the Village of the Holy Ones."

"Okay," says Neely, with a smile. "You three really are in sync with each other, aren't you?"

Yakov and Liling both smile and nod in agreement.

All three close their eyes and open their hearts to what is going on with Eve Elli, Tafari and Emeka in the depths of hell. Immediately, they hear words which they too have never heard before but are imprinted on their souls: *The Lord is my shepherd, I shall not want.*

And the fiery beast from hell appears before them.

* * *

"Bravo!" says Master Howard, enthusiastically applauding Kookie who has just finished serenading them with his treasured tuba. He looks at

Kookie and at his son and comes out with the next rehearsed verbiage. As he begins, once again Kookie notices a tiny, split-second flash of a red light at the base of Master Howard's throat.

"John. Kookie. There is something that I must tell you both," Master Howard says. "The Council is planning one more incident as part of Operation Pied Piper, and they have sent me here to enlist both of you to help with this."

The Major is *really* flummoxed. What on earth is the old man up to?

"In my Cloudtransporter," continues Master Howard, "I am carrying enough neurotoxins to poison the fresh water supply of the entire world. The UC, of course, already has their own pure water supply all set up. What will happen when the people drink the water is the same as when they drink the juice and eat the tea cakes at the Coffeehouses. It will drive them mad so that they are driven to kill each other and themselves."

"Why are you telling us all of this, father?" asks the Major.

Kookie is watching Master Howard closely, not at all sure where he is going with this. As far as he knows, the Masters were to have been kept in the dark about the neurotoxins in the water. The Lords and the Council devised their own way of distributing the neurotoxins in the world's drinking water without that Masters knowing about it. He is fairly certain at this point that there is some serious foul play going on, and he just does not have the heart to say anything to the Major, at least not yet.

"What are you wanting us to do?" Kookie asks Master Howard.

"What I want," says Master Howard dropping his guard a little and glaring at Kookie, "is for you to do to the neurotoxins that I brought, whatever it is that you did to the neurotoxins that were sent out to the Coffeehouses, and whatever you did to the Ebola bioweapon. You know, what made it *look* like the real thing when in fact, it wasn't."

The Major and Vi both pale.

"I have a mole," Master Howard continues. "That is how I found out about your involvement in the neurotoxins and the bioweapon. The Council is very suspicious, but they do not have any real evidence. That is why we must work together on the water project, and why I came straight over here."

Kookie is completely thrown by what Master Howard is saying, but he has no time to mentally process further because Yakov, Neely and Liling come rushing back into the living room.

"They're back! They're back!" the three of them exclaim altogether.

Master Howard glances around the room and says, "Who's back?"

"Excuse me, Master Howard, I will get to all of your questions. But first there is another matter that I must attend to." Turning to Liling and Yakov, who can clearly see that something is very wrong with Kookie, he asks them, "So where are they?"

"Um, well," says Liling, "I think they are putting Eve Elli to bed. It is rather late and well past her bedtime."

"Ah, yes," says Kookie. "Then I will go to their room and have a quick word with them."

Turning to everyone else he says, "I'll be right back," and he scurries off to see Mimi and Ryan.

The Major is left with his father and Vi, and the anxiety of not knowing what is going on. Sadly, the Major can see that his father may be playing a deadly game here, and realizes that he cannot trust him.

"Oh," says the Major, while being *very sure* to catch the eyes of Liling, Yakov and Neely. "Angie went out with some folks a little while ago. Something about *Coffeehouse news*. You know, the news of the people."

"Ah yes. There isn't really all that much on My Buddy, now is there," Master Howard says with a sarcastic chuckle.

"No there isn't," the Major says forcing a smile at his father. He turns to Liling, Yakov and Neely and says, "So did Angie and the others have any news to report from the "Coffeehouse"?! he asks.

The three of them pick up on the Major's cues very easily as Yakov says: "Well, as a matter of fact, things seem to have gotten better lately."

"How so?" asks the Major.

"Yes, how so?" asks Master Howard who is most anxious to hear how things are a bit better. He also knows that the other ears listening; the ones hooked up to his throat would also be very interested in hearing how things are a bit better at the Coffeehouse.

"*We* can tell you that," says Dumaka, as Bem and Nassor nod in agreement. They have been sitting quietly, aware that something suspect is going on.

Everyone turns to Dumaka as he continues: "Things were getting really bad over there for a little while. People would come in as usual, get their coffee and tea cakes, or juice, and the mood changed. There seemed to be an irritability and tension in the air which was very noticeable. And then My Buddy would come on, and when the news and instructions were announced, people just went berserk! There was yelling and arguing and as things got worse, fights broke out and even a few people died."

"Oh my! Good grief! Wow!" and other assorted exclamations of surprise erupt around the living room.

"Yes, well," continues Dumaka, "So the Center Overseer decided to stop broadcasting My Buddy and everything sort of settled down a bit, but not the way it used to be. We are thinking that there is also something else going on, although no one can put their finger on it. Well, at least no one is killing anyone in there for now."

The Major, Vi, Liling, Yakov and Neely all look at each other with great sorrow, realizing that the neurotoxins have indeed gotten to the Coffeehouses in Johannesburg.

Kookie reappears with Angie and Tafari, and sees the sad faces of the rest of the group.

Master Howard turns to Kookie and says, "Like I said, I don't know how you subverted the neurotoxins and the bioweapon, but I need your help now to do the same with the water, son."

Before Kookie can say anything, Tafari says to his friends, "I think it is time for us to leave." To Liling he says, "Thank you, My Lady, and everyone, for the honor of having us here as your dinner guests."

"Oh yes, you are so welcome!" says Liling. "The pleasure has been all ours. Do come again."

They all bow to her with hands across their chests.

Turning to Dumaka, Lady Liling says, "May I walk you all back to your huts?"

Dumaka is enchanted with her. "The pleasure is all mine, My Lady," he says. And the five of them leave.

Kookie turns to Master Howard and all eyes in the room are laser-focused on the two of them. Looking at the bottom of Master Howard's throat, Kookie knows exactly who else is listening, and that he must choose his words very carefully.

"Sir, I am so grateful that you came to me with this information. I will do my best to honor your request and help you with the water situation. It is definitely something that could be a very serious problem. Did the Council tell you how they plan to have their own clean water supply once the neurotoxins are released?"

Master Howard replies, "Not exactly, Lord Kenneth. Something about their own supply line, which they say will be available for the entire UC."

"I see," says Kookie. "And you say that you have the neurotoxins with you; *ALL OF THEM* . . . which you want me to do *what* with?"

"Change them into something harmless while making them register through the Council surveillance scanning system, as the real thing." Master Howard is getting a bit irritated with Kookie's evasiveness.

"You mean, trick the surveillance system," says Kookie, "So that it scans as something harmful when it is in fact not harmful at all."

"Yes, yes!" exclaims Master Howard, as he is losing his patience and about to lose his temper. "You know, like you did with the Ebola bioweapon!"

The red light on Master Howard's throat flashes again and this time the Major notices it. The Major says nothing and merely stares at a dream that has been crushed.

Doing his best to be remain cool as a cucumber and annoyingly evasive, Kookie just smiles and says to Master Howard, "Let's go to your Cloudtransporter first thing in the morning and I'll see what I can do. As for this evening," he looks lovingly at Angie, "It is time for us to retire."

The others all hastily agree, and they go off to their rooms for the night.

* * *

Arriving at the garden of Bem, Tafari, Dumaka and Nassor, each man expresses his gratitude to Lady Liling and wishes her a good night. Three of them return to their respective huts except Dumaka who stands in the starlight alone with Lady Liling.

Bowing in deference to her, he looks into her eyes and says, "I hope you will accept my humble words of praise to you, My Lady. If I may say so, your gentle soul and loveliness are the most enchanting of all women."

Crossing her hands over her chest and bowing to Dumaka, Lady Liling says, "Thank you kind sir. Your words are most appreciated." Smiling into his eyes she adds, "You are most welcome to attend our dinner tomorrow evening, if it pleases you, sir."

Dumaka has just jumped off the planet and landed on one of the twinkling stars overhead. "Oh yes, ma'am! That would please me very much!" he says.

They bow to each other again and say good night.

Kookie, Yakov and the Major wait until they see Master Howard go down the hall to his suite and lock himself in for the night. Then, Kookie motions to the other two with his index finger and the three men quietly sneak back into the study. When Liling returns to the Big House, Kookie catches her coming in. With the Holographic Imager already going full swing in the study, the three of them are waiting there for her.

Kookie, Yakov and the Major proceed to fill Liling in on everything that has happened with Master Howard. As much as they all want to share the wonderful news about Little Lord Emeka and Eve Elli, and the rescue of Ekene, they know all of that will have to wait until the situation with Master Howard and the Council has been dealt with.

"We can do this!" the Major says, stuffing his disappointment and sadness down inside the recesses of his childhood broken heart.

"You bet we can, bro'!" Kookie agrees. "From the little I heard so far about what Eve Elli did this evening, we can do anything!"

"Wow," Yakov says, "What did you hear?"

"Our little three-year-old Chrysalene looked the beast straight in the eye and blasted him with the words of our Heavenly Father!" says Kookie with all the pride of a father whose daughter just stood up to a bully.

They all laugh, and the Major says, "She sounds even tougher than me when I was a kid!"

"Well, now there is no excuse for us *not* to deal with whatever the Council tries to bring down on us. Not with Eve Elli and Little Lord Emeka on our side," Liling joyously interjects.

All of them reply, "Amen to that!"

Putting all their super-intelligence together, combined with the Major's understanding of his father, they stay up late into the night until they come up with a plan.

* * *

The next morning Kookie, Yakov, Liling and the Major meet up with Master Howard and head over to his Cloudtransporter.

"So," Master Howard says to Kookie, "are you going to tell me how you sabotaged the neurotoxins and the bioweapon?"

"Actually," says Kookie, still trying to be as evasive as he can, concealing and protecting Metatron from the Council, "I will simply *show* you how such things can be done. I will do as you ask to the neurotoxins that you brought and make them safe."

"Ah!" says Master Howard clapping and rubbing his hands together. He is quite excited to see this.

As soon as they get inside Master Howard's Cloudtransporter they all start "dancing" to the choreographed number they rehearsed the night before.

Kookie says to Master Howard, "Okay, let's get those boxes of neurotoxins out here, every last one of them."

"I'll help you father," says the Major."

"And I will help you too," says Yakov.

In the time it has taken for them to get moving to where the boxes are stored, Liling has taken out her Lord's Communication Device and turned on the Holographic Imager. Kookie has downloaded it onto all their devices.

Liling sits in the plush chair of the Cloudtransporter and putting on a show for the Council's surveillance system, she appears to be very relaxed, waiting for the men to get back.

They return shortly with several boxes and Kookie sees that Liling is sitting in the plush chair, as rehearsed.

"Well," he says, "Let's open up one of these boxes and check the contents."

Speaking to Master Howard he says, "I need to have one bottle to set my program correctly."

"Okay," says Master Howard and hands the bottle of neurotoxins to Kookie.

The others create a little distraction by thanking Master Howard for doing this wonderful thing and joining them in their mission.

"Of course, my son," he says to the Major. "You do know how I truly feel."

With a sigh, trying to hide his sadness, the Major says, "Yes father, I *DO* know how you truly feel."

Kookie is ready and he approaches each box one at a time. He holds up the small, grey Metatron so Master Howard can clearly see it. However, thanks to the Holographic Imager, the little grey box is appearing as a little *red* box to the Council as they are watching through Master Howard's throat implant.

Kookie holds Metatron against each box and turns on the 369-Program, zapping each one with an old download that was actually used by the Council a very long time ago. It was at a time when the earth's waters were so toxic that they had to come up with something to clean it all up, or it would have been the end of all life on earth. Since it was specifically created to purify *seriously* toxic water, it is an easy remedy for this situation, without Kookie having to reveal anything about Metatron and the 369-Program to the Council. However, the added effects of the 369-Program will give the bottles even greater benefits, as did the DNA transformation of the Ebola bioweapon.

As Kookie zaps each box, they all start to pulsate green.

"That's it!" he says to Major Howard. "Your bottles of neurotoxins are all quite harmless but will appear to be fully toxic when they are inspected."

"Thank you, thank you!" says Master Howard. "I must now get these back to the plant and set the gears in motion. They will be disbursed first thing tomorrow, *allegedly* infecting every reservoir and major source of drinking water across One World. Only we will know that it is truly harmless."

He winks and nods at the Major. "And when I get back in a few days, we can discuss further ways in which I can help you and your mission."

"Thank you, father. Thank you. I shall look forward to your return."

Looking at the others, Liling says, "Well then I guess we had better get back to all that file work of the Ekene estate in the study."

"I'm with you Sister," says Yakov.

"And a great big lunch as well," says Kookie. "Got any chocolate chip cookies?"

* * *

Three screens activate and the incoming message from PA is accepted:

PA: "Greetings Brethren!"

SPA &ES: "Greetings!"

PA: "You have both been watching Master Howard's most excellent progress, no doubt."

SPA: "Yes Brother!"

ES: "Most definitely!"

PA: "My technicians tell me that they were easily able to observe what Lord Kenneth was doing including the equipment he was working with."

SPA: "Yes, my technicians concur, it was quite a simple thing to follow Lord Kenneth's every move."

ES: "And my technicians tell me that Lord Kenneth is apparently using some old transformational system that was developed a very long time ago. The red box that he held up is very distinctive."

SPA: "Well, that would certainly explain how he changed the structure of the bioweapon."

ES: "And the neurotoxins."

SPA: "Yes, it does! We should have thought of that one ourselves!"

PA: "And Lord Kenneth does *not* know about all the other boxes of neurotoxins back at Howard Pharmaceuticals."

SPA: "Yes, that is correct. Lord Kenneth and the others seem to have fallen for Master Howard's story completely."

ES: "So, we now have Lord Kenneth's secret as to how he ruined Operation Snake Bite and the Ebola bioweapons."

SPA: "Our technicians can easily track down and destroy all of those remaining red boxes, so Lord Kenneth and his allies cannot cause any further damage with them."

ES: "And we also now have a trusted mole to help us uncover and destroy all of Lord Kenneth's allies."

PA: "Excellent, my Brethren! Most excellent! I shall now give Master Howard the orders to proceed with the disbursement of the neurotoxins to all of the major reservoirs throughout One World."

SPA: "Let the final solution of the termination of the useless eaters begin!"

ES: "One World will become OUR World!"

In the depths of the underworld, an angry pair of red eyes narrow with pleasure, making its presence felt by PA, ES and SPA.

PA: "And the dark lord shall reign over all!"

The transmission is terminated.

* * *

Master Howard is on his way back to the main facility in California. He messages his Overlord to let him know that everything is in place and ready to go.

The screen on the Overlord's Communication Device is activated and Master Howard's incoming message is accepted.

Master Howard: "Greetings, My Overlord. My apologies for disturbing you at this hour in your time zone. But what I have to tell you is most important."

Overlord: (Rubbing his eyes and yawning) "You may continue, Master Howard."

Master Howard: "It is all done, My Lord! My mission in Johannesburg has been accomplished!"

Overlord: (Fully awake now) "Most excellent, Master Howard. Thank you for letting me know right away."

Master Howard: "I am sending word immediately to all of our distributors throughout One World to begin distribution of Operation Clean Water."

Overlord: (Trying not to let on that he is shocked and dismayed to hear this) "Very well."

Master Howard: "I shall give you further updates as we progress, my Lord Jackson."

Overlord: "Yes, you do that. Most excellent of you Master Howard."

The transmission is terminated.

Lord Jackson is thoroughly bewildered and quite worried.

Rolling over he says to his sleeping sweetie by his side, "I'm sorry to wake you at this foolish hour, my lovely Rita, but I think we may have a problem. We need to send #33, through the pigeon network, to Johannesburg immediately. There is an urgent message we need to send them.

"Mm. . . " Rita yawns, trying to wake up. "So, what's the message, honey?"

* * *

Master Howard has arrived back at the plant. Everything looks like any normal day. His instructions from the Council are to take the boxes that Kookie zapped and send them immediately to the lab for analysis. As the operation is covert, no one in the lab is even aware of what is going on or exactly what they are supposed to be looking for.

Master Howard finds the Lab Overseer and says, "I am having boxes brought into the lab that contain bottles that need to be examined for possible contamination. You are to put aside whatever else you are doing and take care of this. As soon as you have everything analyzed, report back to me immediately. Is that understood, Lab Overseer?"

"Yes sir, Master Howard. That is understood. I will report back to you immediately sir," says the Lab Overseer.

Returning to his office suite, Master Howard sends messages out to several thousand Master Commandants connected to the Howard Pharmaceutical plants all across One World. Each Master Commandant accepts the incoming message, and Master Howard gives the speech that has been ordered down from PA. He begins his transmission:

My fellow Masters of the Upper Crust, I have just found out that the terrible traitor among us who has been helping the slaves toward insurrection has been apprehended. Glory to the highest, PA, ES, and SPA for delivering us from the evil ones. They will be judged and dealt with in due time. But for now, there is another crisis on our hands. We have just discovered that a ring of evildoers who wish to do harm to the people and the UC have tainted the water throughout every reservoir in One World with a neurotoxin.

The Council has learned of this and is having water purifiers that we at Howard Pharmaceuticals created many years ago, delivered to your compounds. You will see several boxes marked Operation Clean Water. The safety of our drinking water is now in your hands, Master Commandants. You must take those bottles, fly over the reservoirs, and empty their contents, to restore the waters to safety.

I give you this command directly from PA himself. Go and restore our waters immediately or our people will die!

The transmission is terminated.

* * *

Kookie and the whole group are in the study of the Big House. The Holographic Imager is going all the time in that room, making it the one safe place where any of them can go and talk day or night. They simply give the impression to the Council's surveillance system that they are helping Lady Liling manage the estate as she was called to do. Even though they know the Council is pretty much onto Kookie, they are not quite sure exactly what the Council thinks is going on with the rest of them, or how far the so-called "treachery" extends.

"I believe," says Kookie, "that the Council feels we are all in this together, and that they probably would have killed us all by now if not for one thing."

"What is that?" asks the Major.

"They probably know that we are getting all kinds of help, and if they kill us now, they will never know who is helping us or what kind of help we are getting."

"Or what kind of force they are dealing with," says Mimi, and everyone nods in agreement.

"Yes," continues Kookie. "So being vague and keeping up a good front is actually our best form of defense right now."

"And what about our best form of *offense*" asks the Major. "I mean, is it enough that we just continue to dodge their bullets, so to speak?"

Ryan has been sitting quietly, lost in thought when the Major's last question suddenly strikes a chord. Somewhere inside of Ryan, words that he has never heard before, yet somehow are imprinted on his soul whisper to his heart, *Pride goes before destruction, a haughty spirit before a fall.* [11] Then he hears other words from a time long past when some talked about the power of *peaceful, nonviolent, noncooperation.* Though he never heard those words either, he hears a voice in his heart saying something about a *"Mahatma", whatever that is,* Ryan thinks to himself.

And suddenly, it all becomes clear, as Ryan says, "Yes, and no . . ."

Everyone goes quiet and turns to Ryan, who explains:

"We have the Monarch Butterflies, the pigeons, the Chrysalenes, the natural world, and some very loving people, even children, on our team. What does the Council have? They have fear, mistrust and unstoppable, unquenchable greed. Love is about life. Fear is ultimately about death. If we just step out of their way, yes, they will ultimately self-destruct. But that is not enough. We are human, too, and subject to the same fears and greed that the Council and much of the UC have fallen victim to. The rest is about finding our own love and courage to live in harmony with each other.

---

[11] *Proverbs 16:18 NIV*

"We can do this, I know. We were born to do this and now we *must* do this. We must show the world a better, kinder way. The way of love, not fear. The way of the Chrysalenes. If we do that with each other and reject the false power of the Council, they cannot win." Smiling softly to everyone, Ryan finishes one last thought. "And we *shall not lose*, my friends!"

The Major walks over to Ryan, puts his hands on Ryan's shoulders and says to him, "Like I said not too long ago, you are a most righteous man!"

* * *

Lady Liling is preparing a truly wonderful dinner. Kookie is also in the kitchen, having fun learning how to make chocolate chip cookies. The rest are relaxing in a moment of harmony, enjoying each other's company and looking forward to the evening's activities. Liling's new friend, Dumaka will be joining them, and they also plan on going over to visit the Chrysalenes.

Ryan's words rang true for all of them, and they know that they must learn as much as they can from everything that he mentioned: the Monarchs, the pigeons, the natural world including flowers and trees, the Chrysalenes, and each other.

Dumaka arrives and they all have a splendid meal together. Eve Elli is very excited that they will be going to the Village of the Holy Ones to visit her friend very soon.

"I just can't wait to see Emeka!" she says. "He is my *most bestest* friend!" Eve Elli proudly proclaims.

Everyone has a chuckle and Mimi says, "I am sure that you are Emeka's most bestest friend too, sweetie!"

"Yes Gramma," Eve Elli continues, "We are the most biggest, bestest, *BEEESTEST* friends ever!"

"Wow!" Kookie laughs. "Sounds like Angie and me!"

All the lovers, old and new, seated around the table look at each other affectionately, nodding in agreement.

After dinner, as the troop is preparing for their excursion to the Village of the Holy Ones, Lady Liling sees a pigeon coming in for a landing at the coop.

Pointing it out to everyone, Kookie says, "Hmm I wonder who could be calling on us right now?"

"I'll get it," says Angie as she dashes over to the coop to meet the new arrival. The leg band says #25, but the attachment says that it originated from #33. While the others are all gathered outside ready to leave for the Village, Angie reads the message. She suddenly turns wide-eyed and pale, staring at Kookie.

"What is it?" he says in an apprehensive tone when he sees her expression.

Everyone else looks anxiously at Angie as well, as she points to the Big House and stammers, "Um, I, uh, that is, I think we left a bit of unfinished work in the study."

The smiles fade from everyone, and they quickly return to the Big House, heading straight for the study.

Angie hands the message over to Kookie, who reads it, looks up to Heaven and closes his eyes. Then he says to the group, "The message was sent through our global pigeon network originating from #33. I have memorized who all the birds belong to, and #33 belongs to Lord Jackson.

"Lord Jackson?!" howls the Major. "That is my father's Overlord!"

"Yes, so it seems. He is also part of our Alliance, Major."

Turning to everyone Kookie sadly reads the message:

BIG KAHUNA – OPERATION CLEAN WATER UNDERWAY – CONTAMINATION HAS BEGUN – #33 AND

#34 NOT IN LOOP – MASSIVE GLOBAL DEATH TOLL PREDICTED IN NEXT 24-48 HOURS

Choking back tears, Kookie says softly to everyone, "Let me spell that out for all of you, just so we are clear about what Lord Jackson is saying. Master Howard apparently believes that Jackson is in the loop with PA, ES, and SPA. But Lord Jackson is not in that loop, and Master Howard does not realize he gave Jackson information he was not meant to hear.

"Like what?" says Angie, with a sigh.

Kookie looks at the Major with all the compassion he has and says, "Like the fact that everything Master Howard told us was a lie. That what we did to the neurotoxins earlier today was probably a decoy for Master Howard's real mission with us."

"What do you suppose that is?" asks the Major, staring at the floor.

"I believe it is threefold," says Kookie. "The first thing was to discover the secrets of Metatron, which he did not get, thanks to our own diversionary tactics. The second is to find out who our allies are. If not for that, I am sure we would have all been disposed of by now."

"And the third?" asks the Major, still staring at the floor.

"To lull us into a false sense of security so we would think that we have won this round; that the water will be okay, because I didn't even think of the fact that they might have had other bottles of neurotoxins at Howard Pharmaceuticals, just waiting to go. While they have caught us off guard, they have already begun to launch their deadly weapon of poisoning the major reservoirs of One World."

As they are all caught up in hopelessness and despair, they notice little three-year-old Eve Elli on her knees in the middle of the room. She is looking upwards with her arms extended and her hands held out to the heavens above. Eve Elli smiles sweetly, and she begins to glow and become transparent. Turning to everyone she says, "Do not be afraid, everything is gonna be okay."

Stretching her arms out to the heavens she continues, "Angel loves you, and she is saying, *Do not despair, human creatures. We are here to help you."* Then Eve Elli says, "Angel wants us to go to the Village of the Holy Ones at once. She says we must all go, and we must also bring #3, #4 and all the other pigeons that are here."

They all look at each other with a glimmer of hope returning to them.

Mimi picks up her precious granddaughter and hugs her. "Bless you, wakanjeja, bless you."

Eve Elli looks up as if she is receiving another message and says to the group, "That was Angel again. She says, *hop to it, human creatures! Time is a wasting!"*

Everyone chuckles, and collectively say, "Yes, ma'am!" as they begin heading for the Village of the Holy Ones.

Chapter 14 – Sons

"WELCOME, EVERYONE," SAYS MAMA EVE ZULA to the 11 companions and their flock of pigeons. "It is so good to see you all again."

Little Lord Emeka runs out to greet everyone, too, especially his "most bestest" friend Eve Elli. As soon as they meet, the two children hug each other, hold hands and become inseparable.

"Dear people," Mama Eve Zula says. "We were told that you were coming and that your need is very great. Do come inside the Big Hut and let us see how we may serve you."

"Thank you, Mama Eve Zula," Angie says.

She is carrying three pigeons on her shoulders: #3, #4 and #25. Liling is carrying #21 and #22, as all 11 people and 5 birds gather into the Big Hut of the Village of the Holy Ones. The 12 Chrysalenes of the Village come to join them as well. Then the Monarchs arrive; eight inside the Big Hut, including Angel, and many hundreds more perched on the outside of the windows.

Angie introduces Kookie, the Major, Vi, Yakov, Neely and Liling to the Chrysalenes, and the Chrysalenes introduce themselves to the group. They are Eve Amadi, Adam Taj, Eve Deka, Adam Sadiki, Adam Uba, Eve Rukiya, Eve Baba, Adam Kojo, Adam Okello and Adam Paki. Eve Zula and Adam Makena are the Elders, so they are called Mama and Papa respectively.

Kookie looks at all 12 Chrysalenes and says, "Already I can feel a peaceful healing just from being in your presence. Thank you so much for giving me hope."

"Most kind," says Papa Adam Makena to Kookie, "Bless your heart. It is wise as well as loving."

Kookie bows his head at the gift of grace. "Thank you," Kookie says. "Thank you very much, sir."

Mama Eve Zula addresses the group, "We know why you have come to us, dear friends. May we begin by telling you that as we move forward in this journey together you will never be without our help. We are here right beside you to serve in any way that we can."

Angel comes down to the center of the group, perches herself on Eve Elli's head and speaks from her heart to everyone. Her "voice" comes through loud and clear to the hearts of one and all as she says:

Human creatures, do not fear the evil that is in your midst. In time you will come to understand why the beast is among the human creatures of the world and who he really is. But for now, we must not allow his legions to cause further death, damage, and destruction. Have faith, hope, and love, and always know that when your need for our help is at its greatest, that is when we will appear.

"Thank you, Angel," says Eve Elli.

The Monarch kisses Eve Elli on her cheek and snuggles back into her hair.

Mama Eve Zula says, "And the Chrysalenes all over One World are here to serve you and free you from your fears so that you may be filled with Courageous Love. With that you may accomplish anything."

"What do you mean, Mama Eve Zula?" asks the Major.

She nods at Adam Okello who goes over and sits down in front of the Major.

"What is it that your heart desires most my friend?" Adam Okello asks him.

The Major thinks about it for a moment and then he says, "I wish more than anything to see my father help people with his knowledge of pharmaceuticals. Not to be drunk on power and overcome with greed. Not to kill for the sake of evil but be willing to die for the greater good of all."

"Then it is time," says Adam Okello, "for you to lead your father and others like him out of the fear which has taken him down that dark road. He will follow in his own time, as the stronger you become, the more powerful your light of truth will shine."

The Major shakes his head and says, "Oh yeah, sure, just like that, huh?"

"Yes sir, just like that," says Adam Okello, holding his hands out and smiling at the Major.

"Well, just exactly how am I supposed to do that, Adam Okello?"

"By healing your own fear first, my friend. And then you will *know* and *become* Courageous Love. And once you have become Courageous Love you will be able to pass it on to others."

The air in the Big Hut is suddenly feeling very hot and heavy with great anticipation of what is coming next.

All eyes are upon the Major as he says in a somewhat smug manner, "O-*kay,* so what do I have to do then to heal my fears? I mean it will have to happen very quickly don't you think? As we speak, we've got some rather nasty toxins inbound about to wreak havoc with One World's fresh water supply."

Still smiling and happy as a clam, Adam Okello says, "Oh it is truly quite simple."

"Is that right?" snorts the Major.

"Yes, sir!"

"Fine, so show me," the Major says with his arms folded across his chest.

"You wish to be healed of your fears then?"

"Yes, I wish to be healed of my fears then!"

"Then it is already done," says Adam Okello offering his hands to the Major.

As he takes Adam Okello's hands, the Major suddenly feels something melting away. In its place the light of Divine energy is pouring down from the Chrysalene's soul into the soul of Master John, son of Master Howard.

The others look on, amazed to see the Major beginning to glow and become a little transparent. Combined with the healing he received recently from the Chrysalene at Judy's cottage, a light is now shining from within the very core of the Major's being.

He looks deep into the eyes of Adam Okello and says, "Yes. It is done. Praise you, my man!"

Turning to Kookie, Vi and the others, he says, "I now know what I must do and will need some of you to join me."

"We are all in, bro', just say the word," says Kookie as he looks around at the Chrysalenes. Papa Adam Makena nods and Adam Taj sits down in front of Kookie.

"Do you wish to be healed of your fears?" Adam Taj asks Kookie, to which Kookie replies, "Yes, kind sir. I wish very much to be healed of my fears."

"Then it is already done," says Adam Taj with joy as he repeats the process with Kookie that has just been done to the Major.

The rest of the group all look up to the Chrysalenes who pair off and sit down with each one of them. And all around the Big Hut is heard the blessing, "It is already done," repeated to Vi, Angie, Liling, Dumaka, Mimi, Ryan, Yakov and Neely. Each and every one of them is now glowing with the light of the Divine and His Courageous Love.

Last but not least, Kookie goes over to Little Lord Emeka and presents him with his very own Universal Translator pendant necklace. He places it over Emeka's head and shows him how to turn it on.

Then, Eve Elli asks her bestie, "Do you want me to take away your fears, Emeka?" and to everyone's joy, Emeka begins to glow with the light of the Divine as he says to Eve Elli smiling, "You have already done that, little angel."

The Major says, "We must leave now for California and stop my father from what he is about to do. We will take the water purifiers that Kookie has created and are now in Master Howard's possession at the main plant. Then we must each go to separate locations and distribute them throughout the main reservoirs of One World, either preventing the neurotoxins from causing any damage or treating any water that has already been contaminated. I also see a ray of hope in how I might be able to help my father," he says with a smile.

The whole group, including all the Chrysalenes, stand and say, "We are with you, we are here, count us in."

Papa Adam Makena says, "We will be able to distribute the water purifier very quickly once you get the bottle to us."

"How so?" asks Kookie, who is intrigued by what the Chrysalenes are capable of doing.

Adam Taj laughs and says to him, "It is called bifurcation, my friend. I think you will find it quite fascinating."

"I think that is an understatement!" Kookie says. They all have a good chuckle and heartily agree that they can't wait to see what this "bifurcation" thing is.

The 10 companions, including Dumaka, together with 12 Chrysalenes, five pigeons, Eve Elli, and Little Lord Emeka, prepare to leave on the four Cloudtransporters. Once on board, they synchronize the transporters and set their destination. In just a few hours they will all arrive in California at the main plant of Howard Pharmaceuticals.

Angel and the Monarchs flutter off to connect with the hearts of all Monarch Butterflies on the planet. For just a moment all the people on the Cloudtransporters hear a voice in their hearts saying, *Fear not, human creatures. The Heavenly Host will be with you.*

* * *

Master Howard has just finished another transmission with his Master Commandant. The toxins are all in place and ready for distribution. The Cloudtransporters are now loaded with the deadly neurotoxins and the first strike on the reservoirs will commence shortly. Master Howard was told by the Council that his pipeline to clean water is directly connected to the same source as the rest of the UC, and that all the Masters and their servants, as well as the Lords will be safe from the deadly effects of the contaminated water.

The Council also told him that the water would remain contaminated for six months, after which time, the effects will dissipate, and it should be restored to normal. Of course, by that time, there will be untold death, damage, and destruction to the rest of the population, as well as much of the other life on earth.

Master Howard is still waiting for the report from his Lab Overseer who has been charged with analyzing the contents of the bottles that Kookie allegedly transformed into an actual water purifier, *just in case,* Master Howard thinks to himself, *just in case something goes wrong.*

He is wondering what is taking the Lab Overseer so long and decides to go and check up on him.

Walking into the lab, Master Howard is aware of an inexplicable feeling that something is not quite right. The place seems eerily quiet and almost, *deserted,* he thinks to himself. He goes from room to room and sees the AI operators working at their tasks, and although there are not many human servers there, he cannot seem to find *any.* "What the devil is going on?" he says out loud. "Where the devil *is* everybody?"

He arrives at the room where the Lab Overseer serves and where Master Howard left him with the boxes from Kookie to be analyzed. He finds no Lab Overseer and "*NO BOXES!*" Master Howard shrieks, "WHERE ARE YOU?" He yells running in a blind panic from one room to the other. "LAB OVERSEER! WHERE THE DEVIL ARE YOU?"

Master Howard stops cold when he hears a faint voice coming from an area near the rear exit of the building.

"I am here, sir," a calm voice says, sounding a bit like the Lab Overseer.

Master Howard makes a dash for the rear exit of the building and when get gets there, he sees the Lab Overseer sitting on the ground with, *a child!* They are, *holding hands?!*

Am I going crazy?! Says Master Howard to himself.

"Excuse me Lab Overseer, I don't mean to interrupt this, um, whatever the bleepity bleep[12] it is that you are doing here, but, um, *WHAT THE BLEEP IS GOING ON! AND WHERE THE BLEEP ARE THE BOXES THAT YOU WERE SUPPOSED TO BLEEPING ANALYZE?!"*

Then as an afterthought, he looks at the child and says, *"AND WHO THE BLEEP IS THE KID?!"*

The Lab Overseer smiles at Master Howard and says in a blissful voice, "I am receiving energy from the Light to release my fears, the boxes are outside, and the child is Emeka, gracious sir."

Turning to Emeka (who is wearing his Universal Translator), the Lab Overseer says, "You remind me so much of my own son who perished in the recent Ebola pandemic. So sweet, so innocent." Tears begin to well up in the Lab Overseer's eyes.

Emeka says to him, "It is alright, Reggie, sir. Your son is in a beautiful place now. I have seen it. My father is there too."

"May I call you 'my son,' Emeka?!" Reggie says all weepy.

"Yes, Papa, I would like that very much," Emeka says with much affection as he leans over and gives Reggie a hug.

Master Howard stares at the two of them stupefied. Then he remembers where he has heard that name, little Lord Emeka, and he is

---

[12] *Reader has liberty to imagine preferred angry word.*

about to hit the roof when in walks the Major, followed by Vi, Adam Okello and Eve Elli.

"We have come to take the water purifiers father," says the Major.

"Oh, you *have*, have you?" Master Howard retorts. "Well, I suppose it doesn't really matter anyway, does it? There is nothing you can do to stop it now. Even if those bottles *are* any good, by the time you get them to the reservoirs the water will already be contaminated and dispersed throughout the populace. You are too late. And you have exposed yourself as a traitor to the Council. And for what, John? For what?"

The Major looks at his father with all the love a son can have, as he says, "For the same reason that I came back in here instead of taking off without your even knowing I was here or what happened."

He hands his father one of the bottles and says, "In case your local water has already been contaminated, you are going to need this. I wanted to give it to you myself so that you will know the truth."

Master Howard looks at his son with a sadness that is welling up inside of him. "What truth, John, what are you talking about? The Council has given all of the UC a special pipeline to the fresh water which serves *them*."

"Not *all* the UC, father. Only the Lords. The Masters are considered to be expendable and useless, just like the people. They mean to kill us too."

"*THAT'S A LIE!*" screams Master Howard.

"I'm sorry, father. Check your pipeline. You will see that the source of your connection is the main reservoir of the people."

Master Howard is in tears as he feels his whole world crumbling, "*NO! NO! IT'S A LIE! IT'S A LIE!*"

"I'm sorry, father."

Looking at the others the Major motions that it is time for them to leave. As they all start to walk out of the back exit, Eve Elli goes over to the stricken Master Howard. He has collapsed on the floor, rocking back and forth, sobbing, and repeating over and over, to himself, "It's a lie! It's a lie!"

Eve Elli reaches out her arms to him with tenderness and compassion and she says, "It's okay Master Howard, don't cry. Your son loves you. Everything is gonna be okay. Don't cry. We *all* love you. Everything is gonna be just fine."

Adam Okello says to Master Howard ever so gently, "When the time has come that you want to let go of your fears, kind sir, just call out to us and we will be here to help you."

But Master Howard is inconsolable.

They all turn to leave, and Reggie smiles at Emeka and says, "Take care, my son, and remember that your Papa loves you."

Little Lord Emeka is so happy, "And I love you too, Papa!"

The last one to leave is the Major, who looks at Master Howard and says softly, "And I love you too. . . Papa."

Moments later Master Howard looks up wanting to say something kind to his son, but the Major has already left.

* * *

The Chrysalenes have instructed the Major, Kookie, Yakov and Lady Liling to take their Cloudtransporters out over the ocean where they will go straight into the next phase of their plan: the bifurcation process.

There are four Cloudtransporters in all. Each one is carrying three of the twelve Chrysalenes from the Village of the Holy Ones.

"Okay!" says Kookie, all excited, furiously tapping the tips of his fingers together. "Now I get to see what this bifurcation thing is all about! I am especially intrigued by anything that can beat technology!"

Adam Taj laughs and is delighted to share the knowledge with Kookie and the others.

In the Major's Cloudtransporter, Vi, Mimi and Ryan help him take out their supply of the water purifiers from their boxes, placing them in the center of the floor, while Adam Okello, Adam Kojo and Eve Deka sit down around them. Eve Elli and Emeka are seated nearby and are watching with great delight.

The Chrysalenes lie down, connecting to each other's head and feet, forming a triangle on the floor around the bottles of water purifier. Their palms are facing upwards, and their eyes are staring up at the heavens. The Chrysalenes begin to glow and grow transparent. When their brightness becomes intense, they start singing their sweet, angelic song. Every Chrysalene in One World is connected in spirit to the 12 Chrysalenes in the four Cloudtransporters just off the coast of California. They are singing the same angelic song in chorus with the 12.

Throughout One World, all the awakened people can hear in their hearts the voices of the angels singing. Judy is witnessing Adam Nelson, Adam Tate and all the other Chrysalenes sing together with the angelic song. As she watches #9 and #10 bopping and cooing to the music, her heart is overflowing with love. Lisa, Kenny, Doc, Phil, and Suzie of the Seashells also witness the singing of the Chrysalenes at Bear River Farm, as well as the joyful noise of a myriad of pigeons cooing in Kenny's large coop.

The hearts of all people everywhere are filled with joy and hope as they hear the angelic singing. Those who are not yet awakened can also feel something peaceful and soothing in their souls with a voice inside their guts telling them that freedom on its way.

* * *

Master Howard is still sitting on the floor with his Lab Overseer Reggie seated nearby. He is looking down at the bottle of water purifier that his son gave him still clutched in his hand. He slowly brings the bottle up to his chest.

Reggie is listening to the song of the Chrysalenes and smiles brightly with the Light of Heaven shining on his face. Although Master Howard hears nothing, he watches Reggie as a trace of a smile begins to appear on his own face.

Master Howard finally says, "Reggie? I didn't know your name was Reggie."

The two men just sit there on the floor staring at each other. And then, Reggie and Howard have a chuckle together.

* * *

A terminal activates in Panamerica. A message goes out from PA to ES and SPA:

EMERGENCY ALERT!
ACCEPT MESSAGE! EMERGENCY ALERT!

But, before ES and SPA can accept and receive the incoming message from PA, Angel and the Monarchs have heard PA's cry. All over One World, the Monarch Butterflies flutter across the transmitting signals of PA, jamming their frequencies.

PA's transmission is terminated.

* * *

Liling and Dumaka watch the wonderous sight in their own Cloudtransporter and are filled with love from the heavenly music. Dumaka notices something and exclaims with awe to Liling, "Look, My Lady! Look at the bottles!"

"Yes, Dumaka," Liling laughs with tears in her eyes. "I can see it."

The same event is taking place in the other two Cloudtransporters. Yakov says to Neely, "Look honey! Can you see it?"

"Yes," Neely says as she smiles at him, "I can see it, my darling!"

Kookie turns to Angie and is beside himself with joy. "Wow, sweetie! Take a look at that, will you?! Hooray for low tech!"

Angie is enthralled as #3 and #4, perched on her shoulders, are cooing with delight at what they are all witnessing.

The liquid inside the bottles of water purifier is going down. It is as if the bottles have all been plunged into the major reservoirs of One World and their contents are now being injected directly into the water. When the bottles are all empty, the Chrysalenes slowly return to their opaque form. They sit up and look peaceful, as if their hearts are at rest.

Kookie's brain is exploding with questions, and although he is trying hard to sit in deference and gratitude for just a little while, showing respect for what he believes has just happened, he absolutely cannot keep his mouth shut. Going from furious fingertip-tapping to full-on hand flapping he finally blows. "So?! Adam Taj! What in the flaming tarnation just happened there, my most excellent man?!"

The three Chrysalenes smile blissfully at Kookie and Angie and say, "We have gone with our ethereal bodies to the reservoirs and poured the healing liquid into them. The water is now safe and pure. And it also spoke to us while we were there," says Adam Taj.

Angie is seated next to the Chrysalenes and is herself filled with the Light of Heaven. "Kind people," Angie says most tenderly, "won't you tell us what the water said to you?"

Mama Eve Zula replies to Angie, "Water is also a living thing sweet lady, and it is very ancient. As ancient as the earth itself."

"Yes, that makes sense!" says Kookie, excitedly tapping the tips of his fingers together.

Papa Adam Makena continues, "It is an element of life and carrier and transformer of life's energies."

"And she also contains and transmits a great wisdom throughout her entire body, that which we call our Mother Earth," says Mama Eve Zula.

Adam Taj continues, "The children of Mother Earth include all the life on this planet. And when her children suffer, our Mother suffers as well. The water of the earth has heard the cries of a Mother in agony."

"Oh my!" says Angie, herself brought to tears. "Do you know why Mother Earth is crying to the water?"

The three of them look at each other and nod. Getting up and forming a circle around Angie, they ask her to stand up with them, and Mama Eve Zula says, "You have been chosen Angie, for a very special task. And very soon, your heart will tell you what that task is and whether or not you chose to move forward with it. Therefore, we are here now to help you and answer all of your questions as best we can."

Papa Adam Makena says, "Mother Earth is crying because her children are suffering, including many of the crops that are growing now in the fields all over One World. They are in great pain because many of them have been harmed with a poison that has altered their genetic structure. And they know that the fruit which they are about to bear will hurt rather than heal those humans who eat it."

"Oh dear!" says Angie, looking at Kookie. "I thought we took care of all that, honey."

"Word did get out," says Adam Taj, "But only to a few of the farmers. And even the seeds that did not get planted and are still sitting there in packages, are crying out in pain."

Angie is weeping and says to the Chrysalenes, "What can be done to help them? Please tell me there is a way!"

The Chrysalenes all smile and say, "It is already done!"

"It *IS?*" Angie and Kookie both shout out together.

The Chrysalenes laugh and Mama Eve Zula says to Angie and Kookie, "The purified water will now transform all of the crops and seedlings all over the earth. The suffering seeds that are still in packages will also be transformed and healed once they are planted and watered."

"You mean, like when it rains?" asks Angie, feeling better.

"Yes, my dear. It is exactly that," Mama Eve Zula says as she, Adam Taj and Papa Adam Makena give Angie a hug. Kookie of course, joins the hug-fest.

Angie laughs. "Oh Kookie! I just can't wait to tell the others the good news!"

Chapter 15 – Rainfall

JUDY IS FINISHING HER DAY'S WORK IN THE GARDEN. It is the first time for as far back as she can remember that she does not have sore knees or an achy back. The angel music of the Chrysalenes was so healing to her body and soothing to her soul that it melted away the usual discomforts she tends to feel this time of day. The Chrysalenes are also retiring for the day, and they prepare for their evening meal and fellowship.

Judy sees her friend Adam Tate. "Thank you so much, my friend. Hearing those songs of Heaven from all of you was so incredibly beautiful," she says.

"You are most welcome, Judy," he says to her. They both look up as they see a pigeon coming in for a landing.

"Well, my goodness!" exclaims Judy, excited to see a messenger bird again. "I wonder who that can be?" Going to the coop, she is just in time to greet the new arrival. "Gracious!" she says. "It is #3!"

Taking the message off #3's leg band it says the following:

INBOUND PASSEL, INCLUDING BIRDS AND FOUR LARGE VEHCLES – BIG KAHUNA

"Woo hoo!" Judy exclaims, with great exuberance. "Come on you guys," she says to #3, #9 and #10. "Let's get some food going in the kitchen! You all can watch and keep me company. There's lots to do!" she laughs, as #9 and #10 bop up and down, catching Judy's excitement.

The Chrysalenes have gone around blessing all the fruits and vegetables that are just about ready for harvesting, sharing the good news with them about the purification of the water. Now they are getting ready to break bread with their fellow Chrysalenes from Johannesburg.

They are especially joyful about meeting little Lord Emeka and both Emeka and Eve Elli together.

Judy starts to bring food out to the tables when she sees four Cloudtransporters coming in for a landing at the nearby open field. Clapping her hands together, she says to the pigeons, "They're here! Oh, my goodness! I better move faster and get the rest of the food out!"

Kookie and Angie are the first to step out of the Cloudtransporter. They have both been working on something together with Metatron and need to share it with everyone right away.

As the others begin to emerge from their respective vehicles, Kookie motions for them to come over. He says, "First, I would like to say to the Chrysalenes, *WOW!*" to which everyone laughs and agrees.

The Chrysalenes bow humbly, and Mama Eve Zula says, "We are deeply honored to serve."

"Thank you," says Kookie, "I don't know what else to say, except thank you." Everyone nods and makes the rounds thanking and hugging each and every Chrysalene.

Eve Elli gets an especially big hug from each person, but nothing as huge as Gramma Mimi who gives her a gramma-sized squeeze. And Eve Elli squeals with delight, "I love you, Gramma!"

"Ooo, I love you too, baby!" says the happiest gramma on the planet.

Kookie says, "Okay everyone, we need to discuss something before we head on over to Judy's Cottage."

"What is it, bro'?" asks the Major. Yakov and Liling look at him with intense curiosity.

"Angie and I have been working on discovering the various properties of the 369-Program and the Metatron device, and one of the things that I have been most concerned about for everyone is our safety and privacy. I am especially concerned now as our defiance towards the Council is making us more vulnerable to them."

Smiling at Angie, Kookie continues, "So, my good Lady and I have put our heads together and come up with something that I must share with you now and download onto all of your Lord's and Master's Communication Devices. And for Mimi and Ryan, you two can start using your Metatron for this."

"YES!" says Mimi. "So, what is it, then?"

"It is a hybrid between the self-cloaking thing that Vi taught us and my Holographic Imager. Basically, when you switch it on, and as long as you are withing 25 feet of your device, you become perfectly camouflaged into your environment. Kinda like a salamander. So, while self-cloaking is a way of avoiding being noticed which we do to ourselves, becoming camouflaged like a salamander is being energetically concealed, or made invisible, by the Metatron device."

"So, we have named it Salamander," Angie proudly announces.

"Whoa!" exclaims Ryan. "That will make me an even *better mole!*" Everyone laughs and Mimi gives Ryan a hug saying, "You will always be *my* best mole, honey!"

"And of course," says Kookie, "We have also built a warning system into it. When a negative force of any kind is around, it will start to vibrate and flash red on the screen."

"Another red-flasher for Kookie!" says the Major. "Bravo, bro'!"

"Thanks, Kookie! Truly awesome!" they all agree, as each one brings over his or her device for Kookie to download the Salamander program.

"And remember," he adds, "That as long as we are in a remote area with plenty of trees, we are naturally protected from the Council's surveillance system anyway."

* * *

Three terminals activate as an incoming message is received and accepted by PA, ES and SPA. Their screens begin to pulsate with a red glow, and the sound of deep booming comes through. An angry voice speaks to PA, ES and SPA:

Voice: You fools!

PA: "Yes, my lord."

ES: "Oh my, yes, my lord."

SPA: "Yes, indeed. We are fools, my lord."

VOICE: ENOUGH!

They are quiet.

Voice: I gave you fools *EVERYTHING!* I gave you untold wealth and power over the simple sheep. And you have allowed them to take away my glory, my victory . . . *MY POWER!*

The three remain silent.

Voice: IT IS NOT OVER YET!

More silence.

Voice: I SHALL REIGN TERROR OVER THEM ALL!

Dead silence.

Voice: YOU WILL DO *EXACTLY* AS I SAY!

PA, ES and SPA: "Yes, yes, my lord! Exactly as you say! Indeed!"

Voice: I *SHALL* have her!

PA, ES and SPA: "Yes, lord, yes, yes. You will have her."

Voice: She *WILL* be mine!

PA, ES and SPA: "Yes, lord. She will be yours . . . *all yours!*"

Then with a snarling growl followed by a long screaming howl that sets PA, ES and SPA trembling with terror, the voice says: *BRING HER TO ME!*

The transmission terminates.

* * *

The sun is setting at the farm. The golden rays cast a brilliant aura around the glowing Chrysalenes as Mama Eve Zula and Papa Adam Makena lead them all to Judy's feast. Judy is just about finished bringing out the last of the bread and chocolate chip cookies to the table when she sees the glowing parade coming towards her. "Adam Tate!" she calls out to him, "Here they come! Quick! Get the others!"

"Yes, ma'am," Adam Tate says. The Chrysalenes of Judy's farm are right behind him.

The Major heads straight to Judy. "Hello there! It's so good to see you again, Judy!"

"Oh, my goodness! It is wonderful to see you folks too!" Judy says to all her friends, as well as to the Chrysalenes from the Village of the Holy Ones. Mama Eve Zula's group finally meets Adam Tate's group. Though they have already met in spirit, now they are most happy to finally sit down and break bread together. And since all Chrysalenes speak the language of the heart, they are able to communicate with each other in their own respective languages while being completely understood.

As they are all about to enjoy an evening of great food and fellowship together, Kookie stands up and addresses the crowd. "It is my most incredible honor to be here among you all this evening, to be a part of the coming new freedom that none of us have ever known. A freedom that our ancestors knew, and perhaps even greater. May we continue to move forward together every day with our hearts full of Courageous Love."

"Here, here!" says one and all, as they raise their glasses of pure, clean water to the heavens above.

* * *

The Coffeehouses all over One World are slowly coming back to life. When it was discovered that My Buddy transmissions were upsetting people and causing violent outbursts, the Center Overseers began to stop the public transmissions. Word has now gotten around as other Center Overseers are following suit. And life at the Coffeehouses is slowly returning to normal; a relaxing evening out and sharing the people's news with each other.

Mimi, Ryan, Vi and Angie are especially anxious to hear what is going on at the Center Coffeehouse, so after dinner they all head on over to the Center nearest to Judy. Kookie, Yakov, Liling and the Major are eager to spend more time with the Chrysalenes. And, last but not least, Eve Elli and Little Lord Emeka are delighting everyone at Judy's farm with their childhood fun and antics.

Mimi and company enter the Coffeehouse and find a couple of tables together. It does not take long before a woman seated next to them says, "Have you folks heard the news?"

"What news is that?" ask Vi, as the others look at the woman with anticipation.

"There is a rumor going around from the local farmers that the crops are almost ready, and the harvest will be the best one ever!"

"Wow! Great news! Fantastic!" the four of them say.

The woman continues, "We are also hearing rumors about the rain."

Now the group is on the edge of their seats. "*REALLY?!*" They all exclaim at once.

"Yes! We are expecting quite a storm this evening. It should continue through the night and into the morning," the woman says. "That should make the crops super happy! Don't you think?"

"Undoubtedly! You betcha! For sure!" the others assert.

News is buzzing all around about the wonderful harvest expected, with laughter and excitement heard throughout the Coffeehouse.

A man stands up and gets everyone's attention. "There should be enough this year for us to have a Harvest Festival! What do you say to that, everybody?!"

"*WOO HOO! YES!*" they all enthusiastically agree.

After hearing all that wonderful news, Mimi, Ryan, Vi and Angie, fill themselves with great coffee before going back to Judy's.

* * *

That night the group of visitors go back to their Cloudtransporters and find a comfortable spot to stretch out. As they are all getting ready for bed, they hear a clap of thunder in the distance, followed shortly by a refreshing rainfall. Kookie, Yakov and Liling waste no time in turning on their devices and getting the analytics going for the water coming down. And to their overwhelming joy, the tests are telling them that the water is the cleanest and purest it has ever been in their lifetime.

Kookie, Yakov and Liling go out into the field and get down on their knees. Getting soaked in the rain, they begin to pray as they have been learning from the Chrysalenes. The others all see what is going on and rush outside to join Kookie, Yakov and Liling, on their knees in the rain, and in prayer. All their friends and all the Chrysalenes and the remaining guests on Judy's farm stream out of their dwellings to join the Sacred Gathering, dropping to their knees to pray, in the rain.

The rain continues, on and on purifying everyone, the crops, and the land, with its Sacred Water.

* * *

That night when everyone is falling asleep, Mimi drifts off into a dream:

She is in a garden with Eve Elli. The Monarch Angel is there and so are #9 and #10. Eve Elli is playing happily in the garden, kissing the flowers, and whispering to the trees. She is saying, "I love you," to all of nature as she radiates the beauty of her little soul.

Mimi couldn't be happier when she joins in with Eve Elli's little-girl playtime. "You just love everything, don't you my little angel."

"Oh yes, Gramma. Eve Elli just loves eeeeverything!" she says while stretching her arms up to the sun.

As she does so, the sun turns into a bright white light. Number 9 and #10 turn into white doves, and the Monarch turns into a large, golden angel. They gently and slowly lift Eve Elli off the ground as a dark tunnel suddenly appears all around her. The angel and the doves are carrying Eve Elli up to the Light at the end of the tunnel.

Mimi is instantly frightened. "Where are you going, my sweetie?!" Mimi cries out to her in a panic.

"Don't cry Gramma. Eve Elli loves you. Everything is gonna be okay. Eve Elli is going home to Heaven now."

Mimi starts to cry, "No! Oh Lord no! Please don't take her! She is only a child." Weeping and pleading to the Heavenly Father, Mimi says, "No! Please Lord, No! Take me instead. Please! Please!"

Eve Elli stands before Heaven's Gate as she turns around one last time. "Don't cry Gramma. We will be together again one day. Eve Elli loves you. Everything is gonna be just fine. Don't cry Gramma. . ."

Mimi wakes up crying. Ryan wakes up at the sound of her sobs and the feeling of her holding him tight.

"Another nightmare?" he asks her.

"I must see her!" Mimi says as she goes over to where Eve Elli is sleeping. Curled up into a little bundle on her sleeping mat, Eve Elli has a peaceful look on her face. Not wanting to wake her up, Mimi touches her ever so softly and whispers, "I love you, baby girl. You stay right down here with Gramma, okay?"

Mimi goes back to bed and curls up against Ryan.

Somewhere in another dimension, a guttural growl resounds with sinister pleasure.

The morning arrives and Mimi is the first one awake. She heads outside and is greeted by the delicious, sweet smell of rain-washed earth and flowers. Mimi is reminded of the Rose Petals and how good they make her feel. She makes a mental note to get some fresh cut Roses at the Center Market.

When everyone else is awake, Kookie announces that they will be going to Bear River Farm shortly, but first they must make a stop at his Kastle.

"There are decisions that have to be made, especially regarding Eve Elli and Emeka," Kookie says, "And I would like us to spend a little time in retreat at my Kabin."

"That sounds like a very good idea, my Brother," says Yakov.

"Yes," says Liling. "There is much we each have to think about and process with all that has been happening."

Everyone else nods at each other and the idea of a retreat for a couple of days at Kookie's Kabin sounds most welcome.

Kookie turns to Angie and says, "Sweetie, would you please get #3 and send a message to Lisa and Kenny? Let them know that we should be there sometime in the next two days, and that we will want to see Phil and Doc too."

"Sure thing, honey," Angie says.

The group shares one last meal with Judy at her cottage. Kookie is also leaving Judy well stocked with food and supplies which she is most thankful for, although she says it really is not necessary. "It is my pleasure to have you all here and to feed you."

"And it is *my* pleasure to eat up all of your chocolate chip cookies!" Kookie exclaims as everyone laughs. "So here are some more baking goods."

"That also includes everything you need for the heavenly bread that you bake Miss Judy!" the Major says with sheer delight.

Judy is reminded. "Oh Yes! Don't let me forget the bread!" She goes into the kitchen and comes out moments later with two fresh loaves of bread for the Major.

"Ahh!" the Major says smelling their fresh aroma. "Thank you, Judy. Thank you, ma'am!"

They all start heading back to the Cloudtransporters when they are stopped along the way by the Chrysalenes. "Come, come good people! Before you leave, come see the miracle!" Adam Tate calls out to them.

"Sure thing," says Kookie a bit baffled as they all follow Adam Tate over to the tomato garden.

"*Whoa!*" Everyone cries out as they see the largest, most succulent tomatoes ever.

"What happened here?" says Vi, completely astounded.

Adam Steve steps forward and Vi instantly recognizes him. "Say!" she says to Adam Steve. "Didn't I meet you a while back at the Howard Pharmaceutical plant?"

"Yes ma'am!" he says.

"Well, my goodness! It is so nice to see you again, Adam Steve!"

"And you as well, ma'am."

"So, what happened here, sir? These tomatoes were barely sprouted yesterday. How did this happen overnight?" Vi asks in amazement.

"It was the rainfall last night, ma'am," says Adam Steve. "The fruit and vegetables have all been blessed with the purified rainwater. And they also have a message for all of you."

Everyone looks at each other and then at Adam Steve anticipating whatever great news he is about to share with them.

"The plants are telling us that wherever it rained last night, the seeds that were suffering have been healed. And they are overjoyed that now they will bear healthy fruit to nourish people."

"Woo Hoo! Yay! Yes! Yeeha! Amen!" and all sounds of praise are shouted with great joy among the crowd. The people all turn to the Chrysalenes and say, "You did it! Oh my goodness! Thank you!"

The Chrysalenes turn to the people and say to all of them with love, "You did it too, my friends. We all did it, together, with help from on High."

They all go back to the Cloudtransporters, cheering and clapping and giving praise to all the help from above. Kookie, the Major, Liling and Yakov are each carrying a sack of fully ripe, sweet, and juicy tomatoes.

In another dimension, an angry beast snarls in the darkness.

Chapter 16 – Harvest

KOOKIE AND ENTOURAGE HAVE ARRIVED at Kookie's Kabin in the woods. Everyone gets settled in for the retreat and a little rest and relaxation while Yakov and Neely go into the kitchen and do what they most enjoy doing together. Yakov is quite the expert with Euroslavic cuisine, and Neely is a whiz at Panamerican fare. Between the two of them they have developed a unique and scrumptious style of cooking. And they prepare an exquisite meal for all their friends. They cannot wait to use the blessed tomatoes from Judy's farm.

Everyone gets comfortable doing what they enjoy most. Angie finds a place to take out her drawing materials and do a little sketching; Liling and Dumaka go outside with #21 and #22; the Chrysalenes go out into the wooded area to commune with the trees; Mimi and Ryan take Eve Elli and Emeka for a nature walk to check out the wildflowers; and Kookie is serenading the Major and Vi with his beloved Tuba Concerto in F Minor.

It is a lovely summer day and all the folks outside are enjoying their communion with nature. Liling and Dumaka sit down on the grass, enjoying the day, the pigeons, and each other's company. Presently, a Monarch Butterfly comes along and alites on Liling's hair.

Dumaka says, "My how beautiful you look, My Lady." Smiling at her he adds, "With or without the Monarch in your hair."

Liling is touched. "That is very sweet of you, Dumaka, and I would ask one thing from you."

"Yes!" he says to her. "Anything, My Lady. You just name it and I will see that it is done."

Smiling ever so gently at Dumaka, Liling says to him, "Kind sir, I wish very much for you to call me Liling, rather than My Lady."

"Bless you, Liling. And thank you for the honor of asking it of me." He smiles and offers his hand to her, and she accepts it graciously.

Liling smiles sweetly and says, "The Monarch here is telling me that you are a kind and gentle man. But I know that already."

They both chuckle.

"Do you talk to them, and do you hear them speaking to you?" Dumaka asks.

"Oh, yes. Everything in the natural world has much to tell us. Even these cute pigeons," she says, nuzzling #21 and #22."

Still grinning, Dumaka asks, "And what is the natural world telling you, Liling?"

Her smile fades and Liling looks down for a moment as she listens to the winged creatures for an answer to Dumaka's question. "The Monarch and the pigeons are telling me that there is much hope for us, but that there is still more darkness ahead."

Looking deeply into his eyes with a touch of sadness Liling says to him, "I believe that they are right."

"How so, Liling?" Dumaka softly says to her.

"I have been experiencing some really bad dreams," Liling says.

Dumaka sits up straight, fully alert. "I believe very much in dreams and the messages that they tell us. Would you share your dreams with me?" he asks.

"Thank you, Dumaka, I am so glad to hear you say that. My dreams seem to be pretty much all the same lately. It is nighttime and I am in a peaceful outdoor setting somewhere. The stars are shining, and I feel contentment in my heart. Then something happens and things go dark; that is, the stars go out and a darkness also comes over my heart. Then the deep booming starts, and a red glow appears beneath my feet. I can feel it calling to me, sometimes trying to frighten me and other times beckoning me towards it.

"It wants something from me, Dumaka. I do not know what. But there is something very scary about it, and I know that it is somehow trying to hurt us all."

Dumaka closes his eyes and feels Liling's words penetrate his soul. "Yes, I have seen the beast too," he says to her. "And I am feeling its anger and hatred. It is an all-consuming, insatiable lust to destroy. It takes pleasure in causing pain and receives thrills from its own brutality."

Opening his eyes and looking directly at Liling, Dumaka says to her, "But it *does* have one weakness."

"Oh, please tell me, Dumaka. What is the beast's weakness?" Liling implores.

"The beast fears that others will find their own courage. The beast fears, *NOT* being feared. Without our fear, the beast loses its power and shrivels to a whimpering puppy. And that is its weakness, my sweet lady. . . I mean, Liling." Dumaka is a bit humbled by the informality.

They are holding both hands with each other now; Liling gazes into Dumaka's eyes and says, "Thank you, dear friend. Thank you."

"LUUUNCH!" Yakov yells from the Kabin as loud as he can.

There is great anticipation about the meal that Yakov and Neely have cooked up, and the aroma emanating from the kitchen is most tantalizing as everyone files in and finds a seat. The food is brought out on platters and served buffet style. Kookie begins by asking everyone to join hands, and he gives thanks for the food, the friendship, and the journey that lies ahead for all of them.

The Major raises a glass of purified water and says, "Many thanks to the chefs of this wonderful meal, Yakov and Neely, and to our host Kookie."

The platters consist of roast turkey, lamb, potatoes, sauteed vegetables of every description, and a fresh garden salad. But the best dish of all is the tomato soup. It is not only sweet and creamy, but it nourishes the soul in a way that is indescribable.

After lunch, the group goes outside and gathers on the grass to share their thoughts and feelings with each other.

Liling begins, "My good friends. I wanted to share with you the conversation I had with Dumaka just before lunch. It is all about the dreams that I have been having."

As Liling recounts what she and Dumaka talked about, the others are all listening intently and nodding.

"And then," Liling continues, "Dumaka told me that the beast has a weakness."

Everyone leans forward to hear this one.

"He says the beast's weakness is that as *we* find our courage and lose our fear, the evil one will lose more and more of *his* power. And that," Liling says emphatically, "is what I propose we focus our emotions on as we move forward in whatever actions we take."

"Yes," agrees Vi, as she proudly turns to the Major. "We have just been a witness to that with the Major and Master Howard."

"And with Eve Elli and Emeka when they rescued Ekene," says Mimi with great pride for her little sweetie.

"And with all of you," says Papa Adam Makena. "You are all showing courage by speaking your truth and acting upon it. This takes *great* Courage, dear people, especially when others do not understand."

"I would like to say something about the dreams," Angie says. "That is, I have been having them too, you know, about the deep, booming sound and the angry red eyes. About being lured to the edge of a cliff with the darkness and red glow below."

"So have I," says Mimi, followed by Vi.

Neely confirms that she too has been having such dreams.

And, last but not least, Kookie exclaims, "Gracious! I have been having that dream too. So, what's going on?"

Dumaka speaks up. "He goes by many names, though I prefer not to utter them. I have simply been referring to him as the beast. He wants something from us."

"Who is he? What does he want from us? Can you tell us some of his names?" everyone asks Dumaka all at once.

Dumaka continues, "I will tell you that he is the lord of the underworld, the beast, the fallen one. And in truth:

It is the beast who would appear to be our true enemy.
Without his power, PA, ES and SPA are nothing!
It is the voice of the beast that causes us to forget our true loving nature,
As we listen to his words of hate and fear.
He tells us that we never have enough,
Never ARE enough,
He tells us that our friends want to take away what we have,
Until out trust in each other is gone.
He makes deals with those who are lost,
 Giving them riches and power to harm the rest.
PA, ES and SPA are merely his disciples,
But the powers of the beast are limited, too.
He has no real power of his own,
Except for the power that our Heavenly Father allows him to have.
And therein lies our strength and our hope."

"And why would our Heavenly Father allow such a thing to have any power at all?" asks Mimi indignantly.

"That is something each one of you will learn when you are ready," replies Mama Eve Zula, with compassion.

Eve Elli pipes up smiling, "I know why," she says, "but I am not supposed to tell you! *Sorry!*"

"Come over here, you!" Mimi chuckles and gives Eve Elli a bear hug.

"So, what about our dreams, Dumaka," Kookie says. "What are they trying to tell us?"

"The dreams are telling us that the lord of the underworld is angry and scared that he is losing his power over us. And for this, he has been attempting to harm us."

The group goes still and quiet. Dumaka says, "I also believe that he is going to try to take one of you women."

They all look at each other sadly and nod as they know Dumaka is speaking the truth. Dumaka adds, "But I do not know which one of you dear ladies the beast wants. Lies, deceitfulness and confusion are how he operates. He thrives on chaos and divisiveness between us. That is why it is so important that we do all we can to bring people together and heal the divide between the people and the Upper Crust of One World."

* * *

The gathering adjourns with a somber mood, and each person finds a quiet space of solitude for respite from the heaviness in their hearts. They do understand that Dumaka is speaking the truth, and they are by no means feeling hopeless. The group of friends feel the love, strength, and courage in their hearts, knowing that they will be faithful and true to one another, no matter what happens and no matter what they are called to do.

The next morning, everyone prepares to leave for Bear River Farm. They are anxious to reconnect with Lisa and Kenny and all their friends over there. They also must decide where the children will go next; whether they will remain at Bear River or go back to Johannesburg. The group will also be arriving in time for the first big harvest after the water purification. If the tomato soup was any indication of what lies ahead for the crops of One World, they all know that the promise of plenty is on its way.

* * *

Suzie of the Seashells is "helping" Phil out in the fields. She is kissing all the fruits and vegetables like Eve Elli taught her while Phil is getting ready to harvest them.

All morning, every available body at Bear River Farm has been out in the fields with baskets and wheelbarrows and anything they can find to collect the fruits and vegetables. There has been so much more produce in the past two days than there ever has been before; the farmers just don't know where to put everything. The fruits and vegetables have grown so large, with tomatoes the size of small cantaloupes.

Word has gotten out to the villagers and nearby townspeople of the yield that is expected today, so folks are coming from all over with trinkets and items to trade. Although the Masters technically own the property and everything that goes along with it, there has never been an issue with excess over the meager allotment that the farmers are expected to fulfill. People have been quietly spreading the word amongst themselves that there will be plenty left after filling the Masters' coffers. They plan to barter and trade for whatever they need with all that is leftover.

A spirit of joy and excitement is in the air when Suzie of the Seashells starts bouncing up and down, flapping her arms and calling out with glee, "EE-Eh-yee! EE-Eh-yee! Yook! EE-Eh-yee!"

Everyone looks up and sees that four Cloudtransporters have landed in the field, with Eve Elli and Emeka emerging from one of them. "EE-Eh-yee!" little Suzie exclaims upon seeing Eve Elli, and she toddles off to greet her best friend,.

"Hi Suzie!" Eve Elli calls out as she runs to meet her, with Emeka right behind. All the people, from those harvesting the crops to the new arrivals getting out of the Cloudtransporters, stop what they are doing to witness the coming together of the three wakanjeja. A Light from Heaven seems to be shining down upon them as if they are, and always have been, Holy Ones.

Phil, Doc, Kenny, and Lisa greet their friends as they arrive in the fields, and Adam Sam and Eve Lydia greet their little Eve Elli, welcoming her home.

"Well!" says Lisa, laughing. "You picked the best day to drop by. Look at all the harvesting we have to do!"

Before she can say another word about letting them *get settled in first, no need to jump right in,* etcetera, the entire crowd from Kookie and his companions to the Chrysalenes of the Village of the Holy Ones, begin picking and packing along with everyone else.

The Major says, "Let's get all of this done so we can eat it all later!" They all have a good laugh considering the mountain of produce that they will have ready to deliver before the end of the day.

People start arriving after the coffers are already full, so Lisa and Kenny invite them to pick whatever they want and give whatever they have to offer for barter.

While all of that is going on, the Chrysalenes are offering healings to whomever needs it and everyone else prepares for the evening's festivities. It is the best harvest that Bear River Farm has ever had, and everyone is overwhelmed and truly grateful for the abundance.

That evening a feast is laid out for the hordes of people who are arriving, including the Chrysalenes from both Continental Territories and all the folks who live at Bear River Farm. It is a gathering of unequaled joy, love, abundance, and hope, for one and all. News is spreading quickly among the people that the same thing is happening all over. Since the rainfall, the earth and its people seem to be coming fully alive again, as if awakening from a very long, deep, sleep. Chrysalenes are singing the songs of the angels, and people are dancing and rejoicing at harvest festivals everywhere as they can feel the passing of an ancient shadow, and a rebirth and coming of the Light.

The tables at Bear River Farm are covered with platters of fruit, pastries, breads of all varieties, and a colorful array of salads. Even the cows and goats have suddenly started to spontaneously lactate, producing milk in excess since the rainfall.

Long ago, the dairy animals started to dry up and they have barely been able to produce enough milk to feed their young. Cows have long since been bred only as meat for the UC, with cheese and other dairy products being the UC's luxury food. Goats have been kept on primarily as pets for the farmers. Lisa and Kenny have a few pet goats and can now start to produce dairy products. Everyone is most excited to see pitchers of goat's milk brought out to the tables.

All the people "ooo and ahh" when they see this nectar of the UC laid out before them.

Lisa stands up and says to the crowd, "I guess we will all have to learn how to make food from this nectar like our ancestors used to!"

The crowd roars with delight and shouts of, "If anyone can figure it out, I know *you* can, Lisa!" and "That should keep us busy for the rest of the summer!" and "What about CHEESE?!"

Kookie, Yakov and Liling are the only ones among them to have ever eaten cheese.

Kookie stands up to get the crowd's attention. "My friends," he begins, "it has been a long time since I have indulged in such exquisite fare, but I promise you this. I shall have my cooks share their recipes with you and then you will all be able to eat cheese, and other wonderful dairy products."

"Yay! Woo hoo! Hooray for Kookie! Hooray for cheese!" the crowd exclaims with mirth.

* * *

The next morning, Kookie and the Major call their group to one last gathering before they head out for their different assignments. Phil and Doc join them along with Adam Sam and Eve Lydia.

Kookie begins, "I guess the first thing we must decide is what to do with these precious children. Adam Sam and Eve Lydia, since you are the parents of Eve Elli, it is entirely up to you what happens to her. And Phil, you must tell us what your wishes are with Suzie of the Seashells."

He turns to Liling and says, "And I suppose the decisions regarding Little Lord Emeka are up to you, as technically he is now an orphan and ward of the state, under your jurisdiction."

Mimi looks on in silence because she knows that she cannot be selfish regarding her little angelic grandchild. However, her heart is aching to be wherever Eve Elli goes, and she will request an assignment accordingly.

Eve Lydia stands up and raises her hand saying, "Good people. Adam Sam and I have talked this over with each other and we know that we will do whatever is best to be of service. And that includes our daughter Eve Elli. Wherever she is sent we would like to go too and serve in the fields as we have been doing here.

"Thank you, Eve Lydia," says Kookie. "I am sure that you will be able to serve in whatever way you like, wherever Eve Elli is."

"Um, does that include me too?" asks Mimi timidly.

"And me?" says Ryan.

Everyone smiles at them and agrees that the five of them will not be separated.

"Whew!" says Mimi. She leans over and gives her granddaughter a big squeeze.

Kookie continues, "It seems that we have all been getting a strong gut feeling that the children are an extremely important part of whatever is going to happen to all of us, and I propose that we keep them together as much as possible."

"I would love to take them all to Johannesburg with me," says Liling, "except I am not sure how safe it will be there now for any of us."

"Please, Liling, they will be welcome and very safe with the gardeners of the estate," says Dumaka. "We know the property well and can keep a watchful eye on the young ones."

"And they are also most welcome, and safe, in the Village of the Holy Ones," says Mother Eve Zula.

Turning to Phil she says, "It is not very different from here, sir, if you would like to join us with Suzie of the Seashells."

Phil looks at Doc and smiles at her. He says, "I'm sure there are all kinds of herbs and flowers there that you can learn about. If you would care to come with us, that is."

Dumaka quickly jumps in, "Oh, my goodness, yes! We would love to have a medicine lady with us, Doc! There is much we can teach each other about herbs and other natural forms of medicine."

Doc is overjoyed to be included. "I would love to come with you and little Suzie, Phil." Turning to Dumaka she says with a smile, "Thank you, Dumaka! I can't wait to learn all about your herbs and flowers!"

"Well then!" the Major says to everyone. "I guess that takes care of the kids!"

"I guess so! Sure does! It takes care of most of the adults too!" they all laugh and agree.

Yakov speaks up next. "I have people back at my estate who are quite able to manage without me for a long time. Neely and I have been talking and we feel that it is important for us all to stay together right now."

"So do we," says Angie as she looks at Kookie.

"Liling, would you be willing and able to accommodate us all at the Johannesburg estate?" asks Yakov.

"Absolutely, my Brother," Liling says with a sigh of relief. She feels much safer knowing that Kookie and Yakov will be there, along with everyone else.

Finally, everyone turns to the Major and Vi. "What about you, bro'?" asks Kookie.

Looking at Vi, the Major says, "I know this sounds crazy, but I cannot abandon my father or Howard Pharmaceuticals. Vi and I can go back and forth between Judy's farm and here, if it's alright with all of you," he says to Kenny and Lisa. "We can also move around undetected, if necessary, thanks to Kookie and the Salamander program. I do feel that we are being called to stay on top of whatever is going on over there."

"Okay, bro'," Kookie says. "But you come right on over to Johannesburg if you feel you need us."

"Sure thing, man. Thanks." says the Major.

"So now we just need to decide what we are going to do next." Kookie says, looking around at everyone. "Does anyone have any ideas or suggestions?"

"Yes! I do!" comes a child's voice as everyone looks down at Emeka.

"Me too!" says Eve Elli, all smiles.

"OOO!" exclaims Suzie, with raised eyebrows.

"Well then, My Lord Emeka, what do you propose," says Kookie, smiling away at him.

Emeka says, "I say that we call on people everywhere to gather together and share what we all are learning."

"Oh? And what is that My Lord?" asks Yakov, also smiling at Emeka.

"That once we learn how to stop being afraid, we are free!" Emeka says swinging his arms out to the side. "When we have nothing to be afraid of anymore, we are all free."

The Major nods, "Yes, My Lord Emeka, that is true. And the truth sets us free, doesn't it." he says looking around at everyone.

"Once everybody really knows that, then they will *all* be free!" says Lord Emeka.

"Somewhere in the past," Kookie says "a great Panamerican politician, or should I say a great *American* politician once said that there is nothing to fear but fear itself. And I for one agree with Lord Emeka here. With the help of all our friends including, the Lords who are our Allies, the Chrysalenes, our winged friends, Metatron, and all the technology at our disposal, we can really bring people together with love."

Eve Elli looks at Mimi and says, "Yep! We got this Gramma! Hee Hee Hee!"

* * *

Deep in the bowels of the darkest dimension of hell, the beast is listening to his enemies above. Growling and snarling he says to them: *You have got nothing! Do you hear me, child? Nothing! Oh no little one, it is I who have YOU! You will see. Yes. You WILL SEE! Very soon. VERY SOON, INDEED!*

Chapter 17 – Vengeance

THREE SCREENS ACTIVATE. ES and PA accept a message from SPA.

SPA: Have you received any news, my Brethren?

PA: It is not good news, Brother SPA.

ES: Dear me. What is it PA?

PA: Another failure.

SPA: What now?

PA: Master Howard was unsuccessful in his miserable attempt at contaminating the major reservoirs of the world with the neurotoxins.

ES: I do not understand.

SPA: How is that possible, Brother?

PA: No one seems to know. The neurotoxins were all loaded onto the transporters and dropped into the reservoirs. And just like the Ebola bioweapon, instead of poisoning the water, the water has been improved.

ES: That's not possible! How can that be? What about Master Howard and the information we obtained from him regarding Lord Kenneth?

PA: It was all false information, my Brethren. Our technical people cannot figure out what the devil it is that Lord Kenneth is doing! As long as we do not know what he is doing or how he is doing it, we cannot terminate him.

ES: Why not PA?

PA: Because then we will never be able to find out exactly what powers he has.

SPA: And who else might know his secrets and be using his powers.

PA: Our technical people say it is dangerous to do anything to Lord Kenneth until we know exactly what that power is, and who he is working with. Besides it seems that everything we have tried against him, or his precious "people," has backfired on us with major consequences.

SPA: There is one more way, you know. Something that we have not tried yet.

ES: What is it SPA? Do tell!

PA: Yes! Do tell!

SPA: The way of surrender Brethren. Lord Kenneth must be *convinced,* shall we say, to surrender.

PA: Ah yes, I do see what you mean SPA. It is like the Lords' training from their HOC's; what to do when there is a traitor among them.

ES: But that would mean harming one of his people, and as the technical people say, we cannot do that without risk.

SPA: Ah! But we must trick Lord Kenneth in some other kind of way. Remember what it is that our dark lord desires most.

ES: What is that Brother?

SPA: His desire is to have *her!*

ES: Ah, yes!

PA: So how can we capture her without possibly harming ourselves?

SPA: We need to discuss that with our technical people. But they will only want to do that at our safe place.

ES: You mean the polar location?

SPA: Yes.

PA: Well then, we must all gather there immediately!

ES and SPA: Yes! Immediately!

The transmission is terminated.

* * *

The Major and Vi have returned to Howard Pharmaceuticals' main plant. They search for Master Howard in his office suite, but do not find him there. The Major feels like there has been some kind of change in the place.

"Can you feel it, Vi?" he asks her. "I don't know, something feels very different here."

"I was going to say the same thing, honey. Something is definitely different," Vi remarks.

The Major sees the Shop Overseer and calls out to him, "Hey there, my man! How's everything going?"

"Oh, Major! I am *so* glad to see you!" the Shop Overseer says.

"Why? Is something wrong?" the Major asks him.

"I'll say there is! Do you remember that torrential rainfall we had just the other night?"

"What about it?"

"Your father has been acting very strange ever since that night, Master John."

"What has my father been up to?"

"I can't rightly explain it, sir. Better if I show you."

The Major and Vi look at each other in utter bewilderment as the Shop Overseer takes them down to the lab. The Lab Overseer, Reggie, is there and when he sees the three of them coming, he gives them all a hearty greeting.

"Hello, hello, Master John and his lovely lady! And of course, hello to you too, Shop Overseer. It is good to see you again, Master John. And won't you introduce me to your lady?"

"Well, um, she actually served here not too long ago. Her name is Vi and she—"

"Ah, yes!" he says, cutting off the Major. "Aren't you the woman who helped out with all of those people from the Shelter Hut during the Ebola pandemic?"

"Why, yes. Yes, I am," Vi replies.

"Wonderful!" he exclaims, "So what can I do for the two of you?"

The Shop Overseer explains to him, "They would like to see Master Howard, sir."

"Ah! So, you've come to see you father then, have you Master John? Well, there's a good son, now, yes you are!" says Reggie, patting the Major on the back.

The Major and Vi glance sideways at each other as if to say *what in the blazes is going on here?!*

"He's right over there, in the little office next door. Seems rather comfortable there, yes, he does. Not to worry though, I bring him all the food he needs, and I even had a little folding bed brought in for him to sleep on."

The Major cannot stand it anymore and blasts Reggie in frustration, "My good man! Sir! WHAT IN THE *BLEEPITY-BLEEPING BLEEP* IS GOING ON HERE?"

Laughing, Reggie puts his hand on his chest and says, "Why dear me! I didn't know that *you* didn't know! But of course, you didn't. You have been gone for the past several days.

"Thank you, Shop Overseer. I can take it from here." Reggie says, as the Shop Overseer seems anxious to leave. Then Reggie speaks in a quiet voice as he prepares to open the door and bring the Major and Vi into the office to see Master Howard.

"Since you were last here," says Reggie, "Master Howard has, well, he has not been quite himself." Then Reggie quickly adds, "But that is a *good* thing, you know! Because Master Howard has always been, um, what word did my ancestors like to say in their day—a *SCHMUCK!*"

The Major has to stifle a laugh. "Oh, I see. And has something happened that he is now, *not* a schmuck anymore, Reggie?"

"Yes, I think so," says Reggie, all smiles. "Come on in and decide for yourself."

* * *

Mama Eve Zula and Papa Adam Makena have arrived with everyone back at the Village of the Holy Ones. Their group consists of Mimi, Ryan, Adam Sam, Eve Lydia, Eve Elli, Phil, Doc, Suzie of the Seashells, little Lord Emeka, and the other 10 Chrysalenes. As soon as they settle into their huts, Mimi, Ryan, Phil, and Doc are anxious to get to the Center Coffeehouse to meet some of the locals and get some people's news.

Meanwhile, Dumaka has returned to his gardener friends, Bem, Tafari and Nassor, and is filling them in on all that has happened. He is thrilled to hear that the sudden heavy rains have produced the same magical results with the harvest in their area, too, and that something is also changing with the spirit of the people. They, too, have agreed to meet up with everyone that evening at the Center Coffeehouse.

Kookie, Angie, Yakov and Neely are back at the estate with Liling and are also planning on gathering with the others at the Center Coffeehouse shortly. They are all anxious to hear what has been happening with the harvest, but more importantly, they are hearing and feeling a spirit of courage that is building in people throughout the area. They are ready to take action and begin mobilizing people, with the Chrysalenes and three wakanjeja at the helm.

* * *

PA, ES and SPA have arrived at the polar location with every High Overlord Contact of the Lords, and a technical support team. They too are ready to move into action, with the lord of the underworld at *their* helm. In fact, the very first thing that PA, ES and SPA do after settling into their luxurious accommodations is gather in a secret room to contact *their* highest.

The room has no windows and is lined with mirrors. There is a small, round pool of water in the center. PA, ES and SPA arrive wearing black hooded robes, and no clothing underneath. Once the door is closed and the light is turned out, the room will be pitch black. Therefore, they must take their places around the pool and close the door before using a remote to turn out the light.

In the pitch-black room their chanting begins. It is a low, deep rumble emanating from their gut, with words that go back to ancient times. The language has long since been forgotten, but the dark lord has imprinted the words on the souls of all those who give themselves to him. It is the call that is used to beckon his arrival into their midst.

After a few minutes a faint red glow appears in the pool of water. The glow is coming from a great distance down below, from another dimension. The faint red glow becomes stronger as it begins to pulsate, sending ripples across the water and sounding like a throbbing heartbeat, coming to life.

PA, ES and SPA know that once they hear the heartbeat, it is time for them to remain still as the beast comes up from hell and reveals himself to them. The entire pool fills with the face of the demon and the red glow casts a shadow of his image in the mirrors all around the room. The three are terrified, which is the only way that the beast can appear in all his strength. Without fear to feed upon, the beast is nothing. He begins:

Let this be your final warning. You will not fail me again. You will bring her to me, and I will restore chaos and destruction to the people of your world. With her at my side, I will build an everlasting empire of fear and hate, and all will be forgiven of your clumsiness and stupidity. You three will continue in all your glory with a reign of terror that will be unparalleled to the people of the earth. I will wreak vengeance on those who would try to stop me, beginning with those who are protecting her now. I COMMAND YOU TO BRING HER TO ME, THAT I MIGHT TAKE HER, FOR MY VERY OWN!

And for this, you shall have all the power and riches of the earth laid at your feet. No one will ever dare to challenge your might again as the renegades are doing now. Their simple magic tricks will work no more. Once she is with me, her protectors will all be crushed, and you three will have absolute dominion over every living soul of One World. Now GO! Do my bidding!

The beast descends back into the depths of the dark pool. The pulsating red glow and thunderous beat subside, and the room is pitch-black once more.

With trembling hands, PA turns the lights on with the remote. He looks at ES and SPA and without a word the three of them leave as fast as they can. They race back to their rooms; only ES stops once. . . to vomit violently.

* * *

The Center Coffeehouse is teeming with people. Everyone is full of excitement over the harvest and the wonderful abundance that it has provided. Trading has been going strong and folks can now begin to feel a real hope of freedom just around the corner. After getting the children off to bed and leaving Mama Eve Zula to watch over them, Mimi and company are the first to arrive at the Coffeehouse and grab a couple of tables.

They do not have to wait long when Kookie and company from the Big House show up, including #3 and #4 on Angie's shoulders. Needless to say, Angie and the pigeons make quite a hit with all the Coffeehouse folks when they talk to, pet, and laugh at the hand-shaking antics of the little creatures. The locals are also amazed at Angie's Universal Translator and how easy it makes communication for them with this charming young woman of Panamerica.

Dumaka arrives with Bem, Tafari and Nassor, and Dumaka sits down next to Liling. He takes her by the hand and says, "I have missed you My Lady—pardon me, *Liling*—though we have not been apart for very long."

She smiles warmly at him and says, "And I have missed you, too, my friend."

As they stare affectionately into each other's eyes, Liling says to Dumaka, "There are several empty suites now in the Big House, if you and your friends here would like to take a few of them. I would be more than happy to have you all stay with us."

Dumaka is choked up with joy at the invitation.

Bem replies, "Oh, ma'am! That would be such an honor!" while the others all nod in agreement.

"Thank you, Liling," says Dumaka, "I am now the happiest man in all of One World!"

Unbeknownst to Dumaka, the entire company of friends have been listening to their conversation and upon hearing his last remark they all give a "Woo Hoo!" and a "You go Brother!" amidst much laughter.

Kookie puts his hand out to Dumaka from across the next table and says, "Welcome to the family, Brother!"

Dumaka is having difficulty holding back tears. He simply nods and thanks Kookie and the others.

As an afterthought, Kookie says to the four men, "Of course, I will supply each one of you with a Universal Translator as soon as you arrive."

At this the men are truly honored. They realize that they are about to receive the technology that is typically only given to a Lord.

Phil and Doc are anxious to get to know the people of this small suburban community in Johannesburg, so they stand up and announce to the others that they are going to mill around.

"Perhaps we should do the same," says Mimi. "Then we can share whatever news we get with each other."

Liling has an idea. Since many of the folks at the Coffeehouse already know her from the reception she gave them all upon her arrival, she thinks it would be a good idea to extend an invitation to them. Liling announces that the next day there will be a great gathering at the estate, to celebrate the harvest and to encourage trading and barter among the people.

"What do you think?" she asks Dumaka, Kookie and Yakov. "We can bring people together encouraging their independent, free trade with each other."

"I love it! Sounds great! Amen to that, Sister!" they all say.

"I know that the children need to remain hidden and protected for the time being," says Mimi, "and the Chrysalenes need to remain low key and not attract too much attention to themselves, but perhaps we can ask them how they might also participate in the Harvest Gathering."

"This is true," says Liling. "We need the help of the children *and* the Chrysalenes if we are going to spread Courageous Love throughout One World."

* * *

Reggie opens the door for the Major and Vi. Master Howard has been staying in the little office since they last saw him, which was the night of the great rainfall and the water purification.

The Major and Vi step inside with Reggie right behind them. Master Howard is sitting in a chair with his back to them. He is facing a blank wall.

Without turning around, he calls out, "Is that you, Reggie?"

"Yes sir, it is. And I have brought two others with me."

Reggie nods at the Major who says, "It is me, father. I am here with Vi."

The Major's words are met with silence, and Master Howard does not move. Reggie beckons to the Major to go over to his father. As the Major does so, he sees his father's face and what he is holding in his hand. Master Howard is clutching the bottle of water purifier that the Major gave to him just before he left, seemingly as if he has never put it down.

Upon seeing this, the Major's heart breaks. He gets down on his knees in front of Master Howard and softly says, "What is troubling you, my father?"

Master Howard looks at his son as a light begins to appear in his eyes. Then he holds up the bottle to his son and says, "I didn't thank you for this." He looks at the bottle and pauses for a moment before saying, "my son."

Master Howard can barely speak those two words. But as he does, something breaks through and a floodgate opens in his broken soul. He holds the bottle tightly against his chest, and with his head bowed low, Master Howard starts to sob.

"My son! My son! What have I done? What have I become?" Turning to the Major who is now also in tears he implores, "What can I do, John? I have killed so many! I have destroyed the lives of innocent people and made them suffer!" And then, looking at the Major, Master Howard feels as if his soul is now shattered in a million pieces as he says, "*I* am the one unworthy of life. Please help me, my son! Please forgive me!" he cries to the Major.

At that moment, in the dark dimension of hell, the beast begins to scream out in a hideous, hateful rage, *NOOO! YOU WILL* **NOT** *REPENT!* ***I SHALL HAVE YOUR SOUL! I AM TAKING YOU! NOW!"***

Suddenly Master Howard clutches his chest as a searing pain goes through his heart. He is gasping for air and cries out to the Major, "Forgive me, son, please forgive me!"

In a flash, Vi hears a voice inside of her and sees the answer right in Master Howard's hand. She grabs the bottle of water purifier, removes the top and starts pouring it into his mouth. The Major shrieks as Master Howard sputters and coughs. They all become aware of a red light flashing at the base of his throat.

"What are you doing?!" the Major howls, beside himself with agony.

"Holy Water," Vi says. "A voice came into my head as I looked at the bottle and the voice said, *Holy Water.*"

She pours a little bit more into Master Howard's mouth and this time he is able to drink without coughing or sputtering. Then the red light on his throat goes out, turns to dust, and disappears.

"I don't know what the words *Holy Water* mean, but it sure sounds like your father should be drinking it, doesn't it?" Vi asks the Major.

"It sure does!" he replies, gasping with relief.

Reggie approaches and they all stay at Master Howard's side. Gradually, he finishes the bottle and the pain in his chest subsides. Master Howard begins breathing normally, but he is most certainly not his old self anymore. The Major, Vi, Reggie and Master Howard hold each other. With smiles on their faces, a small laugh escapes from their lips along with tears of joy.

In the dark dimension of hell, a raging beast bellows a violent, explosion of fury. He screams through the endless abyss of darkness, *NOOOOOOO! NOOOOOO! CURSE YOU, MASTER HOWARD! IT WAS TO BE MY HOUR OF VENGEANCE! CURSE YOU!*

A Light from Heaven hears the fallen angel and replies, *"Vengeance belongeth unto me. . ."*[13]

---

[13] *Hebrews 10:30, KJV*

The raging beast is stricken by those words, and the Voice who is speaking to him. He recoils in anger and fear.

Master Howard is breathing fine now, and there is no more chest pain. But even more than that is a renewed feeling deep in his soul.

Looking at his son with all the repentance of a truly loving father, Master Howard says to the Major, "Son, will you please stay here and help me do what I should have been doing my whole life with Howard Pharmaceuticals?"

"What is that, father?"

"I would like to create medicinal products that truly heal people, deeply, as I have just been healed."

The Major looks at Vi and says to Master Howard, "If my lady here will join me in helping you, it would be a great privilege for us to do just that father."

"Of course, I will join you, Major," says Vi. Looking at Master Howard she says, "I will be most honored to join you both and be of whatever assistance I can; especially right here in the lab, if *you* would like that, Reggie." Vi says smiling at all three of them.

"My dear Vi, I would love to have you help out in the lab!" exclaims Reggie. "In fact, the first thing I want to learn about is this thing you call Holy Water, and how it stopped Master Howard from possibly leaving us. And, how it has made him into someone who, well, is not a SCHMUCK anymore!"

The four of them laugh out loud.

Master Howard says, "Why don't we all go over to my house and discuss plans for a whole new line of healing products, over dinner."

Chapter 18 – Taken

PA, ES, AND SPA ARE SEATED AROUND A TABLE in the Great Dining Hall of the Underground Palace of the polar location. Their nerves are frayed after the confrontation they just had with the beast, and they are most fearful about how they are going to execute his command.

"They are always with her. She is never alone. Besides, I just don't see how we are going to take her by any means other than force," says PA. "And we all know that she must come of her own freewill."

"Have the technical people come up with anything yet, Brother?" asks SPA

"They are currently analyzing her weaknesses through the surveillance system," PA replies.

"Well Brother, so what have they come up with?" asks ES.

"Only that she is a very *loving* person," PA says with contempt, to which they all respond in unison, "YUCK!"

"There is no time to waste," says SPA. "We had better come up with something very soon!"

"They are about to have a large Harvest Festival at the estate of the former Lord Ekene. According to our technical team, we might have a chance at making our move on her then," PA says.

"Most excellent, my Brother!" says SPA.

"Yes indeed!" says ES. "Bravo to the technical people!"

"But are they sure that she will be there, Brother?" asks SPA.

"Of that, the technical team is absolutely certain!" exclaims PA.

"Truly excellent, Brother!" ES cries out.

"Yes indeed, it is *most* excellent!" SPA concurs.

PA, ES and SPA adjourn to their private quarters.

* * *

"Good morning, children!" Mama Eve Zula says as the three young ones in her charge come out to greet her at the Big Hut. "Are you ready for your fruit and bread this morning?"

"Yes Mama, we are ready," says Emeka. The three of them help Mama Eve Zula prepare their meal.

Eve Elli says to Suzie of the Seashells, "Come over here Suzie and sit down. You can help me put the fruit on everybody's plate."

"Pate!" says Suzie happily as she picks up a plate.

With Mama Eve Zula and Eve Elli's help they fill the three plates with fruit from the gardens of the Village of the Holy Ones. Mama slices up the fresh-baked bread and places a chunk on each of the children's plates.

"Mmm! Ooo!" says Suzie as she takes a bite out of the bread.

Mama laughs and gives her a glass of water. "Here you go, child. You may wash it down with the blessed water."

Emeka looks on with great curiosity. He asks her, "How is the water blessed, Mama?"

"It is blessed by our Heavenly Father," she replies.

"Oh, I see!" says Emeka. "The Father in Heaven, where *my* father is now." Thinking about it for a moment he says, "That must be very good water then!"

"Yes, Emeka," says Mama Eve Zula, "Truly it is, *very good water!*"

"Then I must drink it all down and not leave a drop!"

Turning to Eve Elli, Emeka says with a great big grin, "You must drink your blessed water, too."

"Oh yes!" she says, and they each take their glasses in hand and clink them together like they have seen the grown-ups do.

"Hee, Hee, Hee!" they all giggle, including Suzie, and they drink their water together.

Adam Kojo comes into the Big Hut and tells Mama Eve Zula that Mimi and her friends will all be going to the Big House today.

"Mimi and the others told us last night that a Great Harvest Festival has been planned for today where people from all over are expected to come. They will bring food from their harvest as well as all kinds of things to trade. Lady Liling has asked us to come, too, and bring the children."

"Blessings on this special day, and thank you for bringing us the news, Adam Kojo." Mama Eve Zula says. She turns to Emeka, Eve Elli and Suzi and says to them, "Well children, I guess we had better get ready for the Great Harvest Festival at the Big House!"

"Yay!" the three of them exclaim as they start jumping up and down. Little Suzie of course catches the enthusiasm of the other two.

The rest of the troops are still asleep in their huts. After they returned from the Coffeehouse they talked well into the wee hours of the morning, and now Doc and Mimi are in the throes of the same troubling dream.

They are in a field of wildflowers. A breeze is blowing through the flowers of many colors. They can see purple, red, blue, orange, and yellow flowers sparkling in the sunlight, spreading their loving energy everywhere. Doc and Mimi reach down and touch them gently as if they are patting the heads of small children. And the flowers sing and laugh along with them as they begin to reveal all their secrets to the two women.

Then the sky begins to darken, and the flowers lose their color. They quickly fade and turn to ash with the breeze carrying away their remains. Suddenly a chasm opens in the darkening field. Doc and Mimi are frightened but feel compelled to walk to the edge of the chasm. They look down into a black void that grows and deepens right before their eyes. A deep, rhythmic booming rises up and everything goes completely black. A few seconds later they can see a pale red glow, deep down in the darkness below. It is moving up closer to them and the two women take each other by the hand.

They are unable to speak when they hear a snarling voice below. Suddenly, the voice goes quiet and all they can see and feel is the frightening red glow. After a few moments the voice suddenly starts up again. Only this time, it is a whimpering sound, as of someone crying. The tearful voice says to Mimi and Doc, "Please help me! I'm so lonely. I'm so scared. Please come down here and keep me company. Please, oh please! Do not leave me all alone in this forsaken place! One of you, kind, dear, sweet ladies, please come down here and join me!"

Instantly Mimi and Doc feel themselves being dragged forward by the chest. They both let out a piercing scream as they swan-dive into the cold dimension of hell bellow.

Mimi and Doc lurch forward, each in her own respective bed, and wake up shrieking with terror.

The Chrysalenes hear their cries from all over the Village of the Holy Ones and they immediately drop whatever they are doing. "Over there," says Eve Amadi, running towards the sound of Mimi's cries.

Eve Rukiya says, "Over there," as she hears Doc wailing.

The rest of them follow, going to each hut and soon both women are surrounded by the comforting presence of the Chrysalenes.

Mama Eve Zula and the children also hear the howling, and Eve Elli says very calmly, "I have to go to my Gramma now, Mama Eve Zula."

"Yes, child, you go to her, and I will wait here with Emeka and Suzie," Mama Eve Zula says to Eve Elli, with a knowing, tender smile.

Eve Elli arrives at Mimi's hut to find her gramma shaking and crying. Eve Amadi is holding Mimi as she and the others are all glowing with loving, healing energy.

When Mimi sees Eve Elli, she puts her arms out to her granddaughter like a frightened child. The three-year-old grandchild takes Gramma Mimi in her arms and says, "Don't cry Gramma, everything is gonna be okay. I'm here, and I love you. Everything is gonna be just fine."

She leans over and kisses Mimi on the forehead. "Don't cry Gramma."

Ryan watches the scene, stunned. Mimi shares the dream with everyone while the Chrysalenes continue to pour healing energy into her. Eve Elli stays close to her gramma's side.

In Doc's hut the same scene is unfolding. The Chrysalenes and Phil are offering her comfort

"Trickster wants to have his way with you, my dear friend," Phil says to Doc. "But he can only do so if you show him fear."

"Can you all help me?" whimpers Doc, looking around at everyone and still quite shaken. "I think I'm almost feeling angry at that horrible thing now!"

Phil chuckles, "You are a very powerful woman already, Doc, or Trickster would not be bothering with you. It is actually his gift to show you how strong and brave you really are."

In Mimi's hut, Eve Elli says, "It must be very sad to be all alone in the dark, forever and ever. I think that is why the growly one has come to you, Gramma. Everybody loves you 'cause you love everybody."

Mimi has stopped crying now and sits smiling at her little angel.

"I think he is really scared of being all alone," Eve Elli continues, "so he has to scare everybody else, to keep him company."

In Doc's hut, Phil says to Doc, "So Trickster will fool you and confuse you, and show you the shadow. It is really your own shadow, though, which you have the power to rise above. And once you do that you will be that much closer to the Creator. You must already be close to the Creator, Doc, and a force for the dark underworld to reckon with."

They all emerge from their respective huts; Doc and Mimi look at each other and shake their heads.

Mimi says, "My goodness, woman! What was *that* all about?!"

Doc replies, "Maybe Trickster was mad that he did not get an invitation to our party this afternoon!"

They all have a good laugh. Mama Eve Zula joins them with Emeka and Suzie.

Ryan says, "Well, I guess it's time that we get *ourselves* to the party."

Mimi adds, "And it is nice to know that the growly one will *not* be joining us!"

In the dark dimension of hell, a guttural voice warns, *Don't bet on it, my dear. Oh no, woman, do NOT bet on it. I DO plan on being there. Yes INDEED!*

* * *

Preparations are underway for the Great Harvest Festival. Everyone on the estate has discontinued their other chores for the day and all energy is focused on making the necessary accommodations for a large crowd of people from all over the region. Tables and tents are being set up and plenty of food is being prepared in the Lord's kitchen. Of course, folks are also bringing their own food for barter.

There is a festive mood in the air that has not been felt in a long time, and it seems to be spreading to other nearby communities.

In the midst of all the preparations, Angie comes out of the Big House with four pigeons sitting on her shoulders: #3, #4, #21 and #22. Kookie emerges with his tuba. The gardeners and various overseers from the estate show up with drums and assorted homemade percussion instruments. They all gather under a tent with Kookie, and they start to make music together. The children come running over to Kookie and the other performers, dancing, laughing, and playing together.

It is just about this time that the entourage from the Village of the Holy Ones shows up. The group had decided the night before that Emeka would be safer spending the day there under the Salamander camouflage program, since the Council still does not know of Emeka's whereabouts, or even if he is still alive. Mimi was instructed to turn on the Salamander program once they approached the perimeter of the estate.

Part of Liling's official job at Lord Ekene's estate has been to try to locate the little lord or ascertain any information that she can about him. Apart from Kookie and the Major, Liling and the others have managed to stay under the Council's radar with no tangible proof of their true intentions. However, they are all suspected of compliance with Kookie by now, and for that reason among others, they are all under heavy surveillance at today's festival.

There is one though, who sees everything. And that one is about to reveal himself. . . to *HER.*

* * *

Gathered around the table in the Great Dining Hall of the Underground Palace, PA, ES and SPA are making their final arrangements.

SPA asks, "Have the technical people analyzed her weaknesses yet, Brother PA?

"Yes, indeed they have," PA replies.

"Good," says ES, "And how exactly do they plan to execute the capture, then?"

"The technical team has decided to send in a mole," says PA.

"And will the lady go for it, Brother PA?" asks SPA.

PA responds, "The mole is planning a truly great feat of trickery, my Brethren, one that is guaranteed to fool even *her* intuitive genius!

As PA explains the plan of capture to ES and SPA, a pair of angry red eyes is listening from the depths of hell. He is smirking with evil pleasure as he knows that the trap being set will be too much for even *her* to discern or resist.

Before this day on earth is over, woman, it is sure to be your last. And then YOU WILL COME TO ME OF YOUR OWN FREE WILL, AND I WILL TAKE YOU AS MY VERY OWN! VENGEANCE **SHALL** BE MINE! he screams, shaking his fist at the Heavenly Father above.

A small spirit above listens to the raging beast and she whispers, *I don't think so, fallen creature!*

* * *

Everyone from the Big House as well as the Chrysalenes, are welcoming people as they arrive. The big field behind the mansion is filling up with folks bearing fruit and vegetables, pastries and confections, and a variety of items to barter with.

Mimi is reminded of her days in Amber Beach and the seashell jewelry that she used to make. "Hm," she says to Ryan, "it would certainly be fun to start up a jewelry trade here!"

"And I would love to try my hand at making percussion instruments," Ryan says, swaying to the rhythm of the drums.

Kookie is in tuba heaven as the locals are enraptured by this strange instrument of his, the likes of which they have never seen. Yakov and Neely are tasting every scrumptious dish brought by the people, asking them for recipes. Eve Elli, Emeka and Suzie are playing with the local children, and eating a few too many confections. Phil and Doc are looking at all the herbs and homemade natural remedies, sharing ideas with the other herbalists.

The Chrysalenes are quietly milling through the crowd, radiating light and healing energy, filling the hearts of all with laughter and love. Liling and Dumaka are enjoying themselves immensely, informing the guests that they will be holding the festival once a week on the back field of the estate. They hope it will grow and catch on to other communities, and everyone agrees that it most definitely will.

And nobody notices Angie . . . except one.

* * *

A Cloudtransporter has just left the polar location. It contains three technical people and one machine. The machine is an older, less effective version of Kookie's Holographic Imager. It is called a Hologram Projector. The Cloudtransporter with its techies and equipment is on its way to Johannesburg.

* * *

Angie is suddenly not feeling very well. Talking to the pigeons on her shoulders she says, "I'm feeling a bit tired, my friends. And a little bit weak. I think I had better go and lie down for just a bit."

She goes inside the Big House and upstairs to her and Kookie's bedroom. Angie closes the bedroom door and lies down on top of the bed.

The pigeons settle on the bed on either side of her and snuggle up close; they know something is wrong.

Instead of feeling better, Angie notices that she is feeling light-headed and faint. She closes her eyes and hopes that this will just pass.

A few minutes go by when there is a knock on the bedroom door.

Angie opens her eyes and says, "I wonder who that could be," still talking to the birds. The pigeons are getting anxious, nuzzling closer to her. "Who is there?" she says, but there is no answer.

A few seconds go by and there is another knock on the door.

"Who is there?" Angie says again. But again, there is no answer.

The door slowly opens by itself.

Angie is dizzy and having a hard time focusing on who or what is behind the door.

A pale light appears from the other side of the slightly opened door, and she hears something very faint. Everything is a blur to Angie as she begins to slip into a dreamlike state. The door opens a little bit more and the light is a bit stronger. The sound becomes more distinguishable, and she can hear someone calling her name:

"Angie, Angie" the voice says.

Angie recognizes the voice of her deceased mother.

The door opens a bit wider; a figure stands in the doorway. It is glowing with a pale light and calling to Angie.

"Mama?" Angie cries out to her with a faint, weak voice. "Mama? Is that you, Mama?" Tears are streaming down Angie's face.

"Angie," the voice says again, "My sweet child. I have missed you so."

"Oh Mama," Angie cries, tears falling onto her pillow. "I have missed you too. I have missed you SOO much Mama!" She is sobbing heavily now; with what little strength she has.

"I have come to you, my sweet child, to warn you," the voice continues.

"Warn me about what, Mama?" Angie is feeling so dizzy and faint that she feels like she is going to pass out at any moment.

"About the Lord Kenneth, my child."

"Kookie, Mama?"

"They want him, baby. They want to kill him. And they would have killed him already except they fear his power with the people of One World. They fear an uprising."

"Oh, Mama!"

"But you can stop all that from happening, sweetheart. They have promised to work together with Lord Kenneth in helping the people, if you give them what they want."

"Oh Mama, I will do anything for Kookie! Anything! I love him!"

"Good, Angie, very good."

"Just tell me, what must I do? What do they want from me?"

The face is now hanging right over Angie's body, glaring down upon her.

Angie's vision is all but gone, when suddenly, a deep, hissing voice comes out of the face saying:

*I . . . WANT . . . **YOU** . . . ANGIE! YESSSS . . . I WANT **YOU**!*

And Angie finally goes under.

* * *

The festivities outside are going strong. Trading is doing very well, and there is much merriment everywhere.

Kookie is about to take a break from playing his tuba and jamming with the drummers, when he looks up and notices two pigeons dive-bombing at him. He suddenly realizes that he hasn't seen Angie for a while. The pigeons slam onto the top of his head. "Ow!" he yelps. "Hey, where's Angie, you guys?"

At the same moment, #21 and #22 fly down to Mama Eve Zula and the children and start circling frantically around their heads. She and Eve Elli put their hands out and the birds land on each one of them. Mama Eve Zula holds #21 against her heart and Eve Elli does the same with #22. They both receive in their hearts the whole story of what just happened to Angie.

Without saying a word, Mama Eve Zula and Eve Elli look at each other, hold the birds against their heads and send them flying to the other Chrysalenes at the festival. Mama picks up Suzie and they all go flying to Angie and Kookie's bedroom.

Kookie also gets the message loud and clear when he sees the frantic state of #3 and #4.

"Oh God! Where is she?!" he repeats in a panic, and the pigeons fly to the Big House so that he will follow them.

Mama Eve Zula and the children are the first to arrive at Angie's side.

She is all alone; her eyes are closed, and she is not moving. When Eve Elli touches Angie, her body feels cool. However, Mama does notice a shallow, irregular breath coming from her.

Kookie and the pigeons come in right behind the others and when he sees Angie he rushes to her bedside and falls to his knees. "What happened, Mama! What has happened to my Angie?" he cries out in agony.

With great sadness and compassion in her heart, Mama Eve Zula says, "It is the unholy one, My Lord. He is calling to her."

"I don't understand!" wails Kookie. "Why would the unholy one want my precious Angie?!"

Just then a flutter of Monarchs and Angel fly in with a whole bevy of pigeons behind them. The other 11 Chrysalenes from the Village of the Holy Ones also arrive. As they all gather around Angie, Angel lands on her forehead and speaks to the hearts of all who are gathered in the room:

Human creatures, the dearest Angie creature is now in the shadow world. She must decide whether to save all of you or save herself. And I am here to see that she does not face that choice alone.

Slowly, Angel begins to fade becoming almost completely transparent. And as she does so, Angie also begins to fade. Then, to everyone's astonishment, Angel flies up into the air and comes down fast disappearing right into Angie's chest.

The Chrysalenes hold hands around Angie's semi-transparent body telling everyone what they see happening to her.

* * *

Angie opens her eyes and finds herself standing on the edge of a cliff. She is overlooking a black tunnel of wind with a tempest raging all around her. There are echoes of voices crying out in anguish, deep in the bowels of hell. Angie's heart is breaking as she listens to the sounds of damnation and despair, feeling the broken spirits of all those for whom hope has been lost.

Then she sees him; her would-be captor is coming up from the abyss of hell. Since the Heavenly Father has given people freewill, the only way that the fallen angel can take Angie is if *she* chooses *him*. So, the Beast cries out to her:

Oh Angie, Angie, hear me, woman! Your good Lord Kenneth needs you as all the people of One World need him. I am only a misunderstood, lonely creature who longs for some comfort in my eternal darkness. Come to me, Angie, and stay with this fallen angel. You shall be my queen and reign with me for all of eternity. I will allow you to walk the earth, like I have done for so many others, like PA, ES and SPA. I will also grant you untold riches and wealth as I have with those three. I will even hold you higher above them as you will be my queen.

Come to me, Angie, come to me my queen, forever and ever. If not, I will have no choice but to save my world from crumbling, by destroying Lord Kenneth and all his followers. That will cause even greater destruction of the people and ALL living creatures upon the earth.

With one last desperate plea coming from the deceiver's hatred and fear of all that is pure and loving, the beast looks Angie straight in the eyes, holding his cold arms out to her saying:

PLEASE ANGIE . . . COME TO ME . . . PLEASE!

Angie's heart breaks for the lives of all people who live upon the earth; her Brothers and Sisters who are just beginning to taste freedom. She thinks of a life of total misery for one and all should she refuse the evil one.

Finally, Angie thinks of her beloved Kookie and all her friends, as the beast wreaks his vengeance on each and every one of them. And this she cannot bear.

Holding her arms out, palms facing upwards, she looks up and sees the Heavenly Light at the end of the tunnel. With tears in her eyes, Angie looks at the Light and says, "I love you, Heavenly Father! Please forgive me!"

And then, looking down at the fallen one she says:

TAKE ME!

Angie leans forward and begins to dive down into the eyes of the beast, when suddenly from out of her back the Monarch Angel rises. The beast looks up at Angel as the Monarch suddenly becomes massive and turns into a golden angel.

WHO ARE YOU? growls the beast, mere seconds away from taking his prize.

Angel says to the fallen one, *I am an Angel of the Lord. And when you take this woman, YOU WILL DEAL WITH ME!*

Angel plunges back into Angie just as they reach the fallen one, and they enter the head of the beast, and hell, together.

The terrified lord of the underworld suddenly releases a piercing scream.

* * *

The Chrysalenes are standing on either side of Angie's transparent body as she lies motionless in bed. Kookie is on his knees by her side, and the rest are bowed in prayer all around her.

Suddenly, Angie's body disappears altogether. Kookie puts his head down on their bed with his arms stretched out in front of him, and weeps.

His beloved Angie has been taken.

Eve Elli says, "Don't cry Kookie, it's okay. Angel is with Angie now, and the Angel of the Lord will protect her. Angie loves you very much. Do not be afraid."

From the darkest night
Comes Courageous Love.

To be continued...

MONARCH RISING

Book 3

ARISE

Acknowledgements

A HUGE Thank You goes out to my Dream Team:

Leanne Sype, thank you for your fantastic editing, constant encouragement, brilliant insights, and wonderful friendship.

Wendy Garfinkle, thank you for your beautiful formatting, incredible patience with me, and all the other things you have helped me with, above and beyond.

Taylor Dawn, thank you for your magnificent, magical graphic design, and the way it makes everyone go, "OOO and AHH" and "WOW" when they see the book cover.

Glenda Nowakowski, thank you for your very much appreciated, long-term friendship, enthusiasm, and excitement over my book, and taking the time to offer me wonderful insights on the tiniest detail.

Pooja Lama of the UPS store in Sherwood, OR, thank you for your help in printing out the preliminary manuscript. I have really appreciated your joyous enthusiasm over the whole concept of the story, as I shared it with you in the early stages of development.

Once again: thank you, thank you, to the truly awesome baristas at the Starbucks in Sherwood, Oregon. You have made me feel like a part of the family in your very special Coffeehouse, setting a whole new standard of excellence for the hospitality and retail industry.

About the Author

Sylvana C. Candela, L.Ac. MATCM, licensed acupuncturist, Master of Acupuncture and Traditional Chinese Medicine, resides in Sherwood, Oregon. She has supervised in community acupuncture clinics in Los Angeles, California, including Samra University and Yo San University of Traditional Chinese Medicine.

She received her bachelor's degree in special education from Queens College of the City University of New York, and taught children with autism at the Sybil Elgar School in London, England.

Sylvana has five children and six grandchildren.

She is the author of *Gently Heal Thyself: Healing the Soul with Energy Medicine*, and *Monarch Rising: Awaken.*

Made in the USA
Middletown, DE
06 March 2022